LOVE AT A FUNERAL AND OTHER AWKWARD CONVERSATIONS

SOPHIE ANDREWS

Love at a Funeral and Other Award Conversation © 2024 by Sophie Andrews

All rights reserved.

Edited by Lisa Hollet of Silently Correcting Your Grammar

Cover Design by Star Child Designs

No part of this book may be reproduced or transmitted in any form without written permission of the author, except by a reviewer who may quote brief passages for review purposes only.

This book is a work of fiction. Names, characters, places, and incidents are either products of the author's imagination or are used fictitiously.

Digital ISBN: 978-1-957580-58-6

Paperback ISBN: 978-1-957580-59-3

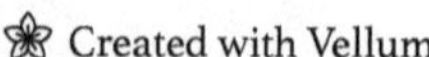 Created with Vellum

CONTENT NOTE

Love at a Funeral and Other Awkward Conversations is a romance. It is also a story about learning how to live and love with grief. Like all romances, this book has a happy ending, but the journey to get there is long and winding, filled with bittersweet moments and some very sad ones. Please read with care.

If you would like more detailed information about the inspiration for this story, please see the author's note at the end of the book.

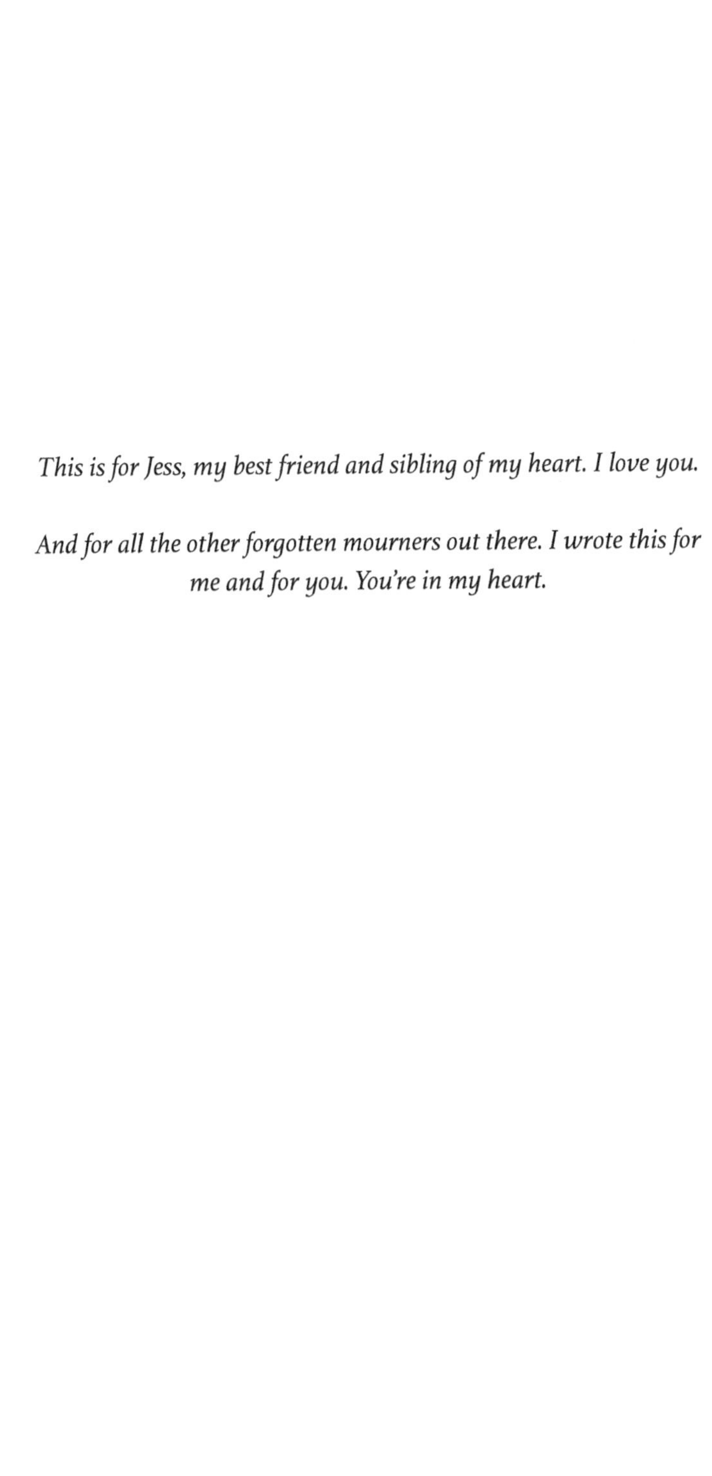

This is for Jess, my best friend and sibling of my heart. I love you.

And for all the other forgotten mourners out there. I wrote this for me and for you. You're in my heart.

"This is all the unexpressed love, the grief that will remain with us until we pass because we never get enough time with each other, no matter if someone lives till 60, 15, or 99."
 – Andrew Garfield, philosopher and superhero

FEBRUARY 14

I never noticed how cold it is in the Northeast on Valentine's Day, probably because I've always been inside. You don't notice the snowstorm while you're bumping uglies, right? But I noticed today. I noticed the freezing ice when my car spurted to a stop as it ran out of gas 200 yards from the station. Did you know no one will stop to help you when it's snowing, even if you're a woman on the side of the relatively busy road at rush hour? Where's the chivalry? I'm an independent woman, doing it for herself (kind of), but would've gladly accepted some 1947 house-wife standards for help today.

Related, the Shell gas station on Clinton Ave doesn't sell gallon containers for gas. They make you walk to the E-Z Mart across the street to buy one, so you have to go back to Shell to fill it up. I can't wait until cars are no longer a thing, and we can all travel in flying buses that run on soybeans and peanut oil.

Come thru, Greta!

I hope everyone's staying cozy today, preferably with a warm body next to them. For me, I'll be spending my

Valentine's Day working to get sensation back in my toes and trying to figure out my brother's Netflix password since he changed it again. Tip: buy leftover Halloween candy in November and store it for February when you want to drown your sorrows on the 14th. You're welcome.

#ValentinesDay #SingleAF #ColdAF #Coldhearted #QueerEyeMarathon #TeamTan #M&MsNeverGoBad #GoGreen #Feminism #ThisIsLivingAtHome #FollowMe

CHAPTER 1

Silver tinfoil crinkles between my fingers as I stuff another drugstore chocolate into my mouth. A fantastic way to spend Valentine's Day, on a daybed in my parents' basement, scrolling through Instagram. At twenty-seven years old, I know I don't have a great grip on this adulting thing, but I *am* trying.

I'm that oft-maligned lost boy and apparent ruiner of all good things. They write articles about me, make fun of my love of avocados and inability to save any money for a house. Though true to form, after living in New York City for a few years, I crawled back home to Mommy and Daddy to live in their basement since my old bedroom had been converted into an exercise room, and god forbid we move the dust-collecting BowFlex machine.

It's arguable that at this stage in my life I should have more than student loan debt and a closet full of black clothes to my name, but as a journalism major and Hellenic Studies minor, I'm qualified for exactly nothing. But when they told me I could do anything I put my mind to, I believed it.

As a kid, I used to read *Rolling Stone* magazine, literally flipped through it with my hands. The same hands that ripped off the covers to tape them to my walls, and I'd dreamed of working there, writing articles on the musicians I loved and funny, lucid pieces on politics and what my generation cared about, things like gun control, equity in the workplace, flying buses that ran on beans and peanut oil.

The problem is, newspapers and magazines don't exist anymore. There are no full-time staff positions, only occasional contract work for pop culture rags that pay pennies. So, instead of living the dream, I spent three years as the assistant to a celebrity whom I cannot name because of the nondisclosure agreement, barring me from discussing the temper tantrums, shoe-throwing, and lesbian affairs. As if the affairs are something to bat an eyelash at and not the shoe-throwing.

But the anonymous celebrity gossip and cheap-living hacks earned me a pretty good Instagram following, almost ten thousand. And yet...

"Cassandra," my mom calls from upstairs. "Will you get up here and clean up after yourself? I'm not your maid."

I cringe at her tone and scoot off the bed like I'm a child being scolded again. My parents aren't making me pay rent, but my mom's made it clear I'm more or less a guest. I've been here about a year, and it still feels like they're waiting on me to check out. But no matter what they think, I've been trying. I haven't even fully unpacked everything, refusing to believe I'm really living with my parents.

By the time I shuffle upstairs to the kitchen, Mom's gone. I hear her in the living room, and I'm happy I don't have to face her questions about what I'm doing or if I've found any other jobs that don't involve a place called Sassie's Lassies with a micro-kilt uniform and bad fried food.

I clean up my single dirty pan and plate from dinner, leaving no evidence of my meal, and then clomp back down to my lair. On the way, I pass framed pictures of me, my parents, and my brother. A family photo in front of some fancy Christmas tree. My eighth-grade school picture with zits and braces. Ray in his high school baseball uniform. Of course, he has the good picture.

I knock it with the side of my fist and take my phone from my pocket. I'm texting my brother before I even sit on the bed, knowing he'll find my episode this afternoon funny. I mean, I guess it's funny now that it's over. But running out of gas on a busy road at rush hour so I had to walk to the gas station in my work uniform of a kilt, knee socks, and tiny white top in freezing temperatures wasn't too funny then.

Ray doesn't respond, although he usually doesn't. He's terrible at texting and prefers to call people. It's strange. I'm not good with interpersonal relationships, but I'm great at social media. Ray thinks *that's* strange. We're three years apart but have always been pretty close, and ever since I moved back home, he's been my only ally.

Which is why when he doesn't answer my text or call me after an hour, I wonder what he's doing. I assume he's fighting with Shayna or out with the girl he's been seeing, but a scream fractures my thoughts into pieces.

I throw my phone on the pillow when the odd, pained scream echoes again. I scramble upstairs, tripping in my haste. "Mom?"

Once, when I was about ten or so, my mom dropped a heavy bowl on her foot and split her toe open. It was disgusting. She'd shrieked so loud I'd heard it upstairs. She sounds like that now, so I grab some Band-Aids from the medicine basket in one of the cabinets in the kitchen and prepare myself for blood.

But there isn't any blood in the living room. Only my mom crumpled up on the floor, her hair matted to her red face, the news on the television, and the remote across the room with the batteries out like it was dropped or thrown. Two police officers stand by the door.

My stomach plummets at the sight, and I freeze in place. "Uh... Everything okay?"

Obviously not. Dumb question. But I'm struggling to rub even two brain cells together at the moment, while Mom moves, only enough to let out the same painful cry.

I glance at the police officers with their sad frowns then back to her. My heart pounds out of my chest, and I wipe my hands on my pajama pants, desperate to understand yet knowing whatever this is, it will hurt.

I tug Mom back onto the couch. "What's going on?"

When she doesn't answer, one of the police officers steps forward. He's bulky and out of place next to the female officer, who appears on the verge of crying herself, blinking rapidly.

"What's your name?"

"Cass." I swallow a lump in my throat. "Cassandra."

"I'm Officer Stone. This is Officer Kwon. This is your mother?" He tips his chin to Mom, and when I nod, he asks, "Do you want to sit down?"

I can't tell, but I think I start to lower down in slow motion, or at least it seems that way, as my mom wheezes next to me. I don't like it. Her cries box me in, and I'm claustrophobic. I step away from her. "No, I don't want to sit down."

"We received a call earlier to respond to—"

"Raymond!" my mom wails. It's worse than when the

neighbor's cat snagged one of the baby rabbits living under our tree in the backyard. The keening cry of the baby bunny is unforgettable.

So is this.

"My baby! My baby is dead!"

My vision blurs, and I stagger back. Officer Something-or-other holds on to my elbow, saying, "I'm sorry to inform you Raymond collapsed outside of the gym and—"

An idea sparks in the back of my mind. The latest season of *Married at First Sight* is available to stream. I love it because I hate it.

"—tried the address listed on his license, but no one was home—"

I need to stop at the store for tampons and set my alarm for tomorrow morning.

"—listed as his emergency contact—"

I really want to paint my nails. This blue's all chipped, and if I don't paint them tonight, I won't have time tomorrow with a double shift at work.

"—couldn't revive him. Your brother died."

Your. Brother. Died.

I pull those words apart in my mind, try to weave them back together in a way that makes sense. They don't. I don't comprehend the language. It's foreign, and I frown in concentration.

"I'm sorry." I finally look up at the police officer. "What's your name again?"

"Officer Stone."

I nod blandly. "Okay."

Mom bawls beside me.

"I don't—" I shake my hands out then wipe my still-clammy palms down my arms. "I don't understand."

"I know it's a lot to accept." Officer Kwon speaks up from

her place at the door like she's afraid to step farther into the house. "Is there someone you want us to contact?"

"Um…" I watch my mother grow more and more hysterical by the second.

Ray is dead.

My brother is dead.

Is there someone I want them to contact?

"I…I'm not sure." I drop my gaze to the floor, kneading the thick threads of the carpet underneath my feet. If I look hard enough, I can find the faint stain of red from a bloody nose Ray gave me when I was nine. He'd been watching wrestling and said he wanted to try a move on me. It wouldn't hurt, he'd said. It's all pretend anyway.

Then he'd dropped me face first onto the floor.

"What happened? To him. To Raymond. What happened to him?"

"They aren't sure yet," Officer Stone says, running a hand over his shiny bald head. "Not until the autopsy."

I focus my attention outside of the window. It's dark already. The thing I hate the most about the winter is how dark it gets. When my brother and I were really little, we used to try to convince Mom it was still light out by piling up a bunch of lamps in his room, as if she'd believe it was daytime and let us stay up later.

"Where…" I squeeze my eyes shut and shake my head, as if I can make any sense out of this. "Where is he now?"

Officer Stone clears his throat. "His body is being transported back to the county coroner's office. That's where they'll do the autopsy."

I imagine all the episodes of *Law & Order* I've watched. My brother's going to be cut open like a frog and dissected like a science experiment. I push my fingers against my eyes as my mind swirls and stomach clenches. I don't usually get carsick outside of a car, but there's a first time for everything.

Like now.

"Cassandra." Officer Stone touches my shoulder lightly. "Does anyone else live here with you both?"

I swallow. "My dad. He works in Manhattan, and sometimes he doesn't get home until late."

"Do you want us to stay here until he arrives? Do you think your mother will need medical assistance?"

I once again look to my mom, trying to think. "I don't— I'm sorry," I say, taking a deep breath. "I don't know."

"It's okay. Take your time. Why don't you sit down, be with your mom for a bit? We'll be right outside."

I nod dumbly as the police officers shuffle out the front door. I don't understand why he keeps telling me to sit down. I don't want to sit down. "Mom?" I reach for her hand, wishing she'd tell me what to do. But she doesn't, and I'm helpless. "Mommy?"

She lifts her head up, her cheeks red and blotchy, mascara all over her face, and her eyes widen like she's seeing me for the first time. "Cassie! My boy! My boy is dead!"

She leaps off the sofa and picks up a framed photo of my brother in his college graduation cap. "He's never coming home again. My baby is gone!"

I watch her, stunned, her wild voice and actions hindering my own ability to do anything other than agree. "I know."

I slowly approach her, gently take the picture away from her and put it back before sitting her on the couch. She wraps her arms tightly around my shoulders, crying next to my ear. Her breaths are loud, shuddering sobs that take over her whole body and dampen my shirt.

"W-what are we going to do?" she stutters out. "What am I going to do now?"

My polished mother with her ironed slacks and pearl earrings—my no-nonsense mother, who has three different planners for any given day—my mother is asking *me* what to do. While she's breaking down, I'm the one holding it together. And I still don't know how to answer her questions.

I have no idea what to do now.

I hear the low hum of my dad's Mercedes, and I tilt my head, catching a glimpse of shadows moving outside. There are soft murmurs and then a muffled sob before a howl. Like a lost wolf crying to the moon, and I cringe as the sound reverberates through my body. The pain invades all of my senses.

With my mother still clinging to me, I'm afraid to move, but I want to see my father. I need something—someone— to help center myself in the middle of this chaos since Mom is lost. Dad raised Ray and me to have a stiff upper lip, and I'm not sure how to do that right now. I need guidance or... or someone to tell *me* it'll be okay.

I unclench my mom's fingers from around my hand as I see my dad retreating to his car. I run outside, waving him down. "Dad!"

He doesn't make a move to stop. Merely drops behind the wheel and takes off.

I bend over, my hands on my knees, out of breath.

"Cassandra, are you all right?" Officer Stone stands me up straight. "You look a little pale."

"Where's my dad going?"

"I don't know," he says. "People take this kind of news in all different ways. I tried to stop him, but..."

I face my house. The front door is open, all the lights on.

My mother's lying on the couch, her face pressed in toward the cushions.

"Your father mentioned Raymond's wife. I assume she was out of the house when we stopped over there before."

I blink a few times, trying to make my way through the fog that's taken up residence in my head. "She takes the girls to gymnastics some nights. I don't remember when... What day is it today?"

"Tuesday."

I nod. "That's probably where they were."

"Would you like us to go back over and talk to her?"

"Uh, yeah, I guess." I rub at the stinging in my eyes.

He assesses me with a squint. "Is there someone you can call to be with you?"

"I'll call my aunt."

"All right. We'll wait until someone gets here."

I head inside, pass Mom, and go to my room. The thread of the texts between me and Ray is up, and for a moment, I scroll back to his last message. **Come on, Cass, I've known you your whole life. I know you're not happy living there, move out.**

How can this be it? The end of the conversation. He's supposed to text me back, make fun of me for being such a child. I'd tell him I want to buy a motorcycle, and he'd send me the side-eye emoji. *This* cannot be how it ends.

I swallow down the urge to throw up and dial Aunt Joanie. She answers after a few rings.

"Hey, Cassie Cat."

It takes me a second to stutter out what I need to say, to even put the words in correct order. "Hi. I, uh, think you should come over."

"Now?" She laughs. "It's almost nine. Isn't your mother going to bed soon?"

My mom and Joanie are sisters but complete opposites. Where Mom is strict, Joanie is loose. Mom sips diet soda; Joanie gulps red wine. Mom's smile has to be earned; Joanie laughs all the time.

"Raymond's dead," I say.

"*What?*"

"My brother. He died. My brother is dead." The words tumble out of my mouth, but I don't believe them. I have to keep repeating them because they don't sound right. The voice is too quiet to be mine.

"Oh my god. I'm getting my shoes on now. I'll be over as soon as I can." She hangs up, and I stare at my phone, wondering what to do next.

So, I sit on my bed for a while, studying everything in my room with new eyes. The dirty clothes piled up on the floor, a T-shirt I sleep in that used to be Ray's. A poster of Harry Styles that I'm way too old to own and my brother makes fun of me for it all the time, even though he constantly sings his songs.

Sang.

He sang those songs.

I rub at the tightness in my chest. It's like I'm filled with cement, every breath difficult to find. Even my arms and legs are heavy as I push off the bed.

"There you are," Aunt Joanie says, rushing to me once I hit the top of the steps. Her normally red-painted lips are plain, and she's wearing sneakers. I'm not sure I've ever witnessed her in sneakers before.

Everything is upside down.

"Oh, honey. I can't believe this happened." She hugs me tightly. "Where's your dad?"

"Drove off somewhere."

She sniffles and holds me at arm's length, telling me,

"We'll get through this. We'll all get through this." Then she clasps my hand in hers and leads me into the living room, where Mom sits, her face free of tears and mascara. "I got her cleaned up a bit. Gave her a Xanax," Joanie whispers to me. "She needed to calm down."

She's certainly calm now, her eyes a million miles away. The only thing moving is her finger twitching on her leg. I wonder what's actually better—this robot version of Mom, or the wild, terrified Mom of a few minutes ago. I'm not sure. They're both unfamiliar to me.

"I'm going to call your grandparents," Aunt Joanie says, furiously typing on her phone. "This is going to kill them." She puts her phone to her ear, gazing over at my mother, then briefly at me before the floor. But I don't miss it, the look in Joanie's eyes. The look that says this has already killed my mother.

I turn away to the windows in the front of the house, where I see Officer Stone leaning on the police car. When I open the door, he tips his chin up to me.

"You're still here," I say, coming to stand in front of him.

"I am. Wanted to make sure your mom was receiving help and you were all right."

"That's nice of you," I mumble, feeling kinda bad about all the Defund the Police stuff I posted. "But my aunt's here now, so…"

He studies me for a long time. It's unnerving, and I glance away, unable to take his scrutiny as if he's waiting for me to break down like Mom or run away like Dad. I won't do either. I can't. It's physically impossible for me to do anything other than stand in shock, accepting each and every blow of this awful thing. It's beating me down, but I'm tethered to a pole, waiting for it to end.

"I know right now this is all new and confusing. It's terrible, but it won't always be that way." He offers a nod before settling into driver's seat of the police cruiser. Officer Kwon is already in the passenger seat. She couldn't handle this.

Funny, me neither.

I stay outside, sitting on the stoop in front of the door. It's cold out, cold enough for my breath to form clouds, but I don't mind. It's nice, a respite from the overwhelmingly warm house. With no idea where my dad is, and my mom gone from completely distraught to weirdly still, I'm not sure what any of this means. Where do we go from here?

I don't have to think about the question long, because in a matter of what seems like minutes, the house fills with people. My octogenarian grandparents arrive with a flourish, my grandmother fainting when she hears the news. My grandfather lets out a string of curses like I've never heard before. A few of my mom's friends show up, making sure she drinks water and eats crackers. One of them even empties the dishwasher and cleans the already-clean kitchen. Another one of them calls a relative who's a funeral director and, as a favor, will be over first thing tomorrow morning. They say my mother won't have to worry about anything.

My closest friend from college lives across the country in Oregon, and we haven't spoken in a while, so I don't have anyone to force me to eat or rub my back. I'm not great with keeping up relationships, especially those from my home-town. Raymond says I don't let anyone get close because I'm afraid to show them my real self. I think he's projecting.

Was projecting.

Was.

Stomaching the gut-wrenching pain is hard enough, but trying to learn the grammar of death is cruel and unusual punishment. I'd rather throw out the English language entirely than try to learn this new version.

Dad eventually shows up, and my earlier disappointment of his leaving morphs to relief now that he's here. We're all present and accounted for—the three of us, at least. He hugs Mom for almost a minute. I know because I time it from my seat on the floor in the corner of the living room.

No one bothers me.

I watch the flurry of action like a movie, some people I know, some I don't. All of them whispering or crying about how terrible this is, how heartbroken they are for my parents.

This is terrible. This is heartbreaking. For me too.

My only sibling is gone. My older brother and first friend has died. And it's as if a piece of me is dead too, but I don't dare say this out loud. I'm almost afraid to think it because being Raymond's sister is so deeply ingrained in the person I am. What am I without that title? Without him?

I slip away to my room in the basement, once more taking some time to admire the pictures on the wall. Raymond in all these photos, with his perfectly aligned teeth, golden skin, and just-this-side-of-wild sandy hair, oozes charm. But there aren't any more pictures to be taken. This is all that is left of him.

CHAPTER 2

After a sleepless night of walking laps around the living room and kitchen—and checking on my mom in my parents' bed and my dad in the office—I shower and change into fresh clothes before the sun is even up. I open the front door, watching the sky above our suburban neighborhood bleed from black to yellow to, eventually, a bright, sunny blue. A new day. A new life.

I hate it. I want my old life. I'd take hurricanes and tornadoes every day if it meant I could have Raymond back.

Listening for any movement from my parents, I force myself to eat half a piece of toast, though it may as well be dirt in my mouth.

Finally, my father stalks into the kitchen, acknowledging me for the first time since yesterday morning. His brown eyes, the ones my brother and I share, are red-rimmed, but he's dressed for work.

"Where are you going?" I ask.

"I've got a lot to do, a lot to handle with death, paper-work that needs to be completed," he says matter-of-factly, like he's talking about one of his business transactions and not Raymond. "Why did the police come here last night?"

The question is harsh, more of an accusation.

I shrug.

"Why would this address be listed, with your mother as his emergency contact and not Shayna?"

I scratch at a divot in the kitchen table. I know why Shayna wasn't my brother's emergency contact. But I don't think I should tell. Even now, after his death.

Ray had divorce papers drawn up. He and Shayna had been separated for the last couple of months, and he'd been sleeping in the basement. He'd even been in a relationship with another woman. And I had to keep it a secret until he found the right time to tell everyone.

My father raises his eyebrows, waiting for an answer, but I won't tell him the truth. I have no particular reason to be my brother's secret-keeper anymore. It just feels wrong to say anything.

"I don't know," I lie.

Dad breathes out deeply and runs his hand over his neck. "I'm going to the bank and then to run some errands."

"Seriously?" I clench my fists. "Do you have to?"

"Yes, Cassandra. I'm Raymond's father. I need to take care of some things."

Like my relationship with my mother, my relationship with my father is strained, but not in the same way. My mom hoped I'd be different, more outgoing, wear more pastel, be more ladylike. She pushed me, while my father avoided me. He had his son, his firstborn, so I was of no use to him, I supposed. We're oil and water, and he doesn't know what to do with me and my *Jesus was a Socialist* T-shirt.

He pockets his keys and is out the door before I can even

ask him to stay, and once again, I'm alone. I check my phone. My social media is lit up with notifications.

It's not even eight o'clock in the morning, the workday hasn't begun, but the local newspaper has run an article on the death of the beloved middle school teacher and high school baseball coach, Raymond St. George.

I have trouble breathing. The cement is back. This time, it fills up my rib cage, sticking to my bones and muscles. I fear I'll snap in half with every breath as I thumb through the posts. Word has traveled fast.

I don't know how time continuums work, but I think I've slipped into one. I've stopped moving, but the world hasn't stopped spinning, and I've somehow fallen backward. I relive last night over and over with every word I read in the article, with every picture and status posted about my brother, *RIP*s and lyrics from his favorite Bruce Springsteen songs. People I haven't heard from in years are tagging me in their heartfelt condolences, as if they know me, as if they know my brother.

Knew.

Knew my brother.

They don't. I'm the only one who knew his stupid grin covered his insecurities about not being the best at everything, that he was absolutely terrified of spiders, and his Mr. Perfect thing was all an act.

I hate every one of them on my social media.

My head aches, and I lay my temple down on the table. It cools my forehead. I close my eyes; maybe it's all a dream. I hope to fall asleep and wake up to a day Ray is still alive.

But then my phone vibrates with reality, Shayna's name on the screen. I can count on my hands the number of times we've spoken on the phone, and I consider not answering because I don't want to talk about what I know we will.

Instead, I cradle my head in my hand and answer with a shaky, "Hello?"

"I've been up all night," she says in place of a greeting.

"Me too."

"The police officer said they went to your house last night too." Her voice shakes on the last syllable.

"Mm-hmm."

"I can't believe RJ is gone."

Her use of the nickname makes me cringe. It's so impersonal, especially at a moment like this. His family—me, Mom, and Dad—calls him Ray or Raymond. His friends, and his legions of fans, call him RJ. He much preferred that name, too cool for a name like Raymond.

"When he didn't come home last night, I figured he was off with that girl he's been sleeping with."

This catches my attention. "You know about her?"

"Of course I know." She sniffs. "I'm not stupid, and your brother isn't as slick as he thinks he is."

I slouch in my chair, afraid to say anything, and we lapse into silence.

So many questions with no answers.

"What am I going to tell the girls?" Shayna asks after a while.

The girls, Lara and Lucy, my twin four-year-old nieces, two miniature versions of Shayna with big blond curls and my brother's brown eyes. My brown eyes. I've never been close to them, but thinking about their futures without their dad makes my heart sink. They don't deserve this. Neither does Shayna.

"What am I going to tell everyone? What are they going to think?" Shayna asks, falling apart. We have nothing in common, save one thing: Raymond. I don't know how to comfort her. We're not friends, but speaking with her is different now. Like we're both in some kind of club...even though I'd really rather not have *this* kind of sisterhood with her. "The last time we spoke, it was a fight," she confesses quietly. "I don't even remember what it was about."

"I'm sure he didn't care," I say after a long pause.

She huffs. "You don't know what this is like for me."

She's right. I have no idea what she's going through, and I bite the inside of my lip to the point of pain to allow myself that much, at least. In the face of so much loss experienced by my parents and Shayna, I can't compare mine to theirs. He was my brother and friend, who gave me nothing other than a couple of black-and-blue marks and more laughs than I can remember. There is nothing left unsaid or incomplete between us. I can't be upset about the life I won't have with him anymore, not like they can. I have no claim to him like mother or wife. I'm only his sister.

"What do we do for the funeral?" I ask. "Did you guys, um, have plans or something? Some people from a funeral home are coming over today. Can you be here?"

"God, Cass." Those two words are not unfamiliar to me and are usually accompanied by an eye roll. She snorts in that superior way—even now, in the middle of this mess— as if I'm not saying the right things.

I know I'm not.

"We didn't have plans...for that. And I can't," she says with a sniffle. "I can't be there. I have no one to watch the girls, and I have to explain this to them somehow. I'm already overwhelmed." That last sentence is barely audible. "I won't be any help to you today, but you can handle it, right?"

"Uh. Yeah. Right." I rub at my breastbone, but the tightness doesn't go away. "Well, I guess I'll let you go."

She squeaks out a few words I don't understand as she cries.

"I'll talk to you later, Shayna," I say and quickly hang up, realizing how wholly unequipped I am to deal with all of this.

By the time I leave the kitchen, two of my mom's friends are back, already making themselves busy. They tell me they're here to help. Aunt Joanie is upstairs helping my mom shower and change, while the friends go about cooking and doing laundry. It's helpful to have them here, I guess. Otherwise, I'd be dealing with my comatose mother alone. But no matter who comes in through the door, no matter how many Tupperware meals are shoved into the freezer, they can't make this better or normal. This isn't supposed to be.

None of this is as it should be.

At about nine o'clock in the morning, after I've aimlessly flipped through every television channel in my parents' cable subscription, two men show up at the door. They're both in suits and, from their physical similarities, obviously related. I don't recognize the older man, but I recognize the younger one.

He's the boy I used to love when I was a girl who had nothing but dreams in her head and hearts in her eyes.

That girl is dead like her brother. But this boy... He's very much alive.

Like Ray, Vince was three years older than me. His hair was always adorably shaggy and often stuck out from under a baseball cap. He usually hung out at our house on Fridays and played video games with Ray while I made up reasons to be around them.

Standing in front of me now, he still has the same dark hair with a cowlick and gently assessing eyes.

"Hi, I'm Robert Mancini from Mancini Funeral Home," the gray-haired man says, his wire-rimmed glasses perched on a big nose. "This is my son, Vincent."

He leans into me. "Hey, Cass. I'm not sure if you remember me."

I blink. Vince is older and slighter broader than I remember, but, "Yeah, yeah, of course I do."

He nods, his lips turned down. My brother and Vince were best friends for years. They played baseball together through high school, and with his hunched shoulders, Vince seems to be taking the loss pretty hard too.

"I'm so sorry to hear about your brother," Mr. Mancini tells me. "My sister-in-law is friends with your mother, and she asked me to meet with you. I couldn't believe it when she called me."

"Thanks for coming over," I say and lead them to the dining room we never use with expensive cream-colored chairs and a dark wooden table. As I sit across from them, my throat tightens. "I'm not sure about what to do with..."

Mr. Mancini smiles sadly and squeezes my hands that are folded together on top of the table. "Don't worry. We'll walk you through this. Are your parents here?"

"My dad's out, and my mom is...upstairs."

"It's okay," he says, understanding we won't be seeing either of them anytime soon, and opens a folder with a notebook in it to begin whatever it is we're going to do.

I want to stop him, shout, and rip the folder away. I don't want to deal with this, with any of this, with or without my parents. But if I have to be here, my parents should be here too. Why do I have to do it alone?

The cement in my chest hardens from resentment, and my skin is tight enough to explode into a million pieces with my next breath.

Vince moves around to my side of the table and takes a seat next to me. "Hey," he murmurs close to my ear, his shoulder brushing mine. "I know how close you were. We're here to help you any way we can."

I swallow down the lump in my throat and look Vince in the eyes. They're a light hazel, a stark contrast to his tall build and prominent nose. "Thanks."

Mr. Mancini spreads out papers on the table with different colors and fonts. "It's hard to plan anyone's funeral, but I can imagine this is especially difficult for you and your family. If at any time you want a break, let me know."

I lay my hands flat on the table. May as well stick a knife through them. It would be less painful.

"We'll start with the program," Mr. Mancini says, and he leads me through an hour-long process of deciding how to bury my thirty-year-old brother. We discuss songs, pictures, poems, prayers, and eulogies. Whenever there's a question I can't answer, Vince offers advice and nudges me along. At one point, he tells me there is no right answer and I should do what I think is best because that's what Ray would do if the roles were reversed.

This makes me laugh. If the roles were reversed, I'm not sure Ray would be sitting here. He was always useless when it came to planning anything, worse than me. He once tried to plan a surprise party for Shayna and never made up an excuse for her to come home from her shopping trip, so by the time she arrived, the pizza was cold and all the guests had left. I ate the birthday cake in silence while they argued over who ruined the party.

"Now," Mr. Mancini starts, opening his planner, "do you have a time when you can come in to finalize everything?"

I pick at my thumbnail and begin to answer *once again* "I

don't know," but my dad walks in the front door. He stops when he sees the Mancinis sitting with me.

"Can I help you?" he asks with a furrowed brow.

Mr. Mancini stands and introduces himself, including, "Our sons played baseball together in high school."

"Right, yes, sorry," Dad says, although he still seems clueless as to who they are. My parents weren't exactly the type to know our friends or our friends' parents.

When Mr. Mancini begins to summarize everything we talked about, my dad holds his hand up. "I'm sure you've got it under control. Let me know what the bottom line is."

I roll my eyes. *The bottom line is I need help planning how to bury your son*, I don't say.

"I was about to ask when you can come in to finalize the last couple decisions about the casket and such."

My dad scrubs at his chin. "My week is pretty full, I'm sure you understand. I'll leave it to my wife and daughter."

"Dad, I think—"

He shakes his head and brushes by me on the way to the kitchen, leaving me slack-jawed. I press the heels of my hands into my eyes as my skin flushes hot.

"I'm going to leave my card here. You call me when you're ready, after you've talked to your mom. We'll figure the rest out later."

I silently agree to Mr. Mancini's calm and tender-voiced instructions, my hands still covering my face. A few seconds pass before I stand up from the table, opening my eyes. Mr. Mancini is gone, but Vince is still here, next to me.

"Okay?" he asks, his hands in his coat pockets. When I shrug, his head bobs up and down. "Yeah, it sucks. Every time, it sucks, but this one hurts a bit more. He was my good buddy."

I can't begin to process my own grief, and witnessing someone else's, like Vince's watery eyes, showers me with guilt. Like I'm doing a bad job of having a dead brother.

He walks with me to the front door, saying, "I know this is hard, but I'll do whatever I can to help you."

It's meant to be kind, but his offer bubbles up a pathetic whine in me. I can't do any of this. I don't want to do any of this. I'm sad, angry, and a tragic mess. "I just want everything to go back the way it was."

"I understand that," he says, as a car rumbles outside. I glance out of the window, where Mr. Mancini is in an old Chevy, one of those cars that is more boat than automobile. Vince bumps his elbow into mine. "My card's on the table too. I wrote my cell number on it."

He gives my arm a squeeze before he opens the door, and a long-ago memory infiltrates my mind. One of him squeezing my arm in the same way, but as we stood outside of the auditorium during the homecoming dance. He was on the court, and I had my heart broken by a boy I can barely remember anymore. Vince told me I looked pretty in my dress and to keep my chin up. Then he walked off with Britney Benson.

It was the last dance I ever attended at school.

Now, I follow him outside. "No hearse?"

"Huh?" He turns, and I gesture with my chin toward his father's car.

"Don't you undertakers all drive hearses?"

The corner of his mouth hooks up in a familiar way that makes me thaw for the first time in what feels like years. "I really prefer funeral director, and we only take the hearse out for special occasions."

"Like first dates and birthdays?"

"Exactly."

I smile, setting aside the fact that he basically held my hand as I discussed my brother's obituary. Vince is almost exactly as I remember him—and nothing like I'd expect a guy who hangs out with dead people to be. Then he waves and hops in the big boat of a car that isn't a hearse, and I head back inside to the house haunted by my brother.

FEBRUARY 15

I never thought I would ever have to write these words, much less think them, but Raymond St. George @Saint-R.J.George passed away last night. It was sudden, and we're still unaware of the cause, but what we do know is how much we will miss him. I know how much everyone loved my brother from all of the well wishes and posts about him, and even though I won't be able to respond to all, I am reading them. For those of you asking, I'll be posting more information about the funeral as I have it.

My family is stumbling to take our first steps without Ray, and I'm not sure how long it will be before our brokenness heals, if ever. This is all so unreal, a bad dream I'm waiting to wake up from. I've been pinching myself, but the reality is, Ray's gone, and it's almost too much to bear. I'd love to have something poetic to say about the fragility of life or about appreciating Raymond for his existence, but I'm far too petty for that. We were supposed to go to trivia Thursday night, and I'm angry about it. I've lost my brother and playmate, constant friend and sometimes foe. He was my light, and I was his shadow. And I'm lost without him.

If you're the praying type, my family will take them. If you have good energy, send it our way. We will need all the support we can get in the coming days. Thank you for the peace and love.

#Grief #RaymondStGeorge

CHAPTER 3

With all the new requests to follow me on social media, I think this must be what it's like for the families of famous people when they die. All of a sudden, everyone's interested and dying—figuratively—for a piece of the macabre glow. Gross.

I assumed I would be consoled by the outpouring, but the connection to the digital world isn't real. The avatars and likes and shares, it's all insincere. I cringe at the link to a YouTube video of Bette Midler's "Wind Beneath My Wings" someone from high school posted and tagged me in. She calls my brother the wind beneath her wings. Whoever Beth Ann Creedy is, she clearly needs attention.

In the past few years, I'd built up my social media following, weaving whatever kind of friendship could be formed over a mutual love of reality television and prickly sarcasm. Now, though, with a dead brother…I'm suddenly more popular. What a life hack. Somebody dies, earn a whole bunch of followers.

Compelled to say something to my new public, I type up

a quick post thanking everyone for their support and well wishes. I refrain from adding *except Beth Ann Creedy.*

It sets off another round of alerts for comments and likes and even more requests. It's overwhelming, and I ignore them, including one from my ex-best friend, Jaya.

We'd broken up during senior year of high school because of her dumbass boyfriend. He was a jerk, and I told her so, maybe in not such nice words, but it still came from my heart. Jaya didn't see it that way. I graduated high school without a best friend. She's now married to the jerk.

She reached out to me when she got pregnant to invite me to her baby shower. A way to mend the fence, I guess, but I was living in the city and made up some excuse not to go. I could've...but I didn't want to. We'd gone in different directions, and our lives felt incompatible with each other. Plus, I'm not great at making conversation, and I hate games, especially when they involve baby things. Although, the pictures she posts of that little girl are cute. Thank god she didn't inherit her father's hairline.

If it hadn't been for our bad history ten years ago, maybe I'd call her now and tell her how shitty this all is. She'd probably say something soothing and maternal because that's the type of person she was, and I'd be mollified. But instead, I have nothing to say.

I hate that my brother is right...was right. I *do* push people away.

Ray would make comments all the time about me being the Tin Man or something. He'd joke that I had a black heart, which was why I always wore so much black. But he wasn't *that* great either. He was cocky and not in the funny kind of way. He liked to be the center of attention and never apologized for *anything*. Even if it was his fault.

But what did I care? What did anybody care? We loved

him just the same for being Mr. Perfect. He was my big brother, I was the little sister, and I played my role, worshipping him with adoration while challenging him whenever I could.

Still, I moved away to find out who I was outside of Ray's sister. I started reading and writing because he was the athletic, outgoing one. Making up stories was my thing. He might have been good at parties, but I was good at school, at writing columns for the school newspaper, extra credit work in English, tutoring other kids, and taking AP courses. I went to Columbia, graduated magna cum laude, and where did it all get me? The basement of my parents' house.

Back to being Raymond's little sister.

My phone buzzes, startling me out of my bitter thoughts. Gary's name is on the screen, the assistant manager at Sassie's.

Work. I'd completely forgotten.

"Hi," I answer, anticipating why he's calling me at three o'clock in the afternoon. "I forgot I had to work today. I'm sorry."

"You're sorry?" he nearly shouts, and I rub at my tired eyes. Gary's actually a year or two younger than me, but he loves to play up his boss role. "You were supposed to be here an hour ago."

"I know. I'm sorry, I—"

"Cass, you better get here now. After the conversation we had the other day about you needing shifts, all of a sudden, you're not gonna show up or even let us know you're not?"

It's easy to slip into bitch mode. Hit that downshift immediately. "Well, no, Gary, I'm not gonna show up, and it slipped my mind to call you while I'm dealing with the sudden death of my brother. I guess you didn't hear the news."

He stutters. He knew my brother. Everybody in this town did. Raymond was the goddamn unofficial mayor.

"Oh Jesus, Cass. I didn't know. I'm sorry. I don't know what to say."

"Join the club," I snap.

"I'll have your shifts covered for the week. But let me know...about things, okay?"

"Yeah, sure." I hang up, and it strikes me again how everyone else is living their lives, people are working, going out to eat, hitting on women in kilts with ridiculous catcalls, but my brother isn't. He won't ever do anything again.

He won't breathe. He won't blink his eyes. He won't feel the rain on his skin or open his mouth to speak. He won't hear music or smell Mom's terrible vinegar cleaning solution. He won't sling his arm around my shoulders or point at me with a stupid wink while belting out "Thunder Road." He won't ever answer my texts by calling me or shake his head at me when I refuse his invitation to watch the new superhero movie out at midnight. As if I'd suddenly change my mind about them.

I don't care about the Avengers or buildings blowing up.

But he did. And I would see those movies one hundred times over with him. I'd do anything if...

My throat closes like I've eaten shellfish.

Ray always got annoyed we couldn't eat out or order in from anywhere with shellfish. Every year when his birthday rolled around, he always asked to go to Red Lobster, but Mom and Dad would deny him because I couldn't go. He'd pout, and they'd buy him an extra slice of cake or an ice cream sundae.

My shellfish allergy never killed me.

Ray didn't even have an allergy.

And I hate him for dying all over again. I hate him because I love him.

The whirl of emotion steals my breath, and I bend over, dropping my head between my knees. It's a while before I'm not so dizzy, and I head upstairs, finding flowers and baskets clogging up every corner of the house. Aunt Joanie's paging through some celebrity gossip magazine on the sofa in the living room, and I sit next to her. She offers me a doleful smile and pets my hair, answering a question I don't ask.

"Your mom is sleeping. Your dad is out," she says pointedly. "And Nana's at church lighting candles." She sighs, and I rest my head on her shoulder. The two of us were always kindred spirits. "Did you eat today?" she asks.

I nod, lying, afraid if I speak the words, she'll figure me out. I don't have an appetite lately.

"How did it go this morning with the funeral director?"

Sitting upright, I shrug. "Okay... I picked a program with, like, a watercolor of a sky and rainbow, and we made a schedule for the service." I pause, gnawing at my bottom lip as I recall the way my dad acted, stonewalling Mr. Mancini, passing everything off to me. I want to talk to Joanie about it, but it's too much like tattletale-ing, so I don't. "I actually know them, or one of them, I mean. Vince was in Ray's grade. They used to be really good friends."

"Oh yeah?" She glances at me before flipping a page in the magazine, and I nod, staring up at the corner of the ceiling, picturing a different time.

"He was the catcher."

"Who? Raymond?"

"No, Vince. I remember he and Ray had this handshake they did before games." I smile at the memory. "Sometimes he'd come over and hang out, and he'd always ask me what new book I was reading. Some of Ray's other friends were...

you know how high school boys are, but not Vince." I exhale deeply, back to the present. "Guess he works for his dad now." I brush my bangs—the bangs my mother hates—to the side and look over to Aunt Joanie, who has her lips pursed. One single wrinkle between her eyebrows.

"What?"

"Nothing," she says after a beat, her questioning mouth and wrinkle gone.

"I still have to go there to pick the casket and stuff." I pull the sleeves of my sweatshirt over my hands and cross my arms as exhaustion slackens my body. I relax against the pillows. "It was too much for me to do it all at once."

She closes the magazine and rubs my knee gently. "You shouldn't have to do all this by yourself."

"Well, Mom isn't..." I trail off. She isn't in the land of the living either. "And Dad hasn't been around." I imagine losing a child might be the worst thing a person can go through, so I can't blame my parents for their reactions to my brother's death.

Can I?

Aunt Joanie's eyes well up, and I close my own eyes, not willing to succumb to the pain of it all. I lean my head back on the couch, although before I can get too comfortable, the house phone rings. I always teased my mother for having a house phone, but I guess it serves a purpose when people die.

"Sit there. I'll answer it," Joanie says and stands to cross the room. I pull my feet up under me and roll sideways into the fetal position as my aunt tells the person on the other line, "It's fine with me, but you'll have to stay in a hotel... Uh-huh, call me. I'll give you my cell phone number."

She's pacing barefoot back and forth along the gray-and-cream patterned rug, and her long hair is up in a ponytail.

She still looks good, even though I assume she's gotten no rest being here, sleeping next to my mom upstairs. I'd heard her tell my mom she'll stay here as long as she needs it, but I can't imagine it's true. She's some bigwig in the medical network, something about marketing and outreach. I was never real interested in her job, more her makeup and wardrobe. Joanie's the one who turned me on to my signature Russian Red lipstick and liquid eyeliner.

As upset as I am that it's Aunt Joanie who sits down and pulls my feet into her lap, I try to be understanding of why my own mother can't be bothered to check on me. I understand that her son is gone, but he's not her only baby. I'm her baby too. And I need my mom, no matter what our relationship lacks in the friendship department.

"That was your aunt Barbara," Joanie says, referring to my dad's sister. "She and David will be coming down tomorrow."

David is my father's estranged brother, and my gut clenches at the possibility of family drama.

More drama. Exactly what we need.

Aunt Joanie rubs my feet. "I'll take care of them. You take care of you."

I clear my throat of the few pebbles there and turn on the television, hoping to shut my mind off for a few hours, and find the Game Show Network. *Press Your Luck* is on. It's not *Price is Right*, but it'll do.

I close my eyes and sleep. Not quite soundly, but not fitfully either. Because of a warm embrace there, a surrounding mix of amber and green. And, somehow, in my dreamland, I know it'll be okay.

CHAPTER 4

*D*eath makes people really popular. It also makes a lot of people argue and *miraculously* lose weight. In the forty-eight hours since I found out my brother died, my clothes are already loose on me.

I laugh morosely at myself as I easily button my previously tight jeans and head upstairs to snag a chocolate-covered pretzel from the new gift basket that arrived earlier today. I think it's the first thing I've eaten since yesterday morning. The house is full again, with my aunts and uncles, cousins, and their kids. My mom is awake, and kind of alive-looking, reading sympathy cards sent to the family as my dad breathes noisily through his nose, his eyes on his brother.

I slump into a chair at the dining room table next to Eileen, my cousin, who's feeding her baby, and she regards me with wet eyes. We haven't seen each other in person in a lot of years since our fathers started feuding, but she's my age and nice, I guess. Of what I remember from some long-ago summer days together.

"You need to stay here is what you need to do," Uncle David says, his hand on my dad's shoulder.

"I need to go out." My father breaks away from him, almost violently. "I found a burial plot. I want to get it taken care of. One less thing," he says, then turns his attention on me. "I'm buying plots for your mother and me next to your brother. Do you want one?"

My breath seizes, and I cough on a piece of pretzel caught in my throat.

"Stephen!" someone cries out, but it doesn't stop my dad from leaning over the dining table toward me. He's clearly preoccupied with this burial plot, and when I can only stutter out a few nonsense syllables, he furrows his eyebrows like he can't understand why I don't have an answer. I can barely process my brother's death, let alone my own.

I look to my mother, who has her face in her hands. Aunt Joanie is rubbing her back, shooting daggers at the side of my father's face. Uncle David is the one to come to my aid. "You can't expect her to make that decision right now."

"Fine," Dad snarls, pushing off the table. He snatches his coat, keys, and wallet like they're weapons. "Fine!"

The door slams behind him, and all eyes fix on me. I force myself to joke. "Must be prime real estate."

My family all sighs in unison, and I break the pretzel up into crumbs. A glass of red wine slides in front of me, and I glance over at another cousin, Mitch. I nod at him gratefully and chug it down. I don't have time for dainty sips. I hold out my hand for the wine bottle, and it's given to me, no questions asked.

Another perk of death.

"Hey, Cassie, how are you?" Aunt Barb sits across from

me, her head cocked to the side. The sad faces are really a little too much. I'd much rather they talk to me as usual.

"I'm fine."

"I think your dad's having a hard time with all of this."

"Okay." I sniff derisively. "I'm having a hard time. We're all having a hard time. Doesn't mean we're all acting like assholes."

Aunt Barb's eyes widen, scandalized. "It's just that—"

"It's just that he doesn't need to act like that," Uncle David interjects, ambling over to the table. Aunt Joanie follows, stealing a sip of wine from my glass.

I'm in the middle of everyone, holding court, like some medieval melancholy tableau. They all begin to talk, voices at an odd whisper as if they'll disturb my mother as she stares at my brother's picture, holding an old, ragged teddy bear. Their eyes constantly cut to me as if waiting for a meltdown. They're here to comfort in the time of need, but there are no words or hugs to help. Nothing they say or do will make any of this better, and in trying to, they're proving how isolating this whole thing is. Even surrounded by family, I'm completely alone in my grief.

Silently standing, I swipe the bottle of wine and head downstairs to my room. I find the business card Vince left for me and type out a text message to him.

Hey, it's Cass. Can I come by tomorrow to do whatever we have to? I need out of this house.

He answers within a minute. **Of course. How about ten tomorrow morning? You know how to get here?**

Sure. I'll look for the mansion with all the dead people.

We don't keep them outside. What kind of operation do you think we're running?

I genuinely smile at his reply, and my fingers pick up

speed, my body recalling what it's like not to drown in misery. **I have no idea. I don't usually hang out with undertakers. Should I bring garlic to ward off the zombies?**

That only works on vampires.

Whatever, I text along with a zombie emoji.

I lean back against the pillows on my bed, attempting to come up with another witty message, but I can't. I'm stuck on the zombies.

I've never known anyone who died, not *really* known them anyway. Dad's parents both passed away when I was younger, and I don't remember them all that well because they lived in another state. Even if I'd had experience with funerals and death, I wouldn't know how to act. It's not like we show a lot of emotion in my WASP-y family.

Because of my inability to "grow up" like my mother always wanted me to, my parents sort of left me to relish my immaturity, my daydreams, and nonsense jobs. Ironic since the thing forcing me to take one giant leap into full-on adulthood is the death of my brother, the mature one. He's the father and teacher, the good-deed-doer. The favorite.

Not like me. I'm not any of those things. I don't know how to be an adult.

I don't even know how to ward off zombies. And isn't that something an adult should know?

CHAPTER 5

I thought all funeral homes were big, old Victorian houses, but the Mancini Funeral Home is a newer white stone and brick building with white pillars in the front. I drive through a portico to a lot on the side where a few cars are parked.

Stepping out of my car, I zip up my coat, taking in the quiet. There are no chirping birds, wind, or cars, as if the immediate environment knows it needs to be silent here, but as I walk to the door, my thick-soled boots land heavily on the macadam, and I cringe. I make even more noise when I open the creaky door, directly interrupting some kind of service as a dozen heads swivel back to me.

I immediately apologize with my hands up and duck back outside, letting the door slam behind me. My face heats with embarrassment. I don't know the etiquette for being in a place like this, but it's obvious I'm breaking it. I shake my head and breathe deeply a few times, suffocated by inexperience and stupidity.

How can I do this for my brother? I don't even know how to get into the damn building.

The door opens again, and Vince pokes his head out, spotting me before stepping outside, gently closing the door behind him.

"I'm so sorry," I say, waving frantically.

He stills my hand between both of his. "It's fine."

"I didn't mean to interrupt. I thought this was another entrance."

"It's fine, really," he says again and lets go of my hand, but I wish he didn't, needing something to cling to. "Come on, we'll go through the front door."

He escorts me around the building, and even with my thick parka on, I feel his hand between my shoulder blades. I reflexively lean into his side as we enter through the double doors beneath the shadow of the pillars, and he ushers me in ahead of him, pointing to the right. "We'll go to my office in the back."

The scent of flowers and antiseptic hits my nose as I shuffle through the lobby area, and I dip my chin down, attempting to cover my nose as I breathe through my mouth. Vince turns in time to catch me wincing at the smell.

"You get used to it after a while," he says, reading my mind, and leads me down a short hallway to what is apparently his office. It's plain beige with no real decorations besides an old black-and-white photo of three men standing in front of exactly what I imagine a funeral home to look like, a tall, slender home with a porch and thick railing. Creepy, almost. It appears to be from the turn of the last century.

"Have a seat," Vince says.

I do and gesture to the photo. "That's what I pictured. Not this."

"Hmm?" He follows my gaze over his shoulder. "Oh.

That's my great-grandfather and his brothers. It was the first funeral home in town."

I raise my eyebrow at him for more of an explanation.

"Funerals were always done in people's houses. The family would take care of the body and host the service right there. It's where the term funeral parlor comes from. It wasn't really until the twentieth century that funeral homes, as we know them, became popular."

I open my mouth to ask him about the family business, but my attention slants to a furry white head that pops up next to Vince on the other side of the desk. I move closer as the dog tilts its head at me, considering me for a few moments before moving so I can fully see it.

"This is Gracie," Vinces says, running a hand down the dog's back, her thin tail wagging in response. "She comes to work me with a lot of days." Gracie twirls as if she knows what he's saying. "We're pretty attached."

I smile at the two of them, and when Vince looks over at me after a few moments, his golden skin flushes like I've caught him naked in bed. "Go say hi to Cass. Go on."

I hold my hand out to the dog, and she slowly walks to me, first sniffing my fingers then my shoes. "She's pretty," I say, petting her neck, covered in short hair. "What breed is she?"

He leans back in his chair. "Lab mix, I think. She was a stray. They found her with a litter of nine puppies."

"Nine babies?" I ask Gracie, eyes wide. "You were busy, huh?"

She rests her head in my lap, and I relax with her weight on me, my anxiety about being here washing away with each of her calm breaths.

Vince watches me for a moment, and I would normally

find that kind of blatant staring off-putting, but there is something about Vince in his assessment of me that's gentle. That always has been.

His eyes aren't filled with the usual sympathy I've experienced lately. It's something more like interest, as if I'm a painting to be studied and admired. I haven't showered and am light-years away from feeling beautiful, yet sitting across from Vince makes me want to be worthy of his gaze.

He leans forward, skimming his finger over his cheek a few times. "So, how are you?"

I huff out a depressed laugh. "I'm not sure how I'm supposed to answer. Everyone keeps asking me." I chew on my lip, actually contemplating the question for the first time in days. "I think they're asking me for themselves. Like they want to know everything is fine so they can go back to normal again."

He shrugs. "Probably."

I wrinkle my nose. "You know, you're not real great at making people feel better."

He raises his thick brows, but his shock melts to a cheeky grin that, for a second, has me forgetting what I'm doing here. There was a reason he was voted Best Smile in high school. "I don't make you feel better?"

And then I remember I'm here because my brother died. "Not about this whole...death thing. Isn't this your job? To make people like me feel better?"

He shifts in his chair, settling back into the exact same position he was in, and I find it oddly soothing I can make him uncomfortable. After a while of what seems like serious thinking, he tells me, "I don't think anyone can necessarily make someone grieving feel better. But it's my job to make their life a little easier in a tough season. I can take care of a lot of things people don't even think about when this time arrives."

I bite the inside of my cheek and look down to Gracie, who lies at my feet.

"How can I make your life easier?"

I have a hard time meeting his gaze. "Is it going to get easier?"

Decades of silence pass, and when I finally lift my head, Vince's eyes are a little red. He clears his throat. "I've never been in your position, but I've seen other people in similar places, and it gets easier. At least, that's what I'm told." He holds a pen between his index and middle fingers, tapping the cap a few times on the desk. "And for the record, there is no right or wrong way to do this. I think you're doing a fine job."

I snort. "That's funny because it feels all wrong. Like everything is wrong." When he doesn't say anything, I push my hair back off my forehead and straighten my shoulders. "So, what's next? What do we do now?"

He aims the pen at me. "You said you needed out of your house, right? How about we take Gracie for a walk? We can figure all the rest out after."

Gracie's ears perk up at the word "walk," and I nod. He grabs a purple-and-pink polka dot leash, clips it on Gracie's collar, and leads us out into the hallway, toward another back door.

With Vince walking next to me and Gracie panting happily between us, it's not so quiet outside anymore, and the sounds, as small as they are, keep me company. I'm not alone with them by my side.

"Gracie's kind of like a therapy dog, huh?" I ask when we reach the end of the sidewalk.

"Not officially, but yeah, she makes people smile when

they come into my office…unless they're allergic. Then it's not great," he says with a smile my way.

From the first moment I'd met Vince when I was twelve years old, I'd been lost to him. Always smiling and affable, he had an easygoing charm, and I would have died—not literally—to be able to spend time with him like this. Now, though, I'm just happy to have someone to talk to.

Overcome with the urge to finally be honest with myself, I blurt out, "I haven't cried. Like, at all. Everyone else around me is, but I…can't."

Vince shrugs. "Everyone reacts differently. Some people cry, some don't."

"But…does it make me a monster?"

He huffs and switches the leash to his other hand so he can tap his index finger to my temple. "It's your brain protecting you. A lot of times when people experience trauma, emotional or physical, their brains disconnect from their bodies to protect them from harm. They detach, like when people talk about an out-of-body experience, it's real. Your brain is protecting you. It's science."

I mull this over. It's logical, but I don't feel any less the Tin Man my brother called me.

The three of us settle into an easy pace that keeps my blood warm on this cold day. It's refreshing being outside. Vince doesn't ask me any more questions or force me to talk, and I find it easier to breathe as he tells me about the obedience class he took Gracie to when he first adopted her and how she sat down, refusing to follow any instruction. Not even for a treat.

I don't have to think about the eulogy I haven't written yet, or that my house has been invaded by people I haven't seen in years, suddenly interested in every detail of our lives, or reflect on the sad reality we all now live in. For this short reprieve, none of that is true, and I'm purely on a walk with a cute guy and his dog.

But it can't last forever, and after a few blocks, we turn around to head back to his office, where we finalize the last, agonizing details of how my brother will be put into the ground at the end of the week to become worm food. With Vince sitting next to me instead of on the other side of his desk, it's easier, but I'm nauseous as images of rotting corpses invade my brain, and I suddenly want to throw up. Vince clearly picks up on this because he offers me a bottle of water and rubs my back in soft circles.

"There's one more thing," he hedges, and I swallow two cold gulps of water before meeting his gaze. "You'll need to pick out an outfit for RJ to be buried in."

The idea of completing this errand is sickening, but the use of his initials makes it feel like it's another person. Normally, I'd be annoyed at the nickname, but I hold on to it for now, pretending we're not actually talking about Raymond.

"Like what?" I ask.

"Whatever you want...maybe something Ray would be comfortable in."

So much for pretending. My mouth goes dry, and the cement is back, but this time, it oozes down my throat, preventing me from taking another sip of water, so I set it aside. "Oh...okay."

He stops rubbing my back to move in front of me, leaning on his desk. "I can come pick it up if it would be easier for you?"

"I'll, uh, I'll get it all tonight and bring it to you tomorrow." I stand and wave vaguely in his direction, hightailing it out of his office. I think he follows me out, but I don't pay much attention, focused on my next task on this never-ending list of How to Throw the Perfect Funeral.

I guess I can understand why my dad wants everything done right away with this stuff. Maybe it'll hurt less, like ripping off a Band-Aid. Stings for only a second, and then it's better. But Dad's not the one who is doing the actual ripping. I am. And this hurt can't be smoothed over with any bandage.

FEBRUARY 17

My mother is impossible to buy gifts for. I call her picky, but she'd argue she's discerning. Nevertheless, department store perfume and flannel pajamas are not her style, so I usually buy her a coffee mug or something. Raymond, on the other hand, is more creative. He stopped buying Mom gifts long ago and now sponsors a farm animal for an international family in need in her name. A cow in Honduras, goats in India, chickens in Senegal, you get the picture. At first, it was a joke, like look at how materialistic we are to laugh at this, but donation after donation, Raymond proved he wasn't joking. He was actively improving lives all over the world in our mother's name. We eventually stopped trying to buy one another gifts, but Raymond kept sponsoring. At one point, he showed me a photo of a family in Cambodia who was thriving because they were able to sell eggs at their local market. Certainly put that leather bag versus suede shoes debate into perspective.

Ray's funeral service will be this Saturday at the Mancini Funeral Home in Plainfield, NJ. The viewing will be at 9 a.m. with the funeral immediately following. In lieu of flowers, please make a donation to World Vision and sponsor an animal in Raymond's name. I don't think there's anything he'd want more than to have an alpaca named Ray living in the Andes Mountains. That, or Bruce Springsteen concert tickets. We might as well give him one of those things, at least.

#Grief #RaymondStGeorge #TheBoss #LonelyValentine #SponsorAPigFeedAFamily #WorldVision

CHAPTER 6

I ring the doorbell at Shayna's house and try not to think about how my brother *used* to live here. When no one answers, I find the spare key Ray had given me "in case of emergencies." Since I've been home, my emergencies have been sleeping off late drunken nights on his couch instead of stumbling back into Mom and Dad's house.

Opening the door, I find Lara and Lucy among a chaos of toys in the normally immaculate front room. They glance up at me, pausing their play with tiny dolls and even tinier clothes and shoes.

"Hey, girls. Where's Mommy?"

"Kitchen," Lucy says, pushing her thick, messy hair back from her face as she goes back to playing. Lara has a knotted ponytail like she slept in it overnight, hair sticking out everywhere, and both girls are still in their pajamas even though it's after noon. All of this is unusual.

"She's crying," Lara says, stealing a miniature brush from Lucy.

I step around them and over a pile of crayons and coloring books splayed out on the floor.

"Mommy says Daddy's gone and not coming back."

Lara's curious voice stops me, and I circle around to them, both staring up at me with their big brown eyes.

I lean down to their level. "No, he's not coming back."

"Mommy says he's in heaven," Lucy says. "Can I go see him?"

Lara nods in agreement. "Me too?"

I bite my lip, completely out of my element. I don't have much interaction with children, including my own nieces, something my brother complained about. It's not that I don't like them—I love them—it's just that I'm not great with kids. I think they can smell my fear, and I have no idea how to exit this conversation without making it worse. "No, you can't go to heaven."

Lara pouts. "I wanna see Daddy."

"I know you do, but you can't." That was the wrong thing to say—both girls' eyes round like they're about to cry. I rub my forehead. "I'm sure your dad wants to see you too, but it wasn't his choice to go to heaven, and it's not somewhere you can come back from. Once you go to heaven, you stay there."

"Why?" Lucy asks.

"Because..." I look around the room, hoping an answer will come to me. "Because heaven is really cool and...fun."

"Fun? Like Disney World?" Lucy asks. "Is that why Daddy wants to stay?"

"Ooh, can we go back to Disney World?" Lara asks excitedly. "We can ride teacups with Daddy!"

Lucy claps and runs for her Moana doll.

"No, you won't be able to ride the teacups with Daddy," I say, floundering in this conversation. "I don't... Maybe you'll go to Disney again." I'd pay for them to go if they would stop asking me questions.

Lara finds her Ariel doll and combs her hair. "Aunt Cassie, know what Ariel's daddy's name was?"

"No, what?"

"King Triton. He has a big stick."

"Mm, interesting." I nod solemnly.

"Aunt Cassie," Lucy says, tugging on my hand, "wanna play with us?"

"I can't right now. I have to talk to your mommy, but maybe later."

"Okay, you can be Snow White 'cause you look like her," Lucy says.

"No! I wanna be Snow White!" Lara snatches the doll, and they begin to argue over who is what princess, and I use it to make my escape. I thought filling out my tax returns was hard, but explaining death to a child may be the hardest thing to do. Besides, possibly, actually dying.

I search for Shayna in the large dining room, recently redone kitchen with granite countertops, and the living room with a huge flat-screen TV, but she's nowhere to be found. Taking a peek out the window to the patio, I finally spot her wrapped up in blankets with a cup of something steaming on the table in front of her. Seeing her alone, looking awfully un-Shayna-like with no makeup and her hair a mess, I'm concerned for her. When I slide open the back door, she keeps her eyes on the brown-tinged grass and the swing set when I say, "Hey."

She has that haunted look. The same one as my mother.

"I didn't think you were home when no one answered the door, and I used my key. Sorry."

She sips her drink but says nothing.

I pick at the grooves in the tiled table. "The girls seem to be doing okay. That's good."

She runs her fingers through her hair, her nails painted a delicate pink, and for once, I wish she'd show me some of her self-indulgent annoyances, some sign of life. It'd be better than this silence.

I can't take it and resort to the question I've grown to hate over the past few days. "How are you?"

She gestures to the swing set. "We bought it for the girls' birthday two years ago. RJ spent almost all night putting it up to surprise them first thing in the morning." She wipes at her eyes. "He came in after midnight, soaked in sweat, cursing up a storm that the directions were wrong. But he finished it."

I focus on the swing set. Its normally vibrant green color appears dull in the overcast gray light.

"He wasn't a great husband, but he was the best dad," she says, and there's a hint of guilt in her voice. She turns to me then. "I'm not sure what I mourn more, his death or my marriage."

"Yeah," I mumble, thinking I should say *something*, but I'm out of my depth. "I have to find some—" I clear my throat of the words stuck there "—clothes for the burial. To pick out what he's going to wear." I assume she's going to have an opinion. Fashion is her thing, but she doesn't move.

"You know where the bedroom is."

I stare at the side of her face, hoping I can shame her into helping me. When it doesn't work, I roll my eyes, opening the door to go back inside.

"Cassandra."

I hate she always uses my full name. Guess it's the way Raymond felt when I used his name. I turn back to her. "Yeah?"

"Pick anything besides the Bruce Springsteen T-shirt or that horrid plaid suit."

I huff out a laugh. That horrid plaid suit is a red monstrosity he bought for Christmas last year, bow tie included.

"Okay," I tell her and head upstairs to their bedroom. It's mostly clean and white, a pristine oasis that I know for a fact caused many a fight between the two of them because Ray was more of a slob than I am. They may have been married for a while, but she could never quite get over his untidiness, especially in the white bedroom.

I slip off my shoes before I cross the threshold, afraid my boots might have microscopic pieces of dirt on them that would drive Shayna batty. A few weeks ago, I might've purposely left tracks to get under her skin, but I don't have it in me anymore. I help myself to the closet, pushing three-fourths of Shayna's pink and cream wardrobe out of the way to get to Ray's. His button-downs and ties are haphazardly hung up, along with a couple of pants and hoodies. A bunch of baseball hats are stacked up on a shelf with scores of sneakers lining the floor.

Carefully examining each article of clothing, I wonder what the purpose of this is. Why put him in the ground in a fancy suit—or any clothing, for that matter? It's not like he needs them wherever he is now. Or wherever he is not. Our parents stopped taking us to church in middle school, none of us particularly religious, so considering what Ray would wear to the pearly gates is silly.

I close the closet and open drawers, looking for something cotton. Natural fibers would be better for the environment, right?

I plop down on the floor, his athletic shorts and baseball shirts surrounding me, remembering the time he convinced me to play hockey with him when we were kids. The game consisted of me standing in front of the garage *without* a helmet for protection as his goalie while he smacked a plastic puck at me. My legs were covered in bruises for weeks. That was when I took up reading books instead of following him around.

Coming across Ray's old but treasured Bruce Springsteen T-shirt, the white one with Bruce in a dark silhouette with his guitar, I bring it to my face. It's soft and worn and still smells like him. I stuff it in my bag, then settle on his coaching shirt and plain black pants to bury him in. I second-guess myself on shoes and boxers—because does he really need those?—but grab them both anyway, just in case his journey to the great beyond requires a clean pair of undies.

Back at home, I find a note in Aunt Joanie's pretty cursive. She's dragged Mom out of the house to get her hair and nails done, and Dad is who-knows-where, so it's quiet for the first time in days.

It's lonely yet not all that different since *it* happened. I play the *White Album* on the vintage record player I bought in Williamsburg, to spite the way Ray made fun of me for being *so cool and different and unlike anyone else*. The bastard.

Then I find the glue and get to work with family photos and pictures of Ray on a poster board. Vince said it would be nice to stick them around the room during the service. I agreed to do it, although they're looking a lot more like a third-grade art project than a "memory board." I place a classic school photo of him right at the top, next to one with the two of us as little kids running through a sprinkler, holding hands. There's one of him dressed as G.I. Joe for Halloween next to self-portrait drawn in crayon from first grade. There's a picture of him grinning in a crown as homecoming king with his arm around Vince, who wore a court sash, and I glue it next to one of him wearing a matching tutu with Lucy and Lara.

Ray was forever taking pictures, and I once asked him what he planned on doing with all of them. He said he'd put them in photo albums eventually, but that eventually will never come around now. Although these piles and piles of photos serve him well today.

I assumed it would be difficult to do this, but I zone out to the point of anesthetization. It's like I'm looking at pictures of strangers. They're happier, living in a different timeline. There is no way that is him or me or my family all grinning on a boat with big orange life vests around our necks. Or, at least, it's not us anymore. These people are all strangers to me.

The house phone rings, and I consider not answering it but pick it up anyway. "Hello?"

"Hi, I'm calling for Donna, please."

"She's not here. Can I take a message?"

"Yes. My name is Janine, and I'm calling from the county coroner's office."

She pauses, allowing enough time for my brain to catch up. "Oh. Hi. I'm Cass, I'm Ray's sister. You can talk to me since, uh, my mom's not really..."

She hums in what sounds like empathy. "Sure. Cass, before I start, let me say how sorry I am to be calling you. Please extend my condolences to your family."

"Sure. Thank you," I mumble, nervous about what she's going to tell me, even though it can't be any worse than learning he's dead.

"I performed the autopsy on your brother and found he suffered a massive heart attack, caused by hypertrophic cardiomyopathy."

I rub my fingers over my forehead a few times, hoping all the information she's giving me sinks in. She talks about gene mutations and genetics, muscle cells, and other science terms I should probably remember from Bio 101 but don't. "This may run in your family, so I would advise everyone to make an appointment with the doctor. This often isn't detected because some people who suffer from it are young and the symptoms of it don't appear any different from the flu. I know—"

"Did it hurt?" I blurt out, cutting her off.

"I'm sorry?"

"Did it hurt?" I repeat, the cement settling in my chest again. "When he died?"

"No, it didn't," she says gently. "It would have been instantaneous, like turning off a light."

I nod, as if any of this makes sense. "Mm-hmm."

"Try to find a little bit of solace in that," she says, and I thank her before hanging up.

The heavy weight of this knowledge settles on me. On top of everything else, I have to explain to everyone how Ray died, although I can't even remember what hyper-trophy-cardio-tappy—or whatever it's called—is.

I Google it, spending hours reading about my brother's condition, falling down a rabbit hole of learning about the human heart. I treat it like I'm cramming for an exam, trying to comprehend the inner workings of the ventricles, as if the more I know, the more I'll be able to grasp why this happened. As if it isn't totally random my brother inherited this particular brand of heart disease, which arbitrarily killed an otherwise healthy young man.

There were no symptoms, no reason for him to get his heart checked. Plenty of people have heart attacks and survive, some of whom are probably older and weaker. But this shouldn't have happened to Raymond. His body betrayed him.

Confusion and fury rip through me, and I step on the memory boards, barely holding back from shredding them. I clench my fingers into fists to stop myself, yelling nonsense to expel the anger from my body. I stomp and jump and throw my arms, but it doesn't help. I want to break something. I want to punch a hole in the wall.

I want to *smash*.

Smash everything to unrecognizable bits.

Maybe then my life wouldn't feel so out of place.

Instead, I grab my phone and pull up Vince's number. I never make phone calls, but my brain is too full, my fingers too numb to text him. When he answers, I offer him a quick "Hi" and then, "It was a heart attack."

"What?"

"Ray died of a heart attack because of hypertrophic cardiomyopathy." I don't give him a chance to ask any more questions because I word-vomit everything I've learned from the internet. I tell him every detail I can remember from the Mayo Clinic, WebMD, the Cleveland Clinic, and Wikipedia. And he stays silent until I finally say, "Did you know Ray owned the reissue of Alanis's *Jagged Little Pill*?"

"The album? By Alanis Morissette?"

"Yeah."

"No, I didn't know that."

I flick off my record player. "He always sang her songs in the shower."

"Huh." He laughs.

I do too. Raymond was a great singer. Of course. "So, isn't it ironic that the guy who coached baseball and worked out every day died of a lousy heart? Something he couldn't even prevent. On Valentine's Day, no less."

After a few seconds, he agrees. "Like a fly in your Chardonnay."

I feel the corner of my mouth quirk, and I stare down at the mess at my feet, the pictures of my now-deceased brother, his Springsteen T-shirt, and years' worth of birthday cards I'd saved from him for some unknown reason. "I take it back," I say, toeing one of the boards away so I can sit. "You're good at this."

"At what?" he asks, though it's in a way I'm pretty sure he already knows.

"You're good at your job." He hums quietly in response, and I close my eyes at the sound, curling my arm around my bent legs to rest my forehead on my knees. "You make me feel better."

It's a while before he speaks. "Technically, I'm off the clock for my job, but never for you."

This time, I'm the one who hums in response, and I can't help the goose bumps that crawl up my skin when he says my name.

"Cass, I'm never on the clock for you. I hope you know that. I'm here whenever you need me."

And I hold on to the light peeking up through the darkness in my chest, new grass rising through a crack in the cement.

CHAPTER 7

*E*ven though I'd been to the Mancini Funeral Home already, coming here today is worse than walking into it for the first time. I'm burning up inside, sweating through Ray's Bruce Springsteen T-shirt, even as my fingers are ice cold. My belly churns so much, I regret not putting on makeup this morning, in case my skin is green with nausea. And my heart...

I place a hand over my chest. My heart hammers an unhealthy rhythm against my palm.

Vince and Mr. Mancini are in the foyer waiting for us—Aunt Joanie, my grandparents, Mom, Dad, and me. Vince touches my elbow, his face solemn and despondent, and I almost, *almost* lose it, but I don't. I can't. I keep it together for the day ahead, for my brother, for my parents.

They take our coats and offer us water or coffee, which none of us accepts, then escort us into a room to the right. Vince had previously told me it was their biggest room, and they expect to have a large crowd today. From the number of people who've left me messages, I expect the same.

What I don't expect is the casket. Intellectually, I knew it would be there. Emotionally, I'm not ready. Seeing it—him —takes my breath away. I steady myself with a hand on the chair next to me as I try to breathe, but it's impossible with the way my chest is caving in. I gulp down air like I've run a race. These past couple of days, all of the announcements, sympathy notes, decisions about wood and felt, it's been one long marathon culminating in this, and it's worse than I thought. So much worse, and I'm not prepared.

Those tears I thought wouldn't come suddenly rack my body. I wipe at my cheek, but it's useless.

I'm having the opposite of an out-of-body experience; I'm trapped here. I can't escape the taut skin stretched over my ribs that can barely contain my heart. Everything hurts. I want out of this situation, and I panic. Maybe I'm having a heart attack now, too.

I inhale through my nose, exhale out of my mouth over and over. I try to relieve the weight pushing me into the ground and focus on my surroundings. The walls are painted a light peach, a happy, vibrant color. The playlist I'd made is already on, and "Born to Run" filters in through hidden speakers. The memory boards are all up at different places around the room, among the rows and rows of chairs. And there, opposite me, is the dark mahogany coffin, the top lifted, displaying the lifeless body of my brother.

I go right to him.

I hear tortured whimpers behind me, and I know what my family is experiencing, but I can't take my eyes off my brother to check on them, because in front of me is Raymond John St. George. With his wavy hair and uncharacteristically straight lips, he has his hands folded over his gray-and-blue Panthers baseball coaching shirt. I touch his fingers; they're cool and hard. I touch his chest; it's cool and hard. His ears, cheeks, and arms are the same, cool and hard.

This isn't Ray, rather some weird, sewed-up, wax version, but it's the only version that remains. Wherever he is now, I hope he can hear me.

"Hey, bro," I say, my voice barely audible even to myself. "What'd you do this for?"

He doesn't answer.

"You're leaving me a real shitshow, ya know," I whisper and lean closer to him. "Mom's gone off the deep end, and I haven't seen Dad in so long, I don't remember what he looks like."

He doesn't laugh at my joke.

"I'm wearing your Bruce concert T-shirt," I tell him, tugging on it and then my black skirt. Suddenly my clothes are itchy against my skin.

"This really sucks, you know. Really, really sucks." I fix the collar of his shirt as my whole face begins to hurt from the tension running through my features. "I don't know how to handle all of this. If you're trying to play a trick on me, I give up. You win."

All the times he fooled me into doing something he wanted always ended with a charming smile. It was all in good fun. But this time, he's not smiling. There is no way out of this, no *just kidding* or playful high five. This is the end. And I'm scared.

Without my big brother, I'm afraid to face what comes next. Whether it's the next ten hours or ten years, I can't lean on him anymore. Without him, I'm by myself. I don't have a brother anymore. I'm an only child. I don't like this. I don't want it.

I stand by his side alone for a while until Aunt Joanie steps next to me.

"Handsome, even now."

When I nod at her words, she pushes my hair away from my eyes and kisses my cheek. She wraps her arm around me as we silently stare at Ray lying in front of us until she squeezes my arm. "Come on, let's sit down."

I let her guide me to the front row of chairs on the side, a few feet away from the casket. Mom is zoned out again, probably from another pill. Dad is antsy, walking in loops around the room, inspecting everything in it, passing the casket with a hovering hand, as if afraid to touch it.

Shayna and the girls come in, and she stands in front of my brother, crying. I wonder if, after everything that has happened between her and Ray, she still loves him. She certainly gives the impression of a widow in mourning, and I'm not sure how to comfort her or if I'm even supposed to. Normally, I'd whisper something to my brother about how she's always late—as if I wasn't—then he'd elbow me and roll his eyes. I imagine if Ray were alive, he'd tell me to hug her, so I do. He'd tell me to act like I mean it, so I do.

The girls, in matching purple dresses, hold hands. I hug them too, and they show me the cards they made for their daddy. Their scribbles kill me because I know how Ray held on to every single one of their stupid drawings. He'd crow about the beautiful bunnies and magnificent family scenes, but I don't have it in me to do the same. I don't know how to do it anyway. I take the cards to put them under my brother's hands, his stiff fingers difficult to move over the colorful markings, then hold each girl up so she can see him. Lucy pats his cheek, and I try to choke down the lump lodged in my throat, but it's impossible when Lara kisses his forehead. They're so in love with their dad, oblivious to what any of this means.

Shayna thanks me, and we hug once more before she

puts on sunglasses and sits at the end of the row, on the other side of my parents. The girls follow her, pulling out Moana and Ariel dolls from their bag.

And then it begins.

In a single-file line, people filter into the room. One after another, they all come. It seems like all of New Jersey is here. People I recognize, family and old friends, and people I don't know, but who spend time introducing themselves to me, explaining how they know Ray and how much they love him.

Ray's girlfriend shows up. I only met her once, but I know her name is Nell. She's wearing a black blazer over a Bruce Springsteen shirt, with her brown hair pulled back into a ponytail, and her pale skin is blotchy and red.

For a minute, I fear this funeral will transform into a soap opera, but Shayna has her head down, and Nell scurries through the line. She places something in the casket before taking a seat in the back, far away from us.

RJ's baseball team shows up, all the players in their uniforms, and my eyes are so blurry with tears, they're one big blob of gray.

Dad shakes their hands. Mom can't look at them. I hug and thank each one for coming.

His students and coworkers arrive. I'm told the school arranged buses to bring them over. I accept all of the cards and art projects scrawled with notes written to Mr. George.

By the time I look at the clock, almost three hours have passed, and the funeral hasn't even started yet. We wait until every last person has come inside the room, and then Mr. Mancini tells us we will begin the service.

It's standing room only.

A priest from my grandmother's church is up first, reading and talking about some passage from the bible.

Nana's at the end of our row, burning through her second box of tissues, while Pop is stoic next to her. She demanded the service have some religious elements, and who was I to argue with a woman who, in her words, is "close to meeting God." With the way she's wailing, you'd think she was going to throw herself into traffic to follow Ray into the ground. She's so loud, I'm sure Jesus himself would come down from the cross to tell her to cool it.

Aunt Joanie reads a poem, and then it's my turn to speak.

I lick my lips and crumple a tissue in my hand so it's practically unusable as I stand behind the podium. I clear my throat, look out over the packed room, then clear it again. I sniffle, and it resonates through the microphone. I apologize.

I've written and rewritten this eulogy so many times over the last week that my thoughts are mostly a jumbled stream of consciousness typed on paper, and I tell everyone so. They laugh, and I wipe the sweat dotting my upper lip.

Using my index finger as a guide so I don't lose my place through my hazy vision, I start reading. First, I thank everyone for coming. I thank them for the cards, baskets, and flowers, but make a plea for no more casseroles. "We're out of room in the freezer," I say. "But if your heart tells you to send chocolate, we have plenty of room for that."

The room rumbles with low chuckles again, and I take a breath before I go on. "To say this has all been a nightmare would be woefully inaccurate. This is much worse, but I haven't yet found the word for the horror movie our lives have become. The death of my brother has left all of us, me, my parents, Shayna, and the twins, in what seems like permanent darkness. With Ray gone, he's taken all of our sunlight with him."

I pause to wipe the tissue under my eye, determined to

get through this for my brother. This eulogy is the last gift I can give him, so I will finish it as best I can. "I've never felt pain like this before. It's razor-sharp and cuts like it may never go away because just when it recedes, it comes back, stabbing in a whole new place. I'm in pain, like everyone here is in one way or another. Everyone but Ray. I'm told when he died, there was no pain. He left us in an instant, like he closed his eyes and went to sleep, and that, at least, is something we can be happy about. Or as happy as we can be."

Someone lets out a weepy hiccup, and I think it's my mom.

I tell everyone how much Ray loved teaching and coaching. I tell them how he enjoyed being a dad. How his favorite thing was drinking imaginary tea from plastic pink teacups and dressing as Cinderella when the girls wanted to play princesses. I tell them how fun he was to grow up with and how awful, like the time he locked me in a steamer trunk, convincing me he could perform a magic trick and make me disappear. Everyone laughs.

I read off some of his favorite movies and songs. I tell them about how he sang all the time and never forgot to send me a sympathy card on the anniversary of the death of the hermit crab he'd given me when I moved to New York City. "I can't even keep plants alive, so I don't know why he thought I would keep a crab alive. But it's probably why he got it for me, because he knew I wouldn't, and he'd be able to taunt me about it in perpetuity. I guess now he and Captain Hook may be hanging out together as we speak, so the joke's on him."

I raise my head, met with a sea of sad smiles and red eyes.

I blink, clearing my own eyes, and go on without the

paper. "The past couple of days, I've learned a lot about the heart. I've learned it's the strongest muscle in the body. And that it can break into a million pieces, yet the body will still go on. I've learned one second, the heart can work perfectly normally, and the next, it stops. I was told my brother's heart was enlarged, and you could argue it was literally and figuratively enlarged because he had so much love to give. Although, I'm not so philosophical about it. I'm mad. I'm really fu—"

I stop, realizing I can't say that word here. Not now. I swallow it down and continue.

"I'm really, really mad. Because while Ray's big heart killed him, we're the ones left with a Ray-sized hole in our stupid, normal-sized hearts."

I glance over to the side where Vince is standing with his arms crossed over his chest, but I catch him wipe a tear away from his cheek. He nods in encouragement, and I look back to the crowd in front of me, offering them whatever kind of smile I can muster. "Thanks again for coming today. On behalf of my family and brother, we appreciate and love you all."

I take my seat quickly, sinking into the stiff chair as disbelief settles over me. I just gave the eulogy, the last words, about my big brother. He's gone.

He's really gone.

Mr. Mancini stands and gives instructions to exit. Vince opens the doors and directs everyone to where they should go to line up their cars. Mr. Mancini escorts me and my family out of the room, but I can't take my eyes off the casket, and I stop walking as panic seizes me.

"Is it weird I don't want to leave?" I ask him.

Mr. Mancini shakes his head. "Why don't you stay here? Take your time. Go to the car whenever you're ready."

I step to the side, allowing the crowd to file out of the door next to me. Most of them stop to hug me or tell me what a wonderful job I did. Uncle David informs me he didn't know I could speak so well. I shrug in response, not wanting to tell him I always spoke well; it's only no one knew because my brother hogged up all the air in the room, leaving none for me. I didn't mind, though. I was just as transfixed by him as everyone else was.

Once the room is empty, save for the pallbearers—some cousins and friends, including Vince—I walk over to my brother one more time. I trace his eyebrows, touch his shoulder, and knock my fist to his fingers. "See you 'round, Ray."

Vince makes me aware he's behind me by offering a soft, "You're okay, Cass." When I acknowledge him with a raised shoulder and quivering lip, he slides his hand along my shoulder blades and curls his fingers around my neck, stroking his thumb along the top of my spine. "You did everything you could, and you did it well. There's nothing left except this last part, but it'll be the hardest."

Then, with his free hand, he lifts my left, twining our fingers together, and brings them to the lid of the casket. I feel the heat of Vince's chest against my back, his mouth close to my ear, his breath slow and steady, a reminder for me to breathe too. Together, we close the casket, forever covering Raymond, and I immediately turn into Vince, crying into the lapel of his suit jacket. One of his hands tangles in my hair, cupping my head, while the other smooths up and down my back. He doesn't say anything, simply holds me and lets me cry, while I try to remember what my brother looked like alive. His big smile, his goofy walk with big arm swings, his habit of biting his nails raw, I try to burn it all in my brain. Instead of the casket.

Vince eventually hands me a handkerchief, and it actually draws a soggy smile out of me. "What is this? Nineteen fifty?"

He shrugs, wiping my cheeks and under my nose when I don't move to do it. "It's all part of the vibe."

I breathe out a waterlogged laugh and press my forehead to his shoulder. "It works for you."

"Come on," he says, slipping his hand to the back of my neck again. "I'll walk you to the car."

My parents, Aunt Joanie, Nana, and Pop are already seated inside the funeral car when Vince opens the door for me, and after he tips his chin to me, silently directing me inside, I hesitantly sit down. A few minutes later, we're off on a slow-moving ride toward the cemetery. Out of the back windshield, the line of cars with blinking lights goes on forever, a depressing parade, creating traffic jams at every intersection.

At the cemetery, we make our way out to the spot below a slight slope, where a hole in the ground is waiting. Mr. Mancini tells us to have a seat, but I can't. Not with my eyes trained on the two rows of baseball players lined up on either side of my brother's casket as it is carried toward us.

Vince is right. This really is the fucking hardest part.

I can't.

It's too hard.

I can't breathe.

I can't.

Someone hands me a long-stemmed rose to place on the casket.

How stupid. Ray doesn't care about flowers.

Nana wails next to me.

Mom's hands are wrapped around the sides of the folding chair, knuckles white.

Dad's head is bent, tears spilling down his face.

The crowd is gathered in a claustrophobic circle around us. I need to get away, and I push through them before it's over, not able to stay there one more second. My limbs ache and throat burns as I run down a path to where a statue of an angel stands with huge wings and open arms.

I guess it's supposed to be comforting, a waiting angel.

An angel of death.

I scream.

I scream so loud I hope those angels in heaven hear me.

I tear the stupid fucking rose up into pieces until the petals litter the ground around my feet.

And I scream again.

Someone—I don't know who, but I know it's not Vince, and I fleetingly and bizarrely wish it was—puts their hands on my shoulders, tugging me to a standing position. I cover my eyes, sobbing into my hands, not caring to pay attention to where I'm going. None of it matters.

I'm guided into the car, but I don't want to face my family. Hunching over, I stay hidden, pulling my coat collar up around my neck. I want to disappear.

But I can't, at least not yet.

We arrive at the Italian restaurant I'd booked for the reception to be held, and Mr. Mancini helps me out of the car. It seems like everyone who was at the funeral shows up. The place is packed. People apparently love free chicken parm and ziti.

I'm not hungry but get a small plate of food to push around as different bodies rotate like a merry-go-round next to me. Some offer stories about Ray, some slide me checks for Lara and Lucy to help with their needs, and yet others still act like dicks, especially the aptly named Uncle Dick.

He brushes his finger over his upper lip, a habit I've

come to know over the years, and taps the table next to my elbow. "Good thing it's been a mild winter so we can bury him today and not wait for the ground to thaw, huh?"

"Yeah," I say, dropping my napkin on my plate. "Thank god for global warming."

I stand up, shoving by him and others motioning for me. I've given everyone else everything I have this week—my heart, my mind, my attention. I don't want to do it anymore. I want a bottle of wine, solely for me.

I shout it out loud when I get outside. "I just need some wine!"

"All right?"

I jump a little, startled by Vince lounging on a bench. "What're you doing here?"

"Too hot," he says, tipping his head to the restaurant. "Want to sit?"

"No." Didn't he hear me? "I don't want to sit. I want to get wine. They tried to make me pay in there. I mean, can you believe that? My brother was put into the ground—" I wiggle my arms out. I still can't believe it. "—and then we come here because I put this whole luncheon together, which they are profiting well off of, by the way, and they want *me* to pay for a glass of wine."

Vince shakes his head with an amused smile.

"I'm serious," I say. "Today, of all days. I can't even get a goddamn glass of free wine."

He stands and steps off the sidewalk, gesturing for me to follow him.

"Where are you going?"

He momentarily stops. "To get you wine. You coming?"

"Oh. Yeah."

Vince's car is not a hearse or a big boat, but a rather bland sedan. I drop into the passenger seat, and on the way, we listen to a Golden Oldies channel on the radio, weirdly fitting for Vince with his dark suit coat and sideswept hair, save for the cowlick. The soft crooning is blessedly, pleasantly mind-numbing.

He drives me to the liquor store and tells me to pick out whatever I want. When I point to the Dom Perignon in the special gold package, he laughs and offers wine in a box instead. I settle for a cheap bottle of Zinfandel with a twist-off cap, and he doesn't say anything when I immediately open it after we get back in the car.

As Elvis Presley sings one of his ballads, Vince drives to a park in the next town over with a manmade lake and walkways that would be decorated with blooming trees if it weren't still winter. He tells me to stay put for a minute then gets out of the car to search for something in his trunk. A few moments later, he opens my door and plops a beanie on my head. Then he takes my hand in his and guides me to a bench by the water, where we sit close to each other, sharing body heat. He doesn't say anything, merely sits next to me while I sip straight from the bottle of wine and watch as the sun sets on the saddest day of my life.

FEBRUARY 29

Leap years are stupid. They're in the same category as time changes. Yeah, I know it's science and based on our trips around the sun, but it still doesn't make it any less dumb. Whether we count our days in revolutions in the atmosphere, in cups of coffee, or in inches or miles, we're still counting all of the days. And because of the leap year, I've got an extra day without my brother.

We spent a whole week preparing to bury my brother and then a whole week after that preparing ourselves to go back out into the world. I thought it would be enough time, but it's not. I'm not sure if there will ever be enough time to get over it or move on or whatever it is we're supposed to be doing.

Life is different now. I don't feel like smiling, and if I do, I feel bad doing it. I know it's ridiculous, the internet has told me so, but I can't turn off the guilt. Raymond isn't walking this earth anymore, yet I am, and I'm not sure how to reconcile those two facts. If anyone has any bright ideas, pass them along to me, but please no more "With time, the pain will fade" platitude. Because at this point, the pain is the only thing keeping me sane. I'm afraid if I gave in to the sorrow, it would swallow me whole, so for now, I'm surviving on my rage. Not even the *Rent* soundtrack can move me.

#Grief #Renthead #FiveHundredTwentyFiveThousandSixHundredMinutes #Rage

CHAPTER 8

Lunch isn't my favorite shift. Really, no shift is my favorite, but today is extra hard.

Putting my kilt and knee-highs back on after being away for two weeks felt ickier than usual. The way the guy with the short-sleeved button-down winks at me is more annoying than usual. Everything about working here is worse than usual.

Sassie's Lassies—with its green paint, faux-leather seating fabric, and framed photos of rolling hills, the Loch Ness Monster, and the occasional big-breasted woman—is not exactly a five-star restaurant. But the patrons aren't here for the décor or food. They're here for the early-bird special, cheap alcohol, or the all-female staff in tiny uniforms. I took this job when I moved home to make a quick buck while I tried to find a job at the local newspaper. At the time, the paper only had unpaid internships. Nearly two years later, here I am, still slinging beers in a top that won't cover my stomach or cleavage at the same time.

I place the plates of a plain cheeseburger and shepherd's pie in front of two elderly men. They thank me, and I force a smile while wondering how old they are. One is completely bald, his face covered in lines and sunspots. He's got a weathered tattoo of a pinup girl and a rose on his forearm. The other man's hair is so thin it reminds me of Charlie Brown as he runs a bony hand over it, his clothes hanging loose on him.

It's clear they've been around a while. They've enjoyed their time on earth.

So why are they alive when my brother's not? I hate them for it.

Then guilt fills me up. They appear perfectly nice.

As I return to the kitchen, the guy in the stupid short-sleeved brown shirt, touches my arm. I raise a brow and toss him my best sneer, having no patience for shit today. "What?"

His eyes suddenly change from confident to nervous. "Can I have some ketchup?"

I step away to the bar to grab a bottle of ketchup and thump it on his table. I hate him too.

I hate them all. Every single person here. Why aren't they dead?

They should be, from eating this food.

With a disgusted grunt, I head outside through the back door in the kitchen to take five minutes, but the door barely shuts before Gary pokes his head out.

"Hey, what's with you today?" he asks.

Without my coat on, my skin prickles in the cold air. I clench my hands around my biceps.

"You look like you're gonna kill somebody," he says.

"I'd like to." I pivot to face him and tilt my head. "You volunteering?"

He laughs at me, but I'm not joking.

"You're not wearing your lipstick." He opens the door

wider and moves to stand to his full height, which is well below average. It's a clear power move, as I'm on the pavement, a step below the door.

I put my hands on my hips. "What?"

"You should go back to wearing the red lipstick you usually do. You'd get more tips that way."

"Fuck off, Gary."

"Hey, you can't talk to me that way."

I turn away from him.

"This is your first day back, so I'll cut you some slack after everything, but that was really uncalled for. You disrespect me again, and I'm going to write you up."

"Yeah, sure, Gar." I flip my middle finger at the click of the door shutting behind me. He's an asshole and this job sucks, but I make good tips here. I've thought about applying to grad school, though tuition would only pile on to the loans I've already got. And I've browsed through enough jobs online to know there aren't many available with my experience as a celebrity wrangler. Sometimes I wonder if that unpaid internship is still available.

Nevertheless, none of it matters now. That was *before*.

I'm not sure what to do or where to go now. So, for the moment, I'm here in my kilt. I fix my hair into a bun and head back inside to check on my tables, waiting for the time I can clock out.

When I finally arrive home, Aunt Joanie's bags are stacked by the front door. I put my coat and bag away in the closet then wind around the steps to the kitchen, where Mom and Aunt Joanie are seated at the table. A pizza box is on the stove.

"Cooked again," Aunt Joanie grins, and I snag a paper plate and slice before plopping down at the table with them.

"Hi, Cassie," Mom says, dunking a tea bag in her mug.

"Hi."

Our dialogue since Ray died hasn't been much more than pleasantries.

"How was work?"

"Fine."

She sips her tea, and I look to Aunt Joanie. "You're leaving?"

She rubs my back. "I've got to get back to work. I have no more vacation time to use."

I stick a gob of cheese in my mouth, trying not to pout.

"It's been a week since the funeral," she says, "and I know it'll be hard, but we've got to go on as usual. Ray would want us to."

I rip off a piece of crust to eat while Mom cries silently across from me.

"Where's Dad?"

Mom dabs at her eyes. "Not home yet."

Aunt Joanie tries and fails to hide her eye roll before she explains how she's not looking forward to facing all the work she's missed. She tells us about her colleague who always has lipstick on her teeth and the guy who burns popcorn in the microwave. Mom doesn't attempt to take part in the conversation, and I already dread Joanie being gone.

When I finish my pizza, she motions with her head for me to follow her out to the living room. We relax on the sofa, and she takes my hand in both of hers. "Promise me you'll be okay."

I nod my promise.

"No, really. Your dad's father died of a heart attack, right? You need to go to the doctor and get checked. If Raymond's heart condition was genetic and he didn't know he had it, you might not know either."

I lift a shoulder. "Yeah, okay."

She pinches the back of my hand. "Go. To. The. Doctor."

"Ow." I pull away from her, shaking my hand. "Fine."

"I'm serious, Cassandra Lyn."

"Full-naming me?"

"Yes. Where's your phone?"

I take my phone out from the pocket of my hoodie.

"Call the doctor now."

I bite back a smile, but she snaps her pinchers at me again.

"Fine. Fine. Okay." I open up the Google app on my phone, pausing over the keyboard. "Should I look up heart doctors or...?" I'm genuinely unaware of who I should be calling.

"You don't have a doctor?" When I stare at her blankly, she huffs. "Who do you go to when you're sick?"

"The emergency room."

"You're not serious, Cassie!"

I don't move, and she takes out her own phone.

"You know I work for the hospital network, right? And you don't have a doctor." She grumbles. "What the hell am I going to do with you?" She continues to murmur to herself but is cut off mid-sentence. "You're exactly the type of person we're trying to get health insur—Kate, hey, how are you? Good, I'm all right. Listen. I'll be back at the office tomorrow, but I'm going to need you to make an appointment with Dr. Parikh for my niece." She tugs on the earlobe of her cell-phone-free ear. "I know she's usually full, but tell them my niece is having heart palpitations and that she's recently been made aware of genetic heart disease in the family. Use my name."

Aunt Joanie tosses a victorious glance my way. "Great, thanks. Text me the date and time for the appointment."

She hangs up then holds her phone above her head in triumph. "It's nice to be the boss."

"Head of the hospital mafia or something?"

"I do run my department like Michael Corleone. Minus all the murder." She yanks me to her when she stands, hugging me tight. "I love you."

"Love you too."

She pushes me back slightly to look me in the eye. "I'll need proof you went to the appointment."

"You won't believe me if I say I went?"

"Of course not." She taps my nose. "You are my niece after all." Then she pets my hair and kisses my cheek. "Be brave."

Those two words roll through my body, knocking the reality of the situation into my bones. The unimaginable has happened, and I have to get through it somehow. I have to be brave. Not like face off against a giant with a pebble kind of brave, or even the naked and alone in the jungle brave. No, she wants me to be emotionally brave. Solid. Sturdy. Words no one has ever used to describe me.

I want to laugh at her, but she gazes at me so earnestly, I have no other answer besides, "I'll try."

She kisses me once more then heads to the kitchen, I assume to say goodbye to my mother, but I can't stay to hear it.

I traipse downstairs to my room, where it's quiet. Everyone's gone, and it's all back to normal. Except normal is relative. Normal is broken.

When I lie on the bed, it doesn't escape me that I'm in a basement, well below ground level, on my back. My brother is in the same position right now, underground, on his back.

I squirm and twist onto my side.

CHAPTER 9

I check in at the front desk for my appointment with Dr. Parikh and have a seat in the nonde-script waiting room. I refuse to admit that I'm actually anxious about this and pretend I'm totally cool, flipping through social media posts, randomly liking but not reading any of them. Although, my body can't convince my mind of my supposed calm demeanor, betrayal in my foot shaking back and forth, palms sweating profusely.

Aunt Joanie's been texting me every day for the past three days, making sure I attend this appointment. I was told I'm going to have an EKG, ultrasound of my heart, and stress test. I don't know what these things are, and the unknown adds to my worries. I watch the second hand tick in circles around the brown-and-white clock on the wall for a few minutes before a nurse in pink scrubs and a black cardigan calls me back.

She introduces herself to me, but I'm too tense to remember her name. I can barely follow her directions to remove my clothes from the waist up and put on the blue hospital gown, yet I smile at her before she leaves the room.

I wiggle my fingers, hoping to stop their tremoring, and remove my top and bra, only to replace them with the loose cotton material left for me. I button up the gown and wait again.

This time, it's much longer. By the time the doctor enters the room, I have myself worked up into a ball of nerves, bouncing around the room, literally unable to sit still.

"Cassandra?"

I drop the stethoscope on the counter, caught red-handed in my exploration. "Yes."

"I'm Dr. Parikh," the black-haired woman says in introduction. "How are you?"

I hold my gown closer to my body. "I'm okay."

She nods at me, in that way people have been for weeks, slightly tilted and with down-turned lips. She gestures to the table, and I follow the cue to sit down as she says, "I'm sorry to hear about what happened. I'm friends with your aunt."

"Thanks for squeezing me in," I say.

She waves her hand nonchalantly. "Anything for Joanie." She asks me some general questions, covering what the nurse did, my age, activity level, drug and alcohol use, and types notes on an iPad. "We're going to run a full battery of tests to make sure you don't have the same heart defect as your brother. It'll take about an hour, but you won't leave without seeing me again, okay?"

When I agree, she opens the door to call out two names, Tina, the nurse from before, and Patrick, a baby-faced physician's assistant who appears to have just graduated. "You'll be in good hands," Dr. Parikh says and waits for me to meet her dark and reassuring eyes. "It'll be over in an hour. No sweat."

When she leaves, Tina and Patrick go to work, sticking

pads and wires to my chest, and swiftly strap me to a small machine that measures the electrical activity of the heart. It only takes a few minutes.

"See," Tina says, probably sensing my panic. "Painless."

I force a smile at her as she helps me to sit up and move off the table to a treadmill in the corner.

"We're going to have you run on the treadmill to observe how your heart does when it's forced to work hard," Patrick explains.

"Torture," I deadpan.

"Oh no, we wouldn't," he says seriously as he readies the machine and types on a laptop. "It's against our oath."

Tina laughs indulgently at him while throwing me a look as she stands next to me. She presses some buttons on the treadmill. First, it's a leisurely walk.

"We'll gradually speed up. You tell us when you're going as fast as you can," Patrick directs, scratching at his red hair.

Tina presses an arrow to increase the speed a bit.

"You're so young to be taking these tests," Patrick says after a few seconds, and I think, *you're too young to be giving these tests.* "What brings you in for them?"

Tina pushes the arrow again, and my arms automatically start swinging at my sides as I force my legs to move faster. "My brother died of a heart attack last month."

"Oh." Patrick practically chokes on that syllable as I choke on my breath, and Tina speeds up the treadmill once again. "I'm so sorry," he says.

"It's okay," I pant. "It's becoming harder."

"Can you go thirty more seconds?" he asks.

I don't answer, concentrating on keeping my pace without falling off. I haven't moved this fast in a long time since my favorite form of exercise is finger yoga while I shop online. I gulp down a big breath, wondering what my heart's doing at this exact second. Probably wheezing and coughing.

"Good. Very good," Patrick says, and Tina slows the treadmill down to a stop so I can step off, waving the hospital gown around my body to cool off. She pats my back and tells me to lie back on the exam table. "Patrick and I are done. I'm going to send in the ultrasound tech, and she'll finish up the last test. You're doing great."

A short Black woman with a Caribbean accent and braids introduces herself as Sherry and turns off the lights, getting right down to business in taking internal pictures of my heart. She doesn't speak as she moves the wand thingy around my breastbone. It's awkward when she pushes it under and over my naked breasts, searching for different parts of my heart on her gray screen. I want to make a joke, something about being a cheap date, but Sherry looks too professional to even crack a smirk. Instead, I focus on the circular pattern of the wallpaper next to me. Sherry finishes after about fifteen minutes and turns the lights back on, instructing me to dress.

I do as I'm told after she leaves, and when Dr. Parikh finally returns, she's smiling. "All your tests look great, nothing abnormal."

"I'm fine?"

She nods.

"Completely fine?"

"With a genetic defect, we can never be sure who will inherit it, but you show no signs of heart disease whatso-ever. I'm happy to answer any questions you have. Take a business card from the desk on the way out, but I do have to get to another appointment." She shakes my hand, patting it gently. "There is no reason you shouldn't live a long and happy life."

And as soon as she leaves the room, my smile drops.

Raymond's heart attack was a total fluke. The guy who worked out all the time and drank a protein shake every morning died. Ramen in a cup is one of my main food groups, but I'm still here.

Survivor's guilt is a whole other kind of suffering.

I'm not sure how to process it. Surprise, surprise.

Sitting in my car for a while, I stare at the text thread I have going with Vince. He's been checking in on me for the last two weeks. Usually it goes something like:

Vince: How's it going?

Me: Fine.

Vince: Need anything?

Me: Nope.

Vince: Let me know.

Me: Okay.

Then it all starts again the next day. If I didn't know better, I'd think he actually cared about me. But I suspect he feels bad for me. Like he did back when we were kids. Back when I was the clinger little sister and he felt guilty because Ray was ignoring me. Vince always gave me this look, like he knew how badly I wanted to hang out with him and usually found a way to make it up to me with stolen moments that made my teenage heart flutter. Eating ice cream together right out of the container late one night or tugging on my ponytail as he ducked out the back door to go hop in the car with Raymond. Always checking in with me.

And he's doing the same thing now. Making sure I'm not ignored.

Warms the cockles of my cold, dead heart.

Enough that I contemplate texting him. Telling him I need him. Need someone to talk to about my appointment, but I shove away the idea. We aren't kids anymore.

The last month has thrown me headfirst into adulthood, and I can't put my head in the clouds over texts from the boy I used to love. Instead, I head home and crack open some windows to let in the unseasonably warm spring air.

As usual, Mom's in bed with the curtains closed over the windows, while Dad is tucked away in the office, doing I don't know what. So I leave for work without saying goodbye to either of them, and at quarter of eleven when I get home, not much has changed since I left except Dad has moved to the living room, where he's lounged with a glass of vodka. I only know it's vodka because the bottle is next to his feet.

I drop my purse by the door where I deposit my shoes. "Hey, Dad." He doesn't acknowledge me, but I sit on the couch opposite him anyway. "I didn't know you drank vodka."

"I don't." He rotates his glass upside down, showing me it's empty. "I'm going to go to the store," he says, standing up with a wobble.

"How much did you drink?" I ask because I've never seen my dad drunk before. I've witnessed him have a beer or two in the summertime and a glass of wine here and there, but that's it.

"I don't know," he mumbles, moving toward the closet, his gait loose like he's trying not to melt into the floor.

I easily beat him to the closet, blocking him. "What do you want? Everything's closed now."

He blinks owlishly at me. "No, I need to replace the bottle. Your mother'll be mad."

"She won't even notice," I say, and when he reaches around me, I step in his way again. "Really, you don't need to go out."

"No, Cassandra. Move."

He nudges me out of the way and opens the closet for his coat, which he clumsily puts on.

I hang on to the sleeve. "Okay, well, how about I drive you? Where do you want to go? I'll take you."

"Don't be ridiculous. I don't need you to take me anywhere." He coasts his unfocused gaze over me. "Especially dressed like that."

With St. Patrick's Day coming up, the work uniform has altered slightly from a white top to a green one with shamrocks placed strategically on my chest. I changed into yoga pants before I left work, but apparently it's still not appropriate for my drunk dad.

He pats his coat pockets for his keys, and when they aren't there, he studies the space around him. I skid past him to the kitchen, where a catchall woven basket is on the counter, and I snatch his keys out, hiding them behind my back. Dad eventually lumbers to the kitchen and shoos me out of the way. When he discovers his keys aren't in the basket, his face changes from tipsy annoyance to intoxicated anger while staring at me. He silently holds his palm up, his fingers curling in to gesture for the keys, but I'm not backing down.

"You shouldn't drive like this," I tell him.

"I will drive whenever I goddamn well please."

"No."

He attempts to grab them from behind me, but I hop out of the way like we're playing some kind of game.

"Cassandra, you don't get to tell me what to do."

"Right now, I do. I can smell the vodka on you. And believe it or not, you don't get to drive like this."

He lunges for the keys again, but his balance is all off and he isn't anywhere close to my hand. "Who the hell do you think you are?"

"I am your daughter," I say slowly.

He sidles up to me, the closest he's been in a long time. He didn't shave today, and his shadow of a beard is white, his irises rimmed in red. He doesn't say anything while he wraps his arm around my torso like a boa constrictor. I try to wiggle away, but he doesn't stop until his fingers wrap around my wrist to take the keys out of my hand.

He shows them to me as if he's won some sort of victory, and the fight drains out of me. The past few weeks, he hasn't been around to check on Mom or even cared to ask how I'm doing, so if he wants to kill himself driving because he'd rather be dead like his son, so be it. But he's not going to kill anyone else either.

I hold up my cell phone. "I'll call the cops if you drive like this."

He stares at me in a standoff. We each wait for the other to flinch. I move my hand, ready to dial 9-1-1, and he gives in, slamming the keys back down on the counter next to me.

"I'm going for a walk." He practically spits the words at me, and I exhale as he stalks away. A few seconds later, the front door slams shut.

I know my father's not himself, hasn't been since last month, but I can't find the sympathy in me to forgive him.

I don't bother going to my mother. She's probably been asleep for hours. Instead, I find a spoon and the jar of Nutella that I splurged on during the last grocery store trip. Without consciously making the decision, I flop on my bed with my cell phone and start typing.

I snap a picture of the spoonful of Nutella, post it, and then proceed to devour the entire fucking jar.

The post is one of my most popular.

MARCH 10

My brother and I were always competitive with each other as kids, from Monopoly to school report cards. He was great at everything, and it was all so easy. Or at least it seemed that way to me, a kid who lagged behind him every step of the way. He had tons of friends, he was smart, athletic, funny, he was perfect. King Midas. No matter what I did, I couldn't capture a piece of that gold, and at some point, I stopped trying to.

It was self-actualization for me, but I think to other people, maybe it appeared to be laziness. It wasn't. It was self-preservation. There was no way to live up to Ray, so I needed to do my own thing. That meant giving up the competition. There was no way to win anyway.

But now, after Ray's death, I'm back in competition with him. I'm fighting to keep my family together, fighting for my parents to recognize what I'm doing and that I'm still here. I'm trying my best, but it's not good enough. Again.

I'm walking the tightrope, straining to keep balance of my life. I'm doing it all. I'm doing the hard part. Meanwhile, all Ray did was die. He got the easy part, and he's still winning.

My brother died, and all I got was this jar of Nutella.

#Grief #GriefFood #RaymondStGeorge #NutellaNut #FueledByRageAndNutella

CHAPTER 10

The next morning, I slink into my parents' bedroom. Dad is nowhere to be found, but Mom is still in bed. Crawling onto the mattress, I rub her shoulder until she turns to me.

"You awake?" I ask, taking in her bed head and wrinkled sweatshirt.

"Yeah...yes," she says, sitting up with effort.

"Coming down for breakfast?"

She weighs the question as if I asked her how to achieve world peace.

"I picked up pancake mix. I can make some."

She shakes her head. "I'm not hungry."

My mom had a full-time job as a paralegal, but she hasn't returned to work since Valentine's Day, and I can only assume early retirement has become her new reality. Too bad she's spending it wasting away in bed.

Not that I don't want to do the same.

"I have the day off. We can go get our nails done," I offer, an activity we haven't done together since I was in high school.

She wipes at her eyes. "Do you need something, Cassie?"

I need my mom, but I don't tell her that. How could I? Can I really blame her for acting this way after her son has died?

"No," I murmur, and she slips back down under her covers.

"Close the door on your way out."

Giving up for now, I make my way back downstairs for my keys and purse. Even though I don't have extra money to burn, I go to the mall, or at least what's left of it. Seeing the pathetic, largely useless two-story building that had, at one time, been bustling and is now basically a half-empty husk, fills me with something similar to camaraderie.

I test out lotions at Bath & Body Works because it reminds me of when I was a kid. Of when my worst day was going to school with a perm in sixth grade because I'd been desperate for curly hair, and Seth Abrams told me I looked like a poodle. I try on shoes I'll never buy and admire jewelry I'll never afford because my bank account is barely surviving at this point.

I go into the bookstore and treat myself to a leisurely walk around each and every stack. I used to have time to read books, real ones with old, dog-eared pages from the secondhand bookstore down the street from my apartment in the city. Now, reading is a luxury. Like my time.

Whenever I have a few hours to myself, I usually watch the Game Show Network. I don't have the brain power to open a book, let alone use reading comprehension skills to follow along with words on a page. I'm too mentally exhausted to read, but I find myself pulling different books off the shelf in the self-help section. They all deal with death. When I read the backs, most of them are general volumes on meditation or the mechanics of grief. There are books directed at children losing their parents, parents losing a child, the loss of a husband or wife, even one about the passing of a best friend. No siblings, though.

I wonder why I can't find one written about the death of a sibling, and I consider how people view siblings. We don't pick our brothers and sisters, and yet they're our first friends. We can hate and love each other in the same breath, be adversaries and accomplices. Sibling bonds are certainly complicated, and it seems someone should have a book navigating the grief of losing one. Or, at the very least, acknowledging it.

Then again, maybe I'm the only one who can't get it together. If there were such a need, someone would have filled it already. I'd assume.

I leave the store without purchasing any books and consider going for a walk in the park to clear my head, but it's still a little too cold out for me, so I sit in my car debating where to go next. Not much to do on a Saturday afternoon. By habit, I lift my phone to scroll my social media apps then think twice and, instead, open my text thread with Vince, finally taking the plunge to let him know.

What are you doing? I type.

Hello to you too.

What are you doing right now?

I'm fine. How are you? he replies, and I groan even though he can't hear me.

OMG. You're like my brother, I message, thinking of how Ray had always wanted me to text him like we were having a conversation in person. Weirdo.

Great minds. he responds.

I have the day off, and I'm by myself.

And you're texting me because you need a friend? He

adds a thinking-face emoji, but it doesn't take the sting out of the situation. I do need a friend.

Could you hear the desperation in my texts?

A smidge.

I sigh and sip of my coffee, not wanting to be *that* person. I don't want to be stuck in a hole, unable to dig out. I want out; I just don't know where to find a shovel.

Want to hang out? he asks, and I'm happy he does so I don't have to.

Yeah.

Meet me at the Turf in an hour.

I agree without even searching where or what the Turf is until after I've started my car. Turns out the Turf is a batting cage.

Does he really think I'm the type of woman to go to a batting cage?

I so *obviously* am not. And yet, I drive there anyway, fooling myself into believing I'm going solely because I need a friend—any friend—and not because it's Vince who will be there.

I wait on a blue plastic chair next to the door of the Turf for Vince to show up. The walls are covered in posters of who I assume are professional baseball players, along with a few pictures of little league teams full of the kids' smiling faces. This is exactly the type of place my brother probably frequented, and sadness overpowers me. I pick up a *Sports Illustrated* to take my mind off him. The article about some college basketball coach doesn't do it, but Vince finally strolling in does.

"Hey, Cass," he says like he's been speaking my name every day for the last decade, and I'm unsure of how to greet him. Although, he doesn't have the same problem and opens his arms for a hug.

I hesitate for a moment, and he smiles. That one little lift of his lips on the left side has me wrapping my arms around his torso before I've even consciously thought it. I haven't seen him in almost a month, and we're barely acquaintances. But the way he folds me into him with one arm banded around my waist and the other around my shoulder so his hand can cup my neck, and his head bent down low enough that I can hear him breathing... It's intimate. I lean my chin against the indent of his collarbone, the perfect spot, and he tightens his hold, pushing a breath out of my lungs. He's squeezing the life out of me.

Or into me, I'm not sure.

"Can I help you guys?"

Vince releases me suddenly and my weight moves forward, and I have to rebalance myself as if he'd been holding me up. I try to brush the thought away of how much I needed or wanted him to.

He steps around me to a bearded guy in a polo behind the counter. They exchange a few words, the worker's eyes briefly drifting to me. I'm out of place in my boots and jeans. It's obvious I don't belong here, but Vince doesn't mention anything about the thud of my steps next to him as we walk.

When Vince showed up the day after *it* happened, I hadn't bothered to pay attention to what he looked like, not really. Now, though, I study him in quick side glances. He's handsome in an old-school sort of way, like he walked out of a Rat Pack movie, with his slightly curly sideswept hair and square jaw and long nose. He should always be in his suit with a skinny tie because his sweats and sneakers look so out of place on him. And yet, he's so at ease in his body, it's impossible to ignore his confident gait. Same goes for that nagging little heartache I had for him as a young girl that's suddenly rushing back.

He stops at a stand lined with bats and holds one out to me. "See if you like this one."

I take it between my fingers. It's heavier than it appears.

"Can you swing it? Try."

I sway it in a downward arc around my legs, and he rolls his eyes at me then lifts a gray helmet from another rack. With a plop of it on my head, he smacks the top of it twice. "How's that?"

I wobble my head back and forth. "Peachy."

"Perfect." He retrieves his own bat and helmet and marches up to a netted cage, opening the overlapping netting and motioning inside expectantly. "Wanna go first?"

"No, I'm good," I say, and he raises his brow in a challenge, but I shake my head.

He clucks his tongue like he's disappointed, but his mouth curves my way as he puts on his helmet before walking inside like he's home. He inserts two gold coins into what looks like a plain metal box with a couple buttons, presses the green one on the top, and then takes his place outside of the plate. He wiggles his butt a little—my fourteen-year-old self collapses—and lifts his bat in the air. He swings and hits every ball that flies at him from the other side of the batting cage.

It's clear he's in his element. He's so good at this—perfect, as far as I can tell. I remember him playing baseball with Ray, that he was really good. A catcher, which was why he and Ray, the pitcher, were such great friends. Like they were on one wavelength, spoke another language all their own.

I don't know what happened after high school, probably what happens to a lot of people. They simply lost touch, and I'm suddenly desperate to know what happened for all those lost years. I need to fill in the blanks.

Especially why he's *here*.

With *me*.

I'm intimidated by the whole scene, of this place and of him, but I pretend not to be with one hand on my bat and the other on my hip. When the balls finally stop flying at him, he pivots to me, and I whistle. He saunters out of the cage, grinning. A light sheen of sweat highlights his forehead, his flushed cheeks.

I lean dramatically against his shoulder. "Be still my beating heart. A man who knows what to do with balls."

The line of his lips slowly curls up, his attempt at not smiling eventually failing. He taps my hip twice, the expanse of his hand finding me like it's the most natural thing in the world. "Your turn."

"Eh. I'll pass." I stand upright, putting a few inches of space between us, uncomfortable being so comfortable with him.

"You agreed to meet me here. You've got the bat and the helmet, but you're going to pass?"

I swing the bat over my shoulder, and it haphazardly knocks into my helmet. "Not really my scene."

"Not really your scene," he mumbles in his faux irritation that I remember so well from years ago. Bordering on flirtatious. He curves his hot palms over my shoulders and bodily spins me around, pushing me forward, through the netting, crowding me into the batting cage.

"Stand over there," he says, indicating to place he stood. "Are you right or left-handed?"

"Right."

"Okay." He tugs me by the arm to stand outside of the plate. With light touches on my elbows, knees, hips, and shoulders, he moves me into the position of a real baseball player. Sort of. "You're holding the bat too low. Choke up a bit."

"Huh?"

He slides my hands up higher on the bat and keeps his fingers over mine. "You'll have more control of your swing this way. How does it feel?"

I angle my head so I can turn to look at him. This close, I reacquaint myself with the individual gray and brown flecks in his eyes, the few freckles on the bridge of his nose, the mole he has on the side of his throat, right above his collar. His skin is naturally bronzed, and he smells new yet familiar, like pine soap and that waft of warm air when you first open the door to summer.

When he raises his brow, evidently awaiting my answer, I blink away. "Okay, I guess."

He backs away from me and goes over to the box to insert more coins. With a press of the green button, he directs me, "Keep your eye on the ball and swing as hard as you can."

The ball releases from the chute on the other end with a rattling *shoop*, and it flies right at me. I jump back.

"Don't be afraid of it," Vince says. "Hit it."

"I'm not afraid." I step back into position. "Just scared me."

He laughs and mimes choking up on the bat, and by the time I'm situated in position, another ball has passed by me.

"Eye on the ball," he says, and I take a swing at the next one. Miss.

And the next one, miss.

And the one after that.

I miss every single ball until the machine quiets at the other end. "This is so stupid." I rip off my helmet. "What's the point?"

"The point is to hit the ball." He slides more coins into the machine. "Try again."

I spin around as the balls start flying again. The first one hits the back of the net with a soft *plunk* and falls to the ground.

"You giving up? Already?" he calls out, goading me.

Growling, I put my helmet back on, then take my stance and focus on the machine at the other end, not taking my gaze off it. And the next time a ball comes at me, I swing the stupid bat as hard as I can and hit it. The white ball lobs up to the top of the netting almost straight above me.

Vince claps his hands a few feet away from me, but I don't look at him. I keep focus and swing again. I hit the next ball.

I channel all my pent-up energy into it. My grasp on the bat slickens, my fingers holding on so tight, but I don't stop. The *clang* of the bat meeting the ball is an audible echo for my anger. I yell out on the next swing. It's barbaric, and I don't care. I want to slam all of my rage into the ball and send it flying out into the atmosphere.

And when the balls finally stop coming, I drop the bat to my side, my arms and shoulders exhausted. Vince seems reasonably impressed. I nod at him. "I want to go again."

He grins. "That's what I like to hear."

MARCH 11

I did something different today. I hit things. Balls, to be exact.

I am not what you would call athletically inclined, but something got into me tonight. Whether it was the Holy Spirit or the Devil, I'm not sure, but I stood in the batting cage for half an hour straight, swing after swing, hitting baseball after baseball. I didn't think about anything else, except that small white thing flying at me and how good it felt to smack it away. But good isn't the right word...it was euphoric. The rage normally trapped between my ribs, pinballing between my bones, didn't have a place to go. It's been seething inside me, my temper rising every day, until now. I was able to release, drive it from me, wind it up, and force it out with every swing. Until tonight, I never knew what it was like to hold a metal bat, have it reverberate in my hands off a hit. That vibration spread through my veins like a gong in a Buddhist temple. It was both violent and calming.

In bed tonight, I'm too tired to remember how sad and angry I am. And after these last few weeks, I'm glad for the reprieve, even if it means I worked up a sweat. At least I'm not fighting my tears tonight. Besides, there's no crying in baseball, right?

#Grief #RaymondStGeorge #TheTurf #SmashedIt #ALeagueOfTheirOwn

CHAPTER 11

My last post with the picture of a bat and a ball has gotten even more comments, shares, and likes than the Nutella one. It's earned me a couple more followers too. I click on the grief hashtag, curious about what else there is. It's mostly sad quotes in pretty fonts and even sadder black-and-white photos.

My posts aren't like that. They're angry and frustrated and perhaps a little more real. Maybe it's why people like them. Because grief isn't always pretty fonts and stylized photos of a sunset or a gray sky over a beach.

It's ugly and out of focus and changes on a daily basis.

And I type exactly that with a picture of my middle finger.

Just as I hit post, Mom asks if I'll go with her to the store. I try to temper my shock and awe so as not to scare her away from the land of the living.

"Yeah, sure," I say coolly and slip my feet into shoes. She waits at the front door for me, in her jacket, with her purse over her shoulder. She's even showered and styled her hair. "You look good, Mom," I tell her as we walk to my car.

She doesn't acknowledge the compliment, probably because it's not really one. After almost two months of darkness and sleep, I'm saying she looks like a real human instead of the lump of skin and bones she's become.

I try to keep the conversation light in the car. I want to keep her talking, keep her conscious like they do in the movies, to prove to myself and her that she's still with us. She's still alive. She tells me she wants to make pork chops, green beans, and potatoes, something she'd normally make with her eyes closed.

After parking the car, I wrestle a cart away from the rest and lead the way into the grocery store, noticing she's slowed down since walking from the parking lot. She's lost some of the confidence she had at home as she holds on to her purse with both hands, and I slow my pace to match her timid steps. First, we head to the produce section, where she wearily eyes fresh garlic and parsley before choosing which ones she wants. I notice the slight tremor in her fingers when she places the beans into the cart, but I don't say anything.

When we move to the meat, she clings to the side of the cart, and I can tell her skin is ashen beneath the bit of makeup she's put on. When she can't decide on package of meat, I pick one out.

"You all right, Mom?"

She clears her throat, nods, and positions the cart toward the condiment aisle. This time, I don't wait for her to stand there, lost in whatever thought she's been struggling with, and I reach for a bottle of olive oil. We move farther through the store to the dairy section.

"I've been buying almond milk for myself, so we don't have any regular," I inform her, opening the glass door. "Do you want a gallon?" I ask, glancing over my shoulder.

My mother is bent in half with her hands on her knees.

I drop the milk and run to her. "Mom, what's wrong."

She wheezes, and I try unsuccessfully to stand her up straight. She's completely white, but when I touch her cheek, she's hot. Her hands are trembling in mine when I tug her toward me. "What's wrong?"

"I can't breathe," she pants, clutching at her chest.

Fear tears through me, and I look around for anyone. An older gentleman is at the end of the aisle, and I shout to him, "Help! I need help!"

He cocks his head but scampers away, returning with an employee a minute later as my mother completely gives out on me, and we sink onto the floor.

"What happened?" the employee asks me.

"I don't know. I don't know. I think we need an ambulance."

The older man nods in agreement. "Could be a heart attack."

Mom wheezes, and I'm helpless holding her. I vaguely remember a kid in grade school breathing into a paper bag when he was hyperventilating and think it couldn't hurt. But there are none to be found in the dairy aisle of the supermarket.

More people gather around, and I wave down a young, acne-faced kid wearing the grocery store polo shirt. "Hey! You got a paper bag?"

He wrenches back, apparently frightened by me. "Where would I get one of those?"

"This is a grocery store! Find me one!" He runs off, and I hold Mom's cheeks between my palms. "Breathe, Mom. You're all right."

"The ambulance will be here in a minute," another employee says, and it takes everything in me not to wail.

How is it I'm stuck in this position again? There's nothing I can do for her except try to calm her down as we wait.

I find my cell phone and tap on my father's cell phone number to call him, but he doesn't answer, and I growl in frustration. Just as the high-pitched sirens blare outside, I stick my phone back in my bag. Two paramedics arrive with a gurney, and they ask Mom questions, her eyes fluttering open and closed as they strap her up with oxygen and wheel her outside.

"You can ride with us," one of them says to me. I follow them out with Mom's purse in my hands, our groceries and dinner long forgotten. The gurney clicks and clacks as the paramedics push it into the ambulance. I have to hop up into the back, and no time is wasted as instruments are pulled from compartments. Wires, tubes, needles.

Mom is stuck with an IV.

I hold her hand.

My head bumps against the wall as we take a turn.

It's all horrible.

The paramedic writes something down on a chart. She's so calm as she works; I don't know how or why she could be in this atmosphere, speeding down the road with someone lying in front of her, possibly having a heart attack.

My heart beats out of my chest—maybe I'm the one having a heart attack.

We arrive at the hospital, and the paramedics wheel Mom into the emergency room, leaving two nurses to get her wired up to different monitors. It's all a blur until a doctor enters. "It's not a heart attack."

I breathe out in relief and wiggle my fingers, forcing some sensation back into them after having them shut into tight fists for so long.

"What is it, then?" I ask since Mom is still breathing through a mask.

"Most likely an anxiety attack," he says. "Has anything like this ever happened before?"

I study Mom, completely reclined, and she blinks a few times, tears rolling sideways toward her temples. I answer for her. "I don't think so. My brother died in February so... It's..."

The doctor nods sympathetically and writes something on a prescription pad before typing on a computer in the corner of the room. "I'm prescribing her some antianxiety medication, only a few tablets, but I'm also going to make a referral note about this for her primary care physician." He addresses my mom then. "It's helpful to talk to someone. Anxiety doesn't always go away on its own. Sometimes when family trauma happens, a mixture of counseling and medication is the best solution."

She closes her eyes, and I hang my head.

Something like shame washes over me. Each of us, Mom, Dad, and me, we're shadows of the people we used to be. We're trying not to disappear, and it's impossible to truly confront what happened. Like if we don't admit it, it didn't happen. At least, that's what it's like for me.

When the doctor leaves, I pull out my cell phone and give my dad a call again. He doesn't answer *again*, so I call his office and talk to his secretary.

"He's in a meeting right now," she says.

"Tell him it's an emergency."

"An emergency?" Her voice rises, and I assume she's thinking of the emergency we had two months ago.

"Yeah, my mom."

"Okay, hold on."

The line quiets until my father picks up a minute later. "Cassandra, what is it?"

"Mom's in the hospital," I say. "We were at the grocery store, and she had a panic attack."

"Jesus Christ."

When he doesn't offer anything else, I ask him, "Can you come home?"

"I'm in the middle of a meeting with the CFO."

I huff. "She's in the hospital, Dad."

"It was a panic attack. People have those all the time. Take her home and put her to bed."

"Like I've been doing for the past couple of weeks?"

"Yeah."

When I grumble, he sighs like this is all so difficult *for him.*

"Anything else?" he asks.

"No." I don't give him the opportunity to hang up on me. I instead press the red button before he can. I text Aunt Joanie to tell her, and she says she'll be over after work, but that doesn't help me with getting to *my* work on time.

Gary eyes me when I finally run into Sassie's, and I hold up my hand, but it doesn't stop him. "You know I'm letting a lot of things slide with you, but you're half an hour late."

"I know. There was nothing I could do about it."

He folds his arms and gives me a disappointed-parent look. "I'm going to have to write you up for this. You're on thin ice here, Cass."

I stuff my purse into one of the cubbyholes in the corner and steal a pen from the jar, ignoring him. If I worried about every write-up from Gary at Sassie's Lassies, I'd be lying next to my mother in bed right now. This job is the least of my worries.

After cleanup and shutdown, it's almost midnight by the

time I clock out, but I don't want to go home. I don't want to deal with my parents, with my mom on whatever pill makes her like a zombie. Or wondering what time my father will be home or if he'll be drinking. It's all too hard. People said it would eventually get easier. But when does eventually start?

In the empty parking lot outside, I sprawl back on the hood of my car. It's cool out, and I pull my jacket up around my neck as I open the contacts on my phone to call Vince.

We usually only text, and I'm dazed by his gravelly, bedroom voice saying my name. "Cass?"

"Yeah. Hey."

"It's the middle of the night."

"Not really." I glance at the time on my phone. "Only 12:13."

"Only 12:13," he repeats with a sleepy laugh.

"Did I wake you up?"

"Kind of," he says. "I fell asleep a little while ago."

"I just got out of work," I tell him, imagining his eyes closed and hair sticking up, cheek creased from his pillow and sleep. I don't let myself imagine what he sleeps in.

"Everything all right?" he asks quietly.

I stare up at the dark sky, stars twinkling here and there. I want to talk to Vince in person, with his pretending not-to-smile smile, but I don't know how to ask. More likely, I'm too chickenshit to ask. So I settle for his voice in my ear instead. "What do you think happens when we die?"

"Hmm," he says after a moment of silence. "I don't think there is one answer."

"What's that mean?"

His voice becomes stronger, as if he's sitting up, fully awake. "A lot of people believe different things, and I don't think any one is right or wrong. I think maybe it all kind of happens, like whatever you believe will happen...does."

"As in heaven or hell or one hundred virgins?"

"Yeah. I guess..."

"What if you don't believe in anything? What if you think the end is the end?" I'm sincerely interested in his thoughts. He is the expert.

"I don't know. I haven't really thought about it much."

I sit up. "But you bury dead people for a living. What else is there for you to think about?"

He yawns. "You ever read *Peter Pan*?"

"No."

"It was my favorite book when I was little," he tells me, and I smile. I don't know why, but I like knowing that little factoid about Vince.

"He says 'To die would be an awfully big adventure,' and I guess it's true. It's the biggest adventure of them all. It's inevitable we'll all find out what's on the other side one day, whether it's a big guy with a beard or an island in the middle of the ocean." He pauses for a few moments, building my suspense. "I don't know what it'll be, but I'm okay with not knowing for now."

I'm okay with not knowing for now.

It's not life-changing, yet it's so perfectly uncomplicated. Like Vince, uncomplicated. I want to be like that, like him. Easy like Sunday morning.

I try to push away thoughts about what Sunday mornings would be like with him. Probably lazy and warm, hazy and still. The kind of stuff Pinterest aesthetics are made of.

I'm tempted to confess all that's tumbling around in my head, but I can't. It's physically impossible for me to even form the syllables with my lips, although I think he already knows that about me. Like my brain, my heart, and my mouth don't exist on the same plane. They don't speak the same language.

Before I can begin to explain what's inside me, he says, "I've seen what grief can do to families, and I know you're trying to parent your parents right now."

"Parenting my parents? Is that what I'm doing?"

"Seems like it to me." He clears his throat, his voice coming through louder, and it sounds as if he's right next to me when he says, "I know I've said it before, but you're doing okay, Cass."

"Feels like I'm drowning." I straighten my neck to lift my head higher, keeping it above the water.

"Just breathe," he says. And I do.

I tilt my head back up to the sky, microscopic underneath the vastness of it all, and close my eyes, giving in to my own insignificance in the face of an awfully big adventure.

CHAPTER 12

*N*ormally for Easter, Mom would make a ham, Nana would bring side dishes, and Ray and Shayna would have the girls over for an Easter egg hunt in the backyard after Dad hid a few plastic, pastel-colored eggs. But that was *before*.

Now, I can't get my mother to talk about a holiday without tears. My grandmother is too busy praying for my brother's soul at church to be bothered with making anything. And my father, he couldn't care less.

In an effort to keep things normal, I arrange to pick up catering and set the table for the family, minus one. I even call Shayna and invite her over, but by the time everyone arrives, the food is cold and Dad is drunk.

Pop stuffs himself with chocolate cake as Nana shakes her head at all the uneaten food. "It's a shame," she says over and over, sometimes pausing to frown at me like the family tradition gone sour is my fault. Aunt Joanie sits next to Mom as she picks at the pasta salad she'll never eat. When Shayna finally shows up with Lara and Lucy in tow, I greet her with a grateful hug, shocking the shit out of both of us. The three of them all wear the same patterned leggings with white sweaters. Lara and Lucy both have big bows in their hair.

"Guess who's here!" I chirp.

My mom pastes on a smile and hugs the girls when they go to her. She pets their heads as fresh tears spring to her eyes. "My grandkids, I love you," she says, hugging them both to her. "You look like your daddy."

"Can we have cake?" Lara asks. Lucy dances in front of Shayna, her hands folded in a silent plea.

"One piece."

Nana cuts them each a piece of cake, and we all watch these two little girls scarf down the dessert. It's the most activity we've seen all day.

"Can we look for eggs now?" Lucy asks with a chocolate-covered smile.

I wince, saying, "We don't have any this year," then reach for a chocolate bunny wrapped in gold foil. "But how about you sit with Pop and eat this, huh?"

Lara snatches it from my hand, and they race into the living room, where they flop on the couch next to my grandfather, who's snoring. Aunt Joanie takes Mom into the kitchen, and Nana clears the table, leaving Shayna and me alone.

I haven't seen her since the funeral, and she's back to her old self. "Got your hair highlighted," I note. "Looks good."

She juts her chin at me. "You need yours done."

"Kind of you to say."

She smirks at me, one that's familiar. Her nails are done too, purple with little pink flowers on her index and pinkie fingers.

"It's been over two months," she says. "At some point, I had to get it together."

I can't meet her gaze as she says these words, half because I hate her for not wallowing and half because I'm still wallowing.

"Your mom looks terrible. She must've lost about fifteen pounds."

I shrug and keep my attention down, drawing the same invisible circle over and over with my finger on the dining room table.

"You look terrible too," she adds.

I snap my head up. "Yeah, well, my brother died."

"He was my husband," she enunciates, as if she's winning some contest.

"And you were getting divorced," I whisper harshly. "Did you even love him?"

She rears back as if I've slapped her. "Of course I loved him. What a horrible thing to ask."

Her reprimand only stokes my fire. "You don't act like it. You're not even wearing your wedding ring."

She calmly folds her hands, her elbows on the table. "And what do you want me to do? Wear black every day? Sit in my house all day long, become a shell of a person? Would you prefer I be like your mother?"

I have no retort, my jaw bobbing up and down uselessly.

"Do you want me to pine over a ghost? If he were still alive, he'd still be sleeping with that woman. Am I supposed to forget that happened? Should I pretend we had a wonderful marriage and our life was perfect?" She holds up one delicate finger, a teacher to her pupil. "I loved your brother, I still do, but it doesn't mean I'm not going to move on with my life like I would've done if he were still here. We would have gotten the divorce. I still would have accepted the date to go out with Todd—"

"Todd? Who's Todd?" I ask, my voice unusually high.

"He's the dad of a kid who goes to school with the girls. He coaches their soccer team."

I roll my eyes. Todd. What a dick. I don't know the guy, but I'm offended on my brother's behalf anyway.

"So you're going out with a guy named Todd?"

"Yes, I am. And I suggest you do the same?"

"Find a guy named Todd?" I ask, in my most mocking tone.

She glares at me. "Move on. You don't need to stop living because RJ's not."

"I'm living," I say, the words sounding meek even to my ears.

She challenges me with one single, perfectly plucked eyebrow raise. And she's right; I haven't really been living, merely getting by. Taking care of my parents, working, and watching reruns of *Price is Right*.

She moves from the table to play with her daughters, and I deflate back into my chair.

APRIL 12

Springtime is supposed to be all about rebirth. Flowers popping up from the cold ground, animals being born… that was basically the whole plot of *Bambi*, right? The calendar has flipped to April, spring has officially sprung, and yet I have no daises. I have no sunshine to speak of. I'm metaphorically the Bambi of this story, still bumbling around on the ice after his mother was shot. Side note: what a terrible children's movie.

Just when I think I'm doing okay, I'm putting one foot in front of the other, I look around and realize I've barely made any progress. It's like I'm running a race in mud or quicksand, and I've got to claw my way out while everyone else is passing me by. Or maybe I'm simply not trying hard enough. I don't know. Whatever it is I'm doing or not doing, life seems to be passing me by.

It's been two months since Raymond died, and I can hear him in my head saying, "Get over it already." He'd probably accuse me of using him as an excuse to stay in my hibernation. A reason not to step out of my comfort zone.

He once told me I write the word literally too much in my posts, but this time, I mean it. "Moving on" is literally the hardest thing I have ever had to do, especially when I'm not sure how. But I'm going to try. I'm going to do my best impression of Bambi and learn to walk again. Because if he can become the King of the Forest after humans murdered his mom and his woods are burned down, I can certainly slap on a pair of skinny jeans and try to have some fun. I'm going to find what makes me happy.

#Grief #RaymondStGeorge #KingOfTheForest #BambisMomDeservedBetter #SaveTheTrees

CHAPTER 13

$\mathcal{E}$ven though we've texted and talked on the phone, I haven't seen Vince in about a month, and I need to see him again. Lay my two eyes on him. Feel his smile. Because that's what it's like.

A feeling.

Warmth and sunshine and fresh air.

And if I am going to be self-reflective about my life up until this stage, it wasn't going *great*. Raymond's heart crapping the bed was the worst thing to ever happen to me—will probably ever happen to me. But before that, I hadn't truly been living.

Somewhere along the line, I'd stopped putting myself out there for fear of getting hurt. Though, I now knew there was nothing that could hurt more than losing Ray, so what was the sense of hiding anymore?

If I want warmth and sunshine and fresh air, I should go after it. At least, that was the plan.

While I wait for Vince's response to my text, I check the newest comments on my post with the picture of the missing foot I ate off the chocolate bunny. People are really responding to these new posts, much more than my previous ones, including those I wrote while in New York. I liked living in the city, mostly because I was invisible there, and my posts were written that way. Not much different from what other people are trying to do—claim some kind of space for themselves.

But my grief posts are not mere space, they're a new universe, and they're inspiring others to join me in exploring it. Some followers message me about their own grief and talk about people from their lives who have died, others comment about how relatable the content is. They like and share the posts, tag other people, building a much wider base than I had before. People of all ages, even other continents.

When I couldn't get the type of job I wanted, I turned my journalism degree to social media, assuming it was the new frontier. I was right about that, but my career hadn't taken off with my social commentary and witty one-liners. But with my several thousand new followers, my anger and loneliness seem to be the ticket. Who'd have thought?

Death, the ultimate unifier.

When Vince responds to my message, we skip the banter and get right to it.

You need a friend, and I'm stuck at work today. Why don't you come over? His text reads.

And hang out while you work with dead people?

I have some paperwork to do. You can keep Gracie company.

I don't really want to spend my time at a funeral home, especially *this* one, but if Gracie needs company... **OK.**

The parking lot at the funeral home is empty, but I notice the landscaping is clean and new. A few rosebushes have started to bloom by the front doors. The big building isn't nearly as overwhelming when I'm not here to attend a funeral, but it's still a funeral home.

I make my way down to Vince's office, where he's singing along to the Frank Sinatra coming from the speaker in the corner, barely loud enough for me to hear. I smile. "Hi."

Vince lifts his focus from his computer, his hazel eyes doing a double take. It could be the lipstick or the light-hearted grin I'm wearing. I don't know if he's ever seen either one on me.

"Hey," he says, and Gracie lopes over to me, licking my hand like an old friend. I cross my legs on the floor next to her, making myself right at home by her dog bed. "You're in a good mood this morning."

"Am I?"

He nods, watching me with squinted eyes like he's examining me under a microscope. I am both pleased and unnerved by it, and I do the only obviously appropriate thing. I look away.

Rubbing Gracie's side, I say, "I've got the day off, the sun's out, and there's a sale at Sephora."

"I've been following you on Instagram. Your posts are really good. They're honest and sad but kind of funny."

"I'll have to add that to my profile description...Cass St. George, honest and sad but kind of funny." I venture a peek at him to find his chair turned to face me, his chin in his hand, and I ignore the tingles spreading from my belly, like champagne on an empty stomach.

"You know what I mean. You've got dark humor. I like it."

I'm inordinately happy about that. "You've been reading all my posts lately?"

I sense him staring at the side of my face, and when I angle to him, he tips his chin up. "It's amazing what some people are willing to say behind a screen."

"By some people, you mean me?"

He flicks his gaze over me. "You're not exactly an open book."

My neck warms from his attention. Even though I'm not an open book, he's able to read me perfectly fine.

I'm inordinately happy about that.

"I'm glad to hear you're going to try to find happiness," he says, quoting my post from last night.

"What can I say? Makeup makes me happy."

"That's all that makes you happy?" he asks, clearly daring me to tell him the truth. Not much has made me happy lately, but he does. In his graciousness of answering my midnight phone calls, his never-ending patience, not treating me as only Raymond's little sister but as a woman who put on her favorite pair of skinny jeans, he's shown me not everything in my life is shit.

And he makes me happy. He always did, even when I was a young girl, lost, trying to find my second-period class on the first day of high school. He had handed me a stick of gum and walked with me to Mr. Parker's geometry class. But that's ancient history, and I don't have enough guts to tell him the truth today.

"Yeah," I say in answer to his question. And then when I finally meet his gaze, his eyes call my bluff, but I refuse to answer him in any form. "Can I take Gracie for a walk?"

The dog's ears perk up at the magic word, and Vince hands me her leash. We leave him to his paperwork and head outside for a refreshing stroll. I spend the time imagining what I want my life to look like, what moving on is for me. I'd like a good job, preferably one that involves writing and not kilts. I'd like to move out of my parents' basement, have money to burn, maybe take a trip.

More importantly, I hope my mom will wake up one

morning and want to be my mom. I hope Dad will recognize I'm his only child now and want to spend time with me. I hope I'll stop calling my brother's cell phone number to listen to his voice mail.

Then again, I've heard somewhere that hope is for fools and children. And I am neither a fool nor a child, so today, I'll focus on something I *can* do. I can enjoy my day off.

When we return to the funeral home, we enter in through the back door like we do this all the time. I let Gracie off her leash as soon as we reach Vince's office door, and I lean against his desk. "You know what I was thinking?"

He stares up at me with a soft smile and curious eyes. "Hm?"

"You've got this grown-up Eddie Munster thing going on, and I think we should work on it."

"Eddie Munster?"

"Yeah. The kid from that old black-and-white TV show...? Maybe if we styled your hair differently and you grow a little stubble, you'd be less 1953, know what I'm saying?"

"You know what I was thinking?" he asks as his phone rings. "We work on your emotional defense mechanisms. How's that sound?" His voice is a bit sharp, and I kind of like snippy Vince. He picks up his phone, his eyebrows raised at me in defiance. I can't argue with him because he's on the phone, but also because I don't want to change my defense mechanisms. They've been working fine for me all these years. Although that's the point, and he knows it.

With a resigned huff, I lounge in the chair across from his desk with Gracie at my feet. He's talking about a flower delivery, and I survey his office. He's got binders and a few pamphlets scattered on the shelves, but other than that, there's nothing to show what he actually does all day. When he hangs up, I ask him, "What do you really do?"

He tilts his head, one eyebrow up.

"Ten-year-old Vince Mancini was like 'I want to be an undertaker'?"

"Funeral director," he corrects me, and I playfully roll my eyes.

He plays with a pen, flipping it from one end to the other on his desk. "We're a family business, so I always knew this was what I was going to do. When you're around it all the time, it's not as weird as it is—" he gestures to me with the pen "—for someone like you."

I shift forward and snag the pen from between his fingers. "You really wanted to dress up corpses all day?"

He leans his forearms on his desk. "Sensitivity's not your strong suit, is it?"

I shrug. He already knows the answer.

"No, I didn't want to necessarily work with the deceased, as those of us with empathy would put it—" he eyes me intentionally and steals the pen back "—but it's part of the job sometimes. I don't do it every day. Most of the time, it's mundane stuff like phone calls, scheduling services, filling out paperwork, or meeting with family members."

I shudder. "Still kinda creepy, though."

He props his elbows up on the desk. "Yet you're here."

"I'm curious," I say offhandedly as I stand to peruse a book of poems. "What would you be doing if you weren't doing this?"

He takes his time to think. "I was good at math in school, maybe an engineer. I was offered a partial scholarship for baseball."

I circle around. "You were?"

He nods, his attention on his computer screen as he types something.

"And you still chose this?"

"Like I said, it's the family business. We've been doing this for generations. It was a given."

"For what it's worth, I think you would have been a good engineer."

He turns to me with his gentle gaze. "What makes you say that?"

"I don't know. You seem pretty good with putting puzzle pieces together." *Like me*, I don't say, but I think that part is understood. I go back to the book of poems, and he goes back to typing. We spend the next few hours together, him working, me reading. And it's one of my best days in a long time.

CHAPTER 14

With the days growing longer and longer, my patience for dealing with my parents is shrinking. Dad's rarely home anymore, and when he is, he's facedown in a bottle, while Mom can't function without medication. She, at least, has a routine down of getting out of bed now, but she's gone from one extreme of not eating to the other of eating everything. Unfortunately, she's learned groceries can be delivered to the door, so she doesn't need to leave the house. Aunt Joanie has made appointments for her to speak to someone, but she's only gone to get new prescriptions, not actual help, which has only pissed off the one person who has been around through all of this—Aunt Joanie.

And for as much as I wanted to move out of the house before, I can't now. I'm the only one left. Without any outside help, I struggle to keep the strings of my family tied together. I have to try, though, to keep some semblance of normalcy, because if I lose them, that's it. I'll truly have nothing left. So I stay in my parents' house, hoping one day they'll snap out of it.

I spend most of my free time with Vince at the funeral home and discover he does a lot more than hang out with dead people. With only him, his dad, uncle, and a cousin working there, Vince performs a lot of the grunt work. He does all the landscaping and cleaning of the building's exterior. Last week, I ate a pint of Häagen-Dazs while he power-washed the white siding until it gleamed. I basically follow him around, asking questions all day. He says I'm becoming obsessed with the macabre. I say I merely want to learn more about him. Though, I never go down the back left hall, where the mortuary is. It's where they prepare the bodies, and he offered to show it to me to prove it wasn't as creepy as what I thought. I absolutely refused.

Instead, I repeated what he told me weeks ago. "I'm okay with not knowing for now."

Today, I sit in the back of one of the service rooms drinking pomegranate juice while he prepares for a funeral, laying programs on each chair. "Do you know the story of Persephone?"

He pauses halfway to a chair with a program in his hand. "No, rando, I don't."

I hold up the curvy bottle of juice. "I thought of it because of pomegranate."

He stands up straight, waiting for me to continue, a habit we've picked up—me saying the first thing that comes to mind and him anticipating an elaboration.

"So, okay, long story short, Persephone's the daughter of Demeter, the goddess of fertility and agriculture. Persephone's all beautiful and delicate, and she's picking flowers one day when Hades sees her, and you know Hades? Of course you know Hades. You *are* Hades, god of the Underworld."

Vince shakes his head in amusement, biting back a smile, but I power through.

"Hades sees her, instantly falls in love, and carries her down to the Underworld in his chariot. But Demeter's so upset for her lost daughter, she's wandering around the earth, searching for her, crying because she can't find her, and causes a draught. The earth changes, vegetation starts dying, people are starving, all because she's so depressed. And she creates a new season—winter."

Vince nods along.

"Finally, it gets so bad, Zeus is convinced he's got to do something and sends Hermes down to the Underworld to bring Persephone back. He finds her, but before she leaves, she eats a pomegranate seed."

I hold up the juice once again as if it should all make sense. Vince stares blandly at me.

"It was the pomegranate that sealed her fate. Anyone who eats anything in the Underworld has to stay there. To keep everybody calm, Zeus decided Persephone would spend some time on Earth with her mother, *and* then go back to the Underworld to spend time with Hades, essentially creating the seasons. Summer with her mother and winter with her husband."

Vince considers me for a moment. "You learn that at college?"

I nod. "Knowledge of Greek mythology is evidently not a great skill for a résumé."

He finishes up placing the programs on the chairs and meets me in the back row, reaching for my juice as he sits next to me. He takes a sip of it, no longer uncommon for us to share food and drinks. "A seed made her stay?"

"Uh-huh."

"She didn't ever love him?"

I take the juice back, our fingers skimming in the exchange. "I don't know. There are a lot of versions of the story, but he kidnapped her. I can't imagine she would love him."

"She ate the seed, though," he reasons. "She had to have known it would force her to stay."

"Stockholm syndrome," I suggest.

He raises a shoulder, and the movement causes friction between our arms. "Or maybe she loved him."

I try not to lean into him and glare at him instead. The idea of loving the Underworld is absurd. "No one would actually want to stay there with him."

"Not no one. *Her*."

I don't argue with him since some of the stories do claim Persephone learned to love Hades. "Whatever. It doesn't matter," I say. "The gods and goddesses were all wild. I mean, somebody had sex with a bull and gave birth to the minotaur, so take kidnapping women and falling in love with a grain of salt, I suppose."

He doesn't object and glances down at his grandfather's wristwatch. It's another old-fashioned piece that I've come to learn makes up this old-fashioned guy. I wish I could say there was something about him that extinguished the flame of attraction that began so long ago, but there isn't, and I bury my feelings underneath the reality of my world.

"The family will be arriving soon. Are you staying or leaving?"

I check the time on my phone. I'm closing shift tonight at work, so I have a couple of hours to kill. "I'll stay," I say, and when we both stand, he casually drapes his arm across my back, his hand skating up to my neck, his thumb gently pressing the side of my throat.

I'm not sure if he knows what he's doing by holding on

to me like this, but he's holding me together, and I tuck into his side as we walk back to his office, where Gracie is waiting for us. I set myself up at his desk and open the bottom drawer to nab one of the snack bars he stores there, saying, "Have fun," as he dashes back out of the office with a folder in his hands.

I'm in the middle of making a new post about Persephone and Hades, drawing parallels between the seasons created by Demeter and the stages of grief—I'm a goddamn genius and quite proud of myself—when I receive an email. It's a long message, starting with a reintroduction. Mr. Alvarado is the principal at the middle school where Ray taught and says we met at the funeral. I'm sure we did, but I don't remember. He talks about how the school and Ray's classes are working to keep his memory alive. He has pictures attached of artwork the students have made, along with one of the faculty wearing jeans and Bruce Springsteen T-shirts. Tears cloud my eyes, and I have to pause to blink a few times before continuing to read what Mr. Alvarado has written.

Knowing how RJ felt about teaching and coaching, I wonder if something can be done to fulfill his work. I'm sure you have often thought about this, and I want to let you know some of RJ's colleagues and I would be more than willing to help put a benefit of some kind together, maybe a race or a baseball game to raise money for a charity. I think it would be a wonderful way to honor his memory and keep his spirit alive.

Keep his spirit alive? I haven't thought about it at all. I didn't know I was supposed to. I'd heard of scholarships in the name of someone or charity golf games or something, but I'd never considered I should or needed to do one. Were people expecting me to?

Obviously, Mr. Alvarado was. Rubbing at the pressure in

my chest, I read the whole letter again as panic sets in. I assumed my duties with my brother were finished. Raymond is long since buried, and I have my hands full with Mom and Dad. But now they want more of him? More from me?

"Hey."

I startle and glance up at Vince leaning against the doorframe, smiling at me and Gracie, the two of us practically entwined together on the floor.

"Do I need to have a fundraiser?" I ask.

"Huh?" He unbuttons his suit jacket and eases down to his chair, swiveling it to me so I catch sight of the purple-and-yellow triangle socks he's wearing. The only bit of color with his uniform black suit and white shirt. His closet is full of black suits, white shirts, and patterned socks, or so he told me.

"A fundraiser...for my brother. Am I supposed to do one? To, like, raise money for his team's baseball uniforms or something? Heart disease?"

"Rewind," he says, making the universal "time-out" gesture so I'll regroup my thoughts. I read the email out loud to him, and he reclines in his chair, connecting the dots. "Some people have fundraisers, yes. That's a thing people do."

"But am I supposed to do it?" Guilt courses through me. Why hasn't anyone written an instruction book about what to do when people die? A step-by-step guide would be helpful.

"You can if you want to," Vince says.

"It sounds like this Alvarado guy wants me to."

Vince shrugs, and I'm annoyed at his indifference. It's like, all of a sudden, I'm smearing my brother's name by not doing something. I should open a library or have a street named after him. He was the local hero after all.

I hang my head, whispering, "This is so stupid."

Everyone's created a fairy tale out of Ray like he was this perfect person, changing the world one middle school class at a time. Sure, he was a teacher and a coach, charming, and the life of the party, but so are millions of other people. "Besides!" I shoot up, throwing my arms out. "It's not like he was curing cancer or solving world hunger. I mean, he could be so condescending to me, as if he didn't just luck into everything he got like the quintessential popular guy from some teen movie."

Vince laughs, and I pout.

"I'm serious," I say, raising my voice, forcing the truth out. "I had to work hard! Did you know why I didn't come home summers during college? Because I was interning, subletting in railroad apartments with five other people, eating dollar-slice pizza every day. Meanwhile, he was here, being...you know, given everything from Mom and Dad and everybody else. No one helped me. No one pulled strings to get me a job."

"I know," Vince starts, but I hold up my palm to shush him.

"And he was having an affair. An affair!"

Vince grips my hand, pulling me toward him as he stands from his chair. "Okay. All right. Shh, sweetheart, you're getting really loud. And I don't mean that in the *you can't be loud* way. I mean it in the you'll disturb mourners kind of way."

I exhale, relaxing my shoulders. "I'm just saying, he wasn't exactly a prince."

Vince hugs me the way I love, with one hand in my hair and my face pressed into his chest. He doesn't take away my pain or anxiety, but with him holding me like this, he keeps the hounds from biting at my heels. Just like Hades.

And I could be convinced Persephone knew what she was doing with that pomegranate seed.

After a few moments, I let out a ragged breath. "Ray was my brother. *Mine.*"

"I know." His mouth ghosts over my ear and temple. "That will never change."

I feel him drop a kiss on the top of my head before moving his hands up to my cheeks, and the affectionate touch cracks me in half. I bite the inside of my lip to keep from crying as his thumbs stroke my cheekbones.

"I don't want to share him," I whisper.

He smiles tenderly and pushes me to sit down in his chair. "I can understand that," he says and squats down so we're eye level. "I can also understand why everyone wants a little piece of him too."

I laugh because, yes, my brother was a pretty great son of a bitch.

Vince places one hand on my knee. We've gotten used to touching each other, contact that would normally be friendly, fraternal pats and hugs, but even this—his fingers curling around my kneecap—isn't so platonic.

"No one is perfect," he says. "But I think people want to remember the best of their loved ones. I'm sure this principal feels that way."

"And if I don't do this thing, I'll be the terrible sister who didn't care about her brother's legacy."

He blows me off with a flap of his hand.

"I already think that about myself," I admit, dropping my gaze to the floor.

"Hey." He tips my chin up, forcing me to meet his eyes, so gentle I don't deserve it. He drags his thumb over my jaw.

"Try not to stress out about it. If you don't want to do it, don't. If you want to, then do it. You'll have more than enough help, according to the email."

I hop up, avoiding any more physical contact with him, and grab my things then give Gracie a pat. "I'm going to head out."

"I thought you had time before work?"

Slinging my purse over my shoulder, I keep my eyes anywhere but on his because I don't want him to know how much he or this email have affected me. "I'll talk to you later."

When I shuffle into the kitchen at home, Mom is drinking coffee and eating a doughnut. She's dressed in an old sweatshirt and sweatpants, which has become her standard form of attire. However, she smiles when she sees me, and I know she must've recently taken one of her antidepressants.

"Good day?" I ask, dropping into the chair across from her at the table.

She nods. "I'm making meatloaf and mashed potatoes for dinner."

"Okay. I'm closing tonight, so I won't be home to eat."

"There'll be plenty of leftovers," she says, except with the way she's been eating her emotions lately, the leftovers won't last very long. I am *not* the model for perfect coping mechanisms, but the dramatic swing of extremes over the past few months can't be healthy for her.

"Maybe we can go for a walk one of these days. The weather's been great lately."

She doesn't acknowledge me, not that I expect her to agree to go. Since our last outing into the world ended in a trip to the ER, she's refused to go any farther than the backyard or mailbox at the front of the house.

"Sunshine might do you some good," I say, but she only sips her coffee. I tuck my hair behind my ears, the bangs my mother hated so much grown out now. "I got an email today from Mr. Alvarado."

Mom gazes at me passively.

"He was Ray's principal."

She finishes off the doughnut.

"He wants me to do some kind of fundraiser in Ray's name."

"Oh?"

"What do you think?"

"I think that would be lovely," she says, showing real signs of life for the first time in a long time, and the small glint in her eyes is the final nail in this coffin. I have to do this. Not for me, but for everyone else.

How novel.

APRIL 24

I had a whole other message typed up ready to post. It was about Persephone and Hades and symbolism, and a really great use of my Greek mythology minor, but my day and mind were hijacked by something unexpected. That's the pattern with me—I have plans, I'm moving forward, and then there's a roadblock and I stumble. A punishment from the gods.

I am Sisyphus pushing the boulder up the hill every day.

Albert Camus argued that only when Sisyphus accepts the absurdity of his doomed fate, can he truly be freed of it. Maybe that's the key for me too. I have to accept that this will be my life from now on. I will think I've found my way out of grief, only to be knocked back into the middle of it. Maybe the fate of a grieving person is to never stop grieving, therefore I should stop trying. I only need to live my life day-by-day, giving in to it in order to accept it.

Is that the key to successfully making my way through this? Did I just win the game? I'm not sure. For now, though, I will continue to push the boulder. These ramblings have been brought to you by a confused, absurd antihero, The Myth of Cassandra St. George.

QOTD: Do you ever feel like Sisyphus? What's your boulder?

#Grief #RaymondStGeorge #GreekMythology #Sisyphus #Persephone #ZeusSaveMe #IGraduatedCollegeAndAllIGotWereHighInterestLoans

CHAPTER 15

The little pizza place where we decided to meet isn't fancy, but I still bounce my leg up and down while I wait for Mr. Alvarado. I play with the napkin holder, bopping it back and forth, second-guessing if I should have agreed to this.

A bell over the door chimes, and I turn my head in its direction, like I've done each time it's sounded. But he's finally arrived, in a salmon-colored polo shirt and jeans. He's younger than I expected, with dark, tanned skin and a touch of salt-and-pepper by his temples. He greets me with a grin and open arms. "Cassandra, it's so nice to see you."

I hug him limply as he pounds my back like we're old buddies.

"I wasn't sure if I should reach out or not, but I'm glad I did. We all really miss RJ at school." He utters the last bit like a prayer, his lips losing their affable curl.

"I miss him too," I say, moving to sit down.

Mr. Alvarado stops me with a gesture to the glass case with pizza behind it. "Let's grab something to eat first, huh?"

I follow him to the counter and order one slice of plain along with his two mushroom and pepperoni. "I love this place," he says. "We order from here when we have faculty meetings or parties at school." He pays and accepts our slices with a "Thanks, Joe," then leads me back to a booth.

Mr. Alvarado is so in control, it's hard not to let him lead me, and I'm grateful when he speaks, even if he is a little overeager. There aren't any awkward silences I need to fill up. He talks about how my brother's students are dealing with his death and how they're still getting used to his replacement. He tells me a story about a boy named Sam. "Miss Hale, the teacher we brought into his classroom, started to take down RJ's posters, and Sam lost it. Absolutely lost it. He started arguing with her, yelling at her that she couldn't touch his stuff, and the other kids got into it too. It was a bit of a mess, but it shows you how much his students loved him."

I rip my leftover crust into pieces. "Yeah," I agree. "He was a good guy."

"So," Mr. Alvarado says, "what did you have in mind for the benefit?"

"Um. I was thinking maybe a baseball game, but I'm not sure how to go about setting it all up."

"A baseball game would be great. I'm sure so many people would love to participate. I'd assume his baseball players would want to play. A ton of our faculty would want to get in on this, obviously." He goes on about some pep rally they had at the school and how my brother would usually be the MC, but this year, another teacher did it and something about a mascot, but I can't be sure because my mind wanders.

Ever since I told Mr. Alvarado I'd do this, I've been

feeling knots in my stomach. It's been a few months since my brother passed away, and I've gotten to a place where I don't think about him every minute—down to a few dozen times a day—but agreeing to do this, he's back in front of me. Every step, every sentence, every thought revolves around the memory of my brother. Or the legend, for how Mr. Alvarado talks about him.

"Anyway, have you thought about what the money would go toward?" he asks, and when I don't have an answer, he toggles his head back and forth. "Our computer lab could use some new computers."

He steamrolls me, and it's hard to say no. "Oh? Yeah, okay, we'll buy some new computers for the school."

He claps once, and his excitement builds as he goes on about ticket sales and concessions. He tells me he'll help advertise the event. "I've got forty teachers to help spread the word. You let me know what you need, and I'll be there."

"That's great. Thank you."

"Anything. Anything you need. RJ's death was a big loss for a lot of people, you know. We're all trying to find a way out of this."

His words take my breath away, and my throat closes. It's true. I'm lost, trying to find my way out. He gives me a goodbye hug, but I stay for a while after he leaves, taking out my phone to Google *How to run a benefit baseball game*.

It brings up a ton of websites for baseball teams and fundraisers and benefits, and my brain swirls. I buy the book *Fundraising for Dummies*, hoping it's a good place to start. The knot in my gut pulls tighter. Having an event where people could come together to celebrate Raymond, have fun in his name, would be a perfect tribute, but it's a lot of work. More stress, more grief, most likely more pain.

But in the end, though, it's not about me. It's about my brother, and his students, that Sam kid. It's for his coworkers, his baseball players, his friends. It's for Mom and Dad, and hopefully a jump start to a different future, and our family of three.

MAY 1

Save the date! In honor of my brother, Raymond St. George, we will kick the summer off with a baseball benefit on June 22nd. We'll be raising money to fund new computers for Edison Middle School. Stay tuned for more details!

#Grief   #RaymondStGeorge   #Baseball   #Benefit #Fundraising

CHAPTER 16

With spring growing to summer, the outdoor patio at Sassie's is the most popular place for customers to sit and where they leave the best tips. It's also where Gary catches me leaning in the corner of the door, reading articles about acquiring fundraising sponsors on my cell phone. He tells me he'll write me up if he catches me with it again. I grin at him overeagerly with a thumbs-up before tucking the phone away. At this point, there's not much left for me to be afraid of.

"Got a three-top at thirteen," the hostess tells me as I'm refilling waters for one of my tables. I acknowledge her and roll back around to my left, barely acknowledging the patrons. "Hi, my name's Cassandra, and I'll be your server today." I flip open the beer menu. "Would you like to start off with something from one of our taps?"

I glance up from the list of beers and do a double take. "Vince."

"Cass." His closed-lip smile is secretive, and with his sunglasses on, I don't know where he's focusing, but I self-consciously tug on my skimpy top, trying to cover up as much skin as possible. "Long time no talk," he says breezily.

We haven't spoken in about a week. Not since the winter have we gone without a text, phone call, or me tagging along as he works. "I've been trying to figure out how to put this baseball game together," I say in a flurry, hoping he doesn't catch my lie of omission—that *he* is making me face things I'm not ready for. "You're out in the sun," I tease. "Visiting from the Underworld?"

"Yep." He gestures to the men across from and next to him. "This is my cousin Nick and my friend Ryan."

"You guys in the death business too?" I ask.

Nick, a stereotypical Jersey Italian, shakes his head. "I'm in HVAC, but my brother works there."

"Tony?" I ask.

"Yep." He removes his sunglasses so I can see the bit of resemblance between Vince and Nick. "You know him?"

"Yeah, I ran into him a couple of times while I was hanging out at the funeral home."

"Huh," he says, his eyes toggling between Vince and me. "You like being there?"

I laugh. "That's a stretch."

Vince's mouth quirks to the side, and my joints go loose, my tongue thick. I like *him*. That's not a stretch.

Ryan, with sandy hair and a beard, frowns. "Gives me the creeps."

When I agree, he tilts his head up, smiling at me with one eye closed against the bright sunshine. He hovers his hand over his brow as his gaze drifts over me. It's not gross, more or less curious. "Hey, Cass."

He says my name overly familiarly, and I slant my head back.

"Don't remember me, do you?" he asks.

I shake my head, and he runs his hand over his beard. "We graduated together. You were in my Spanish class freshman year."

"I'm sorry," I say. "I don't remember."

The beard covers up the lower half of his face, but even without it, I don't know if I would be able to recognize him. He shrugs. "Eh, you were too smart for me. I barely passed that class."

I squint, trying to recall the teacher's name. I snap my fingers. "Señora Garcia."

"Yeah." He grins. "You sat two rows over from me. You had shorter hair then," he says, angling his hand by his ears.

I'm shocked he remembers all that, and with the way Ryan leans back in his chair, folding his arms smugly over his chest, I briefly think maybe it means something more than a fleeting memory.

"Drinks?" I ask, peering down at Vince. He pulls his focus away from Ryan and orders a beer. The other two follow, and I'm barely away from the table when I hear Ryan ask, "Is she single?"

Once I return with their beers, there's a weird tension at the table, and I don't try to engage in any more chitchat. I take their food orders and leave, even though I'd really like to stay and talk to Vince. I float from table to table, occasionally sensing attention on me, but every time I turn to Vince's table, they're talking among themselves. I shake off the imagined awareness and drop off the check with quick goodbyes.

When Nick and Ryan leave the table, Vince sticks around, his sunglasses gone. He holds on to my elbow to keep me in place as he hands me the folio. "I think Ryan liked you in school."

It comes out like a quasi-accusation, and my tone is

more defensive than I'd like it to be. "I honestly can't remember him."

"He obviously remembers you."

I lift my brow. "What's that tone for?"

He scratches the side of his head, where his hair is shorter. After a few weeks, I'd finally strong-armed him into a hairstyle from this millennium. "I don't have a tone."

"A little bit, yeah," I say, and he shrinks back apologetically.

"Sorry."

Maybe it's my stress-addled brain or the weird air between us, but I blurt out a long-held secret. "Besides, I wouldn't have noticed other boys. I sorta had a crush on you."

"You what?" His posture changes from the annoyed-shoulders-back thing he does to this one that's forward and amused. "How do you sort of have a crush on someone? You either do or you don't."

"I didn't know there were rules."

He shrugs. "Should've read the rule book. So, which one was it?"

"Does it matter now?"

"Yeah." He leans into my space, his tongue licking his lower lip, capturing all my attention.

I barely resist curling my index finger into the bottom hem of his T-shirt. "Why?"

"You don't know how protective your brother was of you, do you?" he asks, almost like he can't believe it himself, then huffs. "He told all of us he'd murder us if anything ever happened."

"Happened? Like..."

"Like if any of his friends, any of us on the team, thought about you as anything other than his little sister, he said he'd kill us, and…" He lets out a breath, licking his lips again like he's nervous. "He was my best friend. I wasn't about to ruin anything."

I think back to those little moments between Vince and me. Mere seconds I assumed meant nothing to him but were everything to me. Like when Ray let me tag along with them to a late-night Wendy's run, and Vince and I shared the same Frosty. When Vince let me butt in front of him in the cafeteria lunch line anytime we had lunch during the same period. When he saw me in the stands during their play-off game senior year, grinned, and pointed his bat at me with a wink. It was silly and sent my heart straight into the sky.

Maybe those moments meant something to him too.

And the mere idea sends my heart straight up into the sky all over again.

Playing it cool, I knock my shoulder into his arm. "Ray would never have actually done anything. Especially to you."

"That's what you think." He shakes his head. "You were his favorite person. He definitely woulda killed somebody if they ever hurt you."

I inhale sharply. "You saying you would've hurt me?"

"Back then?" He rakes his hand through his hair. "All teenage boys are assholes. Inadvertently hurting people comes with the territory."

I'm feeling bold. Bolder than I have in a very long time. "And now?"

"Now? I hope I'd never inadvertently or advertently hurt anyone, especially you."

I snicker. "Advertently? That's not a word."

He heaves a sigh, though his eyes sparkle in amusement. "You know what I mean." And to drive the idea home, he brushes my hair behind my shoulder, grazing my bare skin in the process. "And I like your long hair now."

I do know what he means. He remembers me from high school, remembers me enough to know how I'm different now. To know how, in some ways, I'm not that different at all. He's telling me he knows me better than Ryan does, better possibly than anyone else, so much so that he's not going to push me on this topic when I don't say anything else about it. About this *thing* between us.

He stuffs his hands into his pockets. "I saw your post yesterday with the pile of clothes. Getting rid of a lot of stuff?"

I wrote another post yesterday in light of my mom wanting to suddenly clear out the house. She's been almost manic lately. Every time I come home, she's got more bags at the front door for me to put in my car and take out. "It's like she's trying to erase something. Or him. I don't know which."

"It's better than her staying in bed all day," he says.

"I guess. But soon, we'll have nothing left. She's even gotten rid of her prized Christmas china." I scuff my shoe on the concrete, defeat curling my spine over. "She's taken down every picture of Ray in the house and moved anything of his to boxes in the closet." It stings not to have evidence of my brother's life around me. I want to remember him any way I can, but she doesn't want to, and I hate it. I press my hand against my throat, tears clogging my windpipe. "I just...I don't get it."

He curves his hand around my neck and squeezes gently. "Breathe."

I inhale deeply through my nose, closing my eyes for a moment as my lungs fill. One side of Vince's mouth is tipped up when I open my eyes to him. It's my favorite of his smiles, the one that feels only for me.

"You're okay, Cass," he says, the sentence I've come to hear over and over in my head when I need reassurance. Hearing it in person, though, is the most potent way to receive it. With his hand on me, I have trouble not melting into him, but I pull myself together.

I force myself to step back from him, his hand dropping from me, and I straighten my spine. The slight movement shifts my uniform, my shirt lifting to show more skin at my stomach than I'd like.

Vince's attention dips there then lower to my legs, quite a bit of them on display because of the short kilt and thin white knee-highs. "You look good."

I bat him away. "Get out of here."

He laughs and walks back inside to exit via the front door. I watch his retreating figure until he's gone, the sensation of his hand on my neck lasting much longer than it should.

MAY 8

"All pitchers are liars or crybabies." Yogi Berra said that. I didn't know who Yogi Berra was, and I assumed it was Yogi Bear spelled incorrectly. Wikipedia informed me otherwise.

Raymond was a pitcher, a pretty darn good one. His being a liar or crybaby is debatable, depending on who you ask. And it's me. If you ask me, he's both, and we're going to honor the liar and crybaby with the Raymond St. George Memorial Baseball Tournament on Saturday, June 22nd. To stay up-to-date with all the details, follow @RSGMemorial on Facebook, Instagram, and TikTok. If you're interested in sponsoring the event, you can message me directly.

Tell your friends, grab your gloves, and we'll see you there!

#Grief #RaymondStGeorge #BatterUp #SeventhInningStretch #HomeRun #Strike #ThatsAllTheBaseballVocabularyIKnow

CHAPTER 17

I position the screen of my laptop toward my mom. "What do you think of this one?"

She ignores me, washing the floor on her hands and knees. She's been cleaning all day. It started with the dining room, vacuuming and dusting, and now in the kitchen, like a middle-aged Cinderella.

"Mom?"

She glances over her shoulder. "Hm?"

"The T-shirt design. You like this one?"

"Sure."

She doesn't really look. I don't know why I thought she'd have an opinion on this when she hasn't given her two cents on anything else. She hasn't been interested in helping like I thought she would be, so I'm stuck organizing this tournament myself. Because apparently one baseball game wouldn't actually raise any money, it's transitioned into a tournament and ballooned into something much bigger than I had originally planned. I called in a favor from my old friend and college roommate, Alma, who came up with a super-simple logo, and I am chugging along, even if I haven't heard back from Mr. Alvarado on sponsorship ideas.

Google and my *Fundraising for Dummies* book say I need to work on securing a location and permits, but I need a bit of money for that. And for money, I need a sponsor or two. I used my long-dormant writing skills to complete a draft of a sponsorship letter but have no idea where or to whom to send it. Making a T-shirt, though, I can handle. I settle on a navy cotton T with white writing and a Springsteen lyric on the back, leaving room for the names of the sponsors. My goal is to have team sign-ups by Memorial Day for the tournament, but the end of May is quickly approaching and the slice of this pie I agreed to is a bit too big for me to eat.

Leaving my mother to her bucket and rag, I shut my computer and stalk out to the living room as I call Aunt Joanie. She picks up after a few rings.

"Hey, Cassie Cat."

"Hi."

"What's up at one thirty in the afternoon on a Wednesday?"

"I've been working all day on this baseball tournament," I say. I'd told her I'd agreed to do this after my first meeting with Mr. Alvarado, but it's only now occurred to me she's a pretty good contact. "You know anyone who might be interested in sponsoring it?"

She hums in thought for a bit. "I could pass the information along to a few people. The hospital won't sponsor, but individual doctors or practices might. Have you tried the school?"

"Yeah, I haven't heard back from the principal yet. I've emailed him twice."

"Call. Always call. It's better to hear a voice than read words."

"Fine," I grumble. The list of people I will actually call on the phone is very short. Currently, two. One, I'm talking to now, and the other is the man who I know will always pick up.

"Have you thought about prizes or food?" Auntie Joanie asks.

"Prizes?" I choke out. "Food?"

She laughs at me. "Cassie, you're putting a sports tournament together. There'll be winners and losers. The teams are going to pay money to sign up, so if they win, they should receive something in return...maybe the top three teams? And you'll need to provide food for the players and anyone who buys tickets to watch. You always need peanuts, right?"

"I guess."

"Food'll be easy. People are always willing to donate juice boxes or soda or whatever. That'll be a—" She cuts off, her voice fading in the background as she speaks to someone else. "Cass, I have to run. Once you have all your information together, send me a digital copy of it all. And make sure you're making physical copies of everything too. Put it in new folders. It's more professional-looking that way."

I make another mental note.

"And don't wear jeans with holes in them when you go to talk to anyone."

"Now you sound like my mother," I say.

Her voice changes, and I can almost picture how her smile drops on the other end. "Love you, Cassie."

"You too."

While it's on my mind, I find Mr. Alvarado's number and dial. He doesn't answer, I'm *sure* because it's the middle of a school day, and I leave a message asking him to call me back as soon as he can. Then I dig out the to-do list I've started in a notebook and add all the tips Aunt Joanie gave me, plus some names of people and places I can possibly ask for donations.

The lined paper is filled with my chicken scratch, and I'm overwhelmed by all the things I haven't accomplished yet...which is basically everything.

Groaning from exhaustion, I put everything away and get ready for work, taking time to style my newly colored hair with purple highlights. Part of me hoped my mother would pick a fight about the color. She used to dislike that I'd dye my hair so dark, almost black, but now she didn't even bat an eye at the purple. My father noticed, though. He rolled his eyes and reminded me, "You're an adult, Cassandra, not a girl playing dress-up."

I tossed him the middle finger behind his back. Ever since I hit my teenage years, Dad had, for the most part, left me alone. It wasn't great, but at least it wasn't this. All of us have changed from Before to After Ray, but Dad has, by far, become the worst. He's just plain mean now.

At work, I constantly check my phone, hoping to hear from Mr. Alvarado, but by close, there's still nothing. I'm sure he's busy with the end of the school year coming up, yet I need some help. I haven't been this frazzled since— since the funeral.

I call Vince from the back of the kitchen. When he answers, I say, "I'm freaking out."

"What?"

"I'm freaking out."

"Why?"

"I have so much to do for the tournament. A tournament... Who said that was a good idea?"

It sounds like he shuffles something, and his voice is hoarse when he says, "You want to grab a drink?"

"On a school night? How wild."

"I could use a stiff drink."

"Yeah?"

He murmurs an agreement and, after a few moments, says, "We buried a little girl today. She was eight years old. Cancer."

I have no words. It's awful. And a stiff drink seems like the right answer, but I don't want to go to a bar after finishing my shift of serving drinks. "How about I bring drinks and some food over to your place?"

"You've never been here before," he says in a voice higher than usual.

"Don't sound so nervous." When he doesn't respond, I grin. "I promise not to take advantage of you."

He huffs out a laugh. "I'll text you the address."

A minute later, his address comes through, and in twenty minutes, I'm on my way to his house. It's small, not too far from the Mancini Funeral Home, but it always strikes me when someone my age lives on their own. They seem so much older, more mature than me...perpetually a child living in my parents' basement.

The porch light is on, shining down on the space in front of the door, and I hold open the screen door to knock. Vince answers wearing dark athletic shorts and a T-shirt that shows off the contours of his chest. He smiles and holds his arm up for me to walk under. The living room to my left is sparse, with a coffee table, TV, and big couch, while a well-worn wooden staircase in front of me leads upstairs. I lean down to kiss Gracie's head.

Vince accepts the greasy paper bag and box of wine from

my hands before leading me to the back of the house. Gracie races ahead of us to the kitchen. It's straight 1960 with teal cabinets, white countertops, and patterned laminate flooring. It's kind of quaint in its older style and totally Vince. When he sets the food and drink down on the kitchen table, I explain, "I got Potter's. It's the only thing open this late."

"I'm not complaining." He sticks a couple of fries into his mouth before retrieving two glasses from a cabinet above the sink. He hands one to me, and I waste no time opening the spout on the box. "Like a pro," he teases.

I fill up my glass, hold it aloft to him in a silent toast then down about half of it. When I wipe my mouth with the back of my hand, all ladylike, he gives me a goofy smile, filling up his own glass. He sits down with the burger, fries, and wine, sighing like it's the best meal he's ever had.

"Sorry about your day," I offer.

He nods, mouth full. I eat a few fries then give some to Gracie, who's at my feet.

"You're going to spoil her," he tells me.

"That's why she loves me more."

"Probably." He stares at me for a thoughtful moment then lifts his cup. "Sorry you're having a tough time with the tournament." After a gulp of wine, he cringes. "This is terrible."

"Yeah." I shrug and fill up my glass again.

I ignore him watching me with his curious eyes until he asks, "You okay?"

He's so goddamn perceptive. I hate it because I love it. "Yeah, why?"

He balls up the paper from his cheeseburger. "You're quiet."

I float my gaze over the room and land on the ceiling, chewing on my lip. With everything I've experienced, and especially with Vince having a funeral for an eight-year-old today, it seems insignificant to be upset over this. Nevertheless, I am. "It's my birthday. I'm twenty-eight today."

"Happy birthday." His words force me to look at him and his smile. He taps his glass against mine.

I take a deep breath, waiting until the sting in my nose goes away. "We're not really celebrating birthdays anymore."

"What's that mean?"

"We used to all go out to eat. But we don't do that anymore...obviously." I push the cold cheeseburger away and finish off my second glass of wine. "Last month for my mother's birthday, I bought her a card she never opened. The next day, I saw it in the garbage, still in the envelope."

Vince's lips tip down, and I force a laugh.

"What're you gonna do, right? Things change, people die, birthday cards get thrown away."

"Yeah, but..." He licks his lips and scratches his eyebrow with his thumb, clearly unable to come up with something to say, even though I don't expect him to. After a moment, he stands abruptly to open the small pantry. He digs around and returns to me with a half-smushed Twinkie in its clear plastic packaging.

When I don't move, he opens it and holds the snack cake out to me, singing an off-key version of "Happy Birthday." Then he takes my hand and places the Twinkie in my palm. We catch each other's gaze and laugh together. It's silly and sweet and cures a little bit of the burn from my family forgetting my birthday. This isn't quite Jake sitting on a table like *Sixteen Candles*, but it's close enough.

"Thank you," I say and rip off the end piece to offer it to him, but he declines.

"It's your cake."

I pop the piece into my mouth, and Vince watches me

with his hazel eyes. It's difficult to pretend I'm completely oblivious to him and the buzzing electricity between us, but I'm not sure I'd know what to do if I ever acknowledged it. It's like I've forgotten how to be a human.

I finish the Twinkie and change the subject, breaking away from the growing pull toward him. "Going to give me the grand tour of your bachelor pad or what?"

"I don't know about grand tour, but if you want to…"

Gracie pads beside me when I wind around the waist-high wall to the other side, which is presumably the dining room. It's empty.

"It's a work in progress," he says, motioning to the whole of the house. "It was built in 1938 and pretty beat-up when I bought it."

I scuff my foot on the hardwood floors. He must've refin-ished them because there are no marks of wear and tear like some other parts of the house. I follow him up the creaky steps to the top floor. He flicks the lights on in all the rooms. The bathroom is nice, and I tell him so.

"It's the first room I did," he says, skimming his hand along the new sink. It's modern, all gray and white. The room next to it is smaller and outlined in painter's tape, with one lamp on the floor plugged into an outlet in the corner. Vince's bedroom is at the opposite end of the hallway, completely finished with shiny wood floors, cream walls, and a comfy-looking green bedspread on the huge mattress. There are even floating shelves on the walls holding succu-lents. As I touch the wood-framed picture of his family on top of his dresser, he says, "I watch a lot of HGTV."

"It all makes sense now."

When I turn around, he's right behind me, close enough I can smell the soap he uses, and I'm tempted to wrap my arms around him. He's the only guy I've been in close contact with for months. The only one I've wanted to be around. And he's an undertaker.

Hades.

I back away from him. "So, what's your deal?"

"Deal with what?" He lounges on the bed with his legs extended, feet crossed at the ankles.

"Why are you single?"

He eyes me suspiciously. "Have you been talking with my mother?" I snort out a laugh, and he glances around the room as if for an escape but makes no move for one. "I don't know," he starts quietly. "I was with this girl for a while."

When he doesn't continue, I lean forward, circling my hand to urge him on.

"Her name was Sandi with an I."

"As opposed to a Y? That's important?"

He offers me a shy grin. "I met her down the shore."

"Ah, where all good Jersey romances start," I joke, but I wrinkle my nose. I hate to admit it, but I'm jealous of Sandi with an I.

Vince shakes his head at me. He can tell I'm judging the woman he used to date. "She's a nice girl, a pediatric nurse, super-Italian family."

"But *you're* from a super-Italian family."

"Yeah," he acknowledges. "And it was too much."

"Too much what?"

"I'm close with my family. She was close with hers. You know...too many Sunday dinners, too many gossipy aunts and interfering mothers. It got to be too much after a while."

My own family is basically the opposite, but I can understand why it might be hard. When I sit next to him on the bed, he elbows me, tossing my own question back at me. "What's your deal?"

I hesitate, glancing down at my hands as I scratch at my nail polish.

"Hey, I told you. Now, you tell me." Vince puts his hand on top of both of mine, his golden tan over my fairer skin, his fingertips a little rough.

I resist curving my palm up, lacing our fingers together, and instead move my hands to tie my hair up in a ponytail. "Well…since I changed my Tinder profile to *Sister to a dead brother looking for the meaning of life*, I haven't gotten many matches."

He huffs next to me. "You didn't."

"I didn't," I say. "I deleted the app after moving home. Living in your parents' basement doesn't make for the greatest opportunities for houseguests." I pick at the comforter, unnerved by Vince's concentration on me. "Besides, I'm sort of a mess anyway."

"I don't mind your mess," he tells me, and I shoot my eyes back up to his. He's so sincere, I have to blink a few times to clear my senses. He doesn't shift toward me, not even a centimeter, simply lets his words settle between us. For as much as I should be warmed and comforted by them, I'm scared. Fifteen years ago, I would have been jumping for joy, melting right into his arms at the first sign of him wanting to be with me. Now, I'm melting, but for a different reason.

Because I don't have the capacity to reciprocate the same honesty.

Vince has been a constant in my life since *it* happened. He's been a friend and my oasis, a chance to forget about everything. It terrifies me that at this moment I want to get lost in his smile for a long time.

"I should go," I say, leaping up from his bed.

"You sure? Are you okay to drive?"

I wave his questions away and leave his bedroom before I change my mind. "Yeah. I'm fine. The wine was basically grape juice."

He follows me downstairs, and I stop next to the front door, where Gracie's lying down. I bend to pet her, and when I straighten back up, Vince is in my space.

Yielding to my instincts, I close my eyes and lean against him. He combs his fingers through my hair, brushing it behind my shoulder, then he presses his lips against my temple, my cheek, and my ear, where he murmurs, "Happy birthday, sweetheart."

Sweetheart.

God, how I love that word.

Though I don't think it suits me very well.

I'm not sweet, and I certainly don't have a working heart.

But I love hearing him say it, love imagining that I am as sweet-hearted as he believes me to be. And for one short moment, I pretend I'm worth his smiles and gentle endearments.

When I finally open my eyes, he's standing back by the thick railing of the steps with his hands in his pockets.

"Talk to you later?"

"Of course," he says in his perfectly easygoing way, and I dash from his house, my insecurities trailing behind me. He doesn't need to carry all of my baggage, even though he would without question. I can't ask that of him.

Besides, I'm too used to carrying it all myself. I don't know how to give it up.

MAY 25

FYI: Team registration for the Raymond St. George Memorial Baseball Tournament is now open! Be prepared to enter the team captain's contact information, number of players, and team name. I will be contacting all captains with more information and paperwork. Registration closes on June 15th.

Don't forget to follow @RSGMemorial on all social media platforms, and see you on June 22nd to relive some glory days!

#Grief #RaymondStGeorge #RSGMemorial #Baseball #Tournament #GloryDays #TheBoss

CHAPTER 18

I park my car in one of the few spots left open and step out into the packed parking lot even though it's barely noon. A couple of teens sit on the curb outside, while a set of small boys run ahead to the building in front of a woman calling after them. I should've expected how busy it would be during this long Memorial Day weekend, but I've had my head down, working on the tournament.

Briefly, I wonder if I should come back later, maybe on a different day, but I shake my head.

No.

There are only a few weeks left, and I need sponsors. Mr. Alvarado's help has been sparse, even though this whole thing was his idea. I've kept him in the loop, telling him everything I've been doing, waiting for him to offer up suggestions on contacts or companies. He's given me neither, although he was the first one to sign up a team. So I guess that's something.

With so much stress, I haven't been sleeping well, and I can only hope after all this is over, I'll be able to sleep for fifteen hours straight. But to even put this memorial on, I need money, so I take a deep breath, double-check my folder, and smooth out my sleeveless black romper.

Sunny's Sundaes is a small business owned by a woman who went to my high school and graduated a few years ahead of Raymond. For my first go at obtaining a sponsor, I thought this might be my best chance. A painted pink, blue, purple, and yellow sign decorates a wide window next to the door. Inside, I'm greeted with cool air conditioning and the distinctive scent of sugar waffles. I haven't eaten dairy ice cream in a long while, but the pistachio almond fudge is awfully tempting.

As I rummage through my purse for lactose pills, a young man behind the counter greets me. "Can I help you?"

I skip the stomachache and tell him, "I'm here to meet with Sunita. My name's Cassandra. She's expecting me."

"Okay, one minute." He walks a few steps to a door that looks like it leads to some sort of kitchen and leans inside. A moment later, a woman with light brown skin and black hair tied up in a messy bun appears, stripping off rubber gloves that look like they're smeared with chocolate. She smiles at me.

"Sunita?"

"Yes, hi. Call me Sunny," she says then directs her thumb over her shoulder. "I was dipping some of the waffle cones."

"Oh, you make everything yourself?" I ask as she scoots around the counter and gestures to a small booth in the corner.

"Everything but the little sugar cones. We always have at least twelve homemade ice cream flavors to pick from. The waffle cones and bowls, the cookies, we make every-thing here. I like to dip the cones myself," she says with a laugh. "When I let the staff or my husband do it, they all end up with different amounts of chocolate." She rolls her eyes. "I can't help that I'm a micromanager. Avyaan and I opened this place two years ago. I'm the creative, he's the business."

"Well, everything looks delicious."

"Is this your first time here?"

I nod, embarrassed to be here asking this business owner for money when I've never frequented her shop. "I've got a bit of a lactose sensitivity, so I mostly stay away from ice cream."

"I have two vegan flavors right now. Do you want to try one? Toasted coconut or dark chocolate peanut butter?"

I squeeze my thumb and forefinger together. "I guess I'll have a smidge of the toasted coconut."

She hops up and goes back behind the counter. In the meantime, I take out the sponsorship packet, which includes an outline of the event, why I am doing it, and the different levels of sponsorship. I keep from nervously chewing my lip, but my palms are moist. I've never asked anyone for money before, not in this sense, at least, and even though I've mentally rehearsed the spiel, it's still nerve-racking.

My hand itches to text Vince. I almost asked him to come with me today, but I stopped myself before I sent the message. I agreed to put this fundraiser together, and I need to take these meetings on my own. If not because it's for *my* brother, then to prove to myself I can do it. Vince's been my crutch through everything, but I want to stand on my own two feet for once. I don't want to need him as much as I do. Plus, I'm not comfortable with how we left things at his house. We've texted a few times about the tournament but nothing too personal. Nothing more than a friend helping out another, a guarantee for a sponsorship from the Mancini Funeral Home.

"Here ya go," Sunny says, handing me a small cup and spoon as she sits down opposite me again.

"Thank you for this and for meeting with me."

She inclines forward, one hand on top of the other on the table. "Of course. I'm happy to help. I didn't know your brother personally, but I can sort of understand what you're going through. My cousin died when she was thirty-two from complications of childbirth."

"Oh my god," I gasp, the spoon of ice cream paused halfway to my mouth.

She frowns, nodding solemnly. "It's amazing that happens in this country, you know? My family came here for opportunity, a better life, right? And then something so preventable happens... It's kind of unfathomable. We were all devastated."

"I'm sorry," I say even though I've come to the conclusion that is the dumbest thing to say to someone mourning. There is nothing I can do for her. There has been no wrongdoing, except maybe death coming too early for this woman and a messed-up healthcare system. "That's awful."

She brushes stray hairs back from her face and takes a deep breath. "So, what do you have for me?"

I hand her the papers and, in between bites of ice cream, explain to her what I'm doing for the tournament and that I need funds for rentals and permits. In exchange for donations, Sunny's Sundaes would receive advertising on all social media platforms, in event emails, signage, and on our T-shirts. She listens intently and smiles encouragingly. I take it as a good sign that we pull out our phones to follow each other, but she doesn't give me an answer now.

"Let me go over all of this with Av, and I'll get back to you."

"Great. Thank you again."

"Good luck with all of this. It's really cool you're doing it," she says as we shake hands. She's so bubbly and friendly, I wonder if I put myself out there more, maybe we'd be friends. When I lived in New York, one of the biggest cities in the world, I didn't go out often. My work schedule as personal assistant didn't allow it, but if I'm honest, I didn't try all that hard. I had a handful of friends yet never made an attempt to meet new people, and now I think it's possible I've lost the ability to make friends. Perhaps that skill fades away if not used enough.

Though, this meeting is a turned corner. Proof I'm not totally inept at people-ing.

Later, at work, I sneak away to check my emails and find one from Sunny. She's in.

JUNE 6

Big hi, hello to all my new followers! Whether you're here for my so-called honest and sad but kind of funny posts about my dead brother or for more information about the memorial tournament for said dead brother, welcome.

The tournament will be held at Hillsdale Park on June 22nd. You can find more information on the park, along with directions, in the link in my profile. And don't forget, team registration closes on June 15th!

I'd like to shout out some of our sponsors: @Sunnys-Sundaes_ @BigAlsBBQ @TheTurfNJ @LilysHair_N_Nails and Mancini Funeral Home. Message me for information on sponsorship packages.

Remember, you don't have to play baseball to enjoy the Raymond St. George Memorial Tournament. Come hang out and have some snacks. There'll be a raffle table and 50/50 tickets. Or if you'd like to skip the event altogether yet still donate, that's okay too.

Keep your fingers crossed for good weather. I don't deal well with heat. I'm more of an indoor cat myself, but I'll be there and hope you will be too!

#Grief #RaymondStGeorge #RSGMemorial #Baseball #Tournament #Summer #TheresNoCryingInBaseball

CHAPTER 19

With less than twenty-four hours before the big day, I'm both relieved that it's almost over and nauseous I still have to put the actual event on. I take my break at an empty booth in the back of Sassie's, double-checking I have the appropriate paperwork for every team registered with my notebook, folders, and binder. I didn't know I needed medical releases for each player until Aunt Joanie told me a few days ago. And now that the local news is covering it, I need media releases as well.

"Hey, what're you doing?"

Buried in my work, I'm startled when Gary appears next to me.

"Taking a break," I tell him, going back to the checklist of names to cross-reference against the paperwork.

"Your break was over ten minutes ago," he says, and I blink at him. He frowns at me in return. "It's ten after two."

"Okay." I peer around the vacant tables. "The place is empty."

"It is not." He nods to a couple of tables at the front of the restaurant where people are seated.

"They aren't my tables."

"Your break's over. You should be working, not doing this." He flaps the edge of my binder up.

"Please don't touch my stuff," I say, righting the papers he's shifted.

He ignores me. "We need the utensils and napkins refilled."

"Come on, Gary. I have a lot to do."

"I'm really getting sick and tired of your BS."

I put my pen down to give him my full attention. "My BS?"

"Yes," he says, a little less bold. "You could have a little more enthusiasm about being here."

"You're right, I could."

My easy capitulation takes the wind out of his sails, and he exhales audibly. He holds his hands out to me, his jaw moving up and down, probably searching for something to say, but I don't let him get that far. "Except this is a *breastaurant* with girls walking around in short skirts and knee-highs, the food is subpar, and the patrons are drunk guys with roaming hands. This isn't exactly a Michelin-star restaurant. I'm here for a paycheck, not the enthusiasm."

I gather up my stuff, leaving him stuttering after me as I head to the back to fold utensils up in the napkins. The rest of the girls who work here are barely legal or wasting their early twenties trying to make it into Sassie's Lassies' calendar. They may be afraid of standing up to Gary, but I'm not. He's a simpering try-hard, who gets off on having the title manager on his name tag and showing the young girls how tough he is, along with those "biceps" he's been "working on."

Gross.

He has his eye on me for the rest of the shift, and I can

almost perceive the reproachful words form in front of him, but I don't let him corner me to release them. Instead, I focus on getting out of here and finishing up what I need to for the tournament.

When I do finally return home, I spend the rest of the night packing up my car with donated snacks and beverages to sell at the concession stand, triple-checking I have the paper tickets for the 50/50 drawing, along with each team's paperwork, all the permits, and throwing together a first aid kit. It's only a plastic bag of a couple of Band-Aids, Q-tips, and a tampon, but it'll have to do.

My nerves don't let me sleep, and I'm up and dressed with the sun. Shockingly, so is my father. We dance around each other in the kitchen as we make coffee, and after all the shuffling, pouring, and stirring is done, silence falls between us.

Ray and Dad never had these awkward moments. They always got along. I'm not sure why. It's not like they had a ton in common. Maybe it was because they both had the XY chromosomes, I don't know. Whatever the reason, Dad and I are missing it.

When he moves to another room, I scrub my hands over my face. I should talk to him. I should tell him I need a father, not like the little girl in the "Butterfly Kisses" song way, but in the *You're my dad, act like it* way. Then again, I should drag my mother to the doctor's office instead of playing into her mood swings, but I don't do that either.

This is the new status quo, and it's my fault. I'm not forcing a relationship, because it's easier to let it go. The road less traveled and such.

I toss back the rest of my coffee and head over to the field. It's oddly satisfying to systematically check everything off my list as I set up the registration table, tie balloons to the fence, and hang the signs. I arrange the snacks in the concession stands, even putting the candy in size order. When Aunt Joanie shows up, I put her in charge of the registrations. Juan, the rental guy, sets up the microphone and sound system as people begin to arrive, and in a matter of minutes, my calm state ratchets up to chaos.

More people are here than I thought would be. They sit in the stands, linger on the fields, and warm up, throwing balls back and forth. A bunch of guys from RJ's high school baseball team greet one another warmly, his coworkers and students mingle, and even more faces I don't recognize continue to pour through the fence.

I spot Vince out of the corner of my eye, dressed to play in what looks like his old high school baseball jersey and hat. The sight of *him*, wearing *that*, without my brother next to him is momentarily earth-shattering. Of course I knew I was doing this for Ray, but being here today is yet another reminder he isn't.

Vince strolls over to me, holding Gracie's leash in his hand as she lopes next to him, and I smile past my melancholy. "Hey, pretty girl," I say, kneeling down to kiss Gracie's face. "I missed you."

She licks my face and hand, and I nuzzle her.

"Didn't miss me?" When I tip my head up to Vince, he smiles like he's joking, but his rough voice gives him away. "I figured you guys would like some time to hang out since you haven't seen each other in a while," he says, referring to Gracie.

I want to apologize for making it weird between us. I can't help it, I want to say. He said he didn't mind my mess, but he doesn't know the extent of my life in disarray. I don't even fully understand the extent of it. It's not you, I should tell him. It's me. *Really.*

"I'm glad you're here," I say instead.

"I wouldn't miss it." He hands the leash to me, checking out the size of the crowd. "You got a really good turnout."

I stand up, shielding my eyes with sunglasses. "Mm-hmm."

"Don't sound too happy." He fixes the bill of his baseball hat and tilts his head, doing his usual wary inspection of me.

"I'm tired," I say, which could be the description of my life since February 14th. "I did it all by myself." I gesture to him. "I mean, you helped, which is amazing. You're amazing. But this took over my whole life, and for what?"

At that moment, Mr. Alvarado shows up, calling my name. He's grinning brightly, with a hop in his step. "Cassandra, this is great!" When I meet his handshake, he uses it to pull me in for a hug. "Wonderful, just wonderful."

"It is," I agree, folding my arms over my chest.

"I'm ecstatic we were able to put this together," he says, and I roll my head over to Vince. He grunts out a laugh. Mr. Alvarado didn't put any of this together.

"Yep." I motion to the parking lot, where my dad's car pulls up. "My parents are here. Gotta go."

I leave Alvarado and Vince behind while Gracie and I not-so-subtly sneak off. My parents are wearing the tournament T-shirts I got them, and they're both smiling.

I never thought I'd see that again.

Mom brings her hands to her lips. "Wow, Cassie."

"I'm impressed," Dad tells me with his hands on his hips. He's got sunglasses on, but I can tell he's crying from the way he sniffs and clears his throat. "I'm sorry I didn't help you with it."

Genuine disbelief has my jaw hanging open. At this

conversation, and because he's suggesting he would've somehow helped me.

"You did good," he tells me. "RJ would be proud."

A jumble of emotions clogs my throat, and I can't separate any of my words into coherent sentences. This is my chance. I can lay it all out. Ask him why he hasn't been coming home, tell him he's a jerk, demand he face what's happened to our family.

But I don't.

I say, "Thank you."

Because I'm a coward.

He pats my shoulder, in a "good game" kind of way. He's not exactly emotional, let alone physically effusive, so this contact—even small—is a step in the right direction for mending our rocky relationship. I can work on telling him the truth later.

Maybe this tournament *did* help my family in some small way. Miracle of miracles.

Mom follows him with watery eyes to the concession stand where they buy waters, and my sudden goodwill toward my dad evaporates when he rolls his eyes at my now-weeping mother after one of RJ's coworkers hugs her.

And I want to scream.

But I can't. I've got a tournament to run.

I tuck my topsy-turvy mood aside as I check the time. Signaling to Juan to lower the volume of the music, I take hold of the microphone. "Hey...hello..." Heads swivel in my direction, and I try again. "Hi, everybody. Over here." I wave my arm in the air, and my stomach churns when everything goes quiet, all eyes on me. I reach for the top of Gracie's head, her fur reassuring under my fingertips. "My name is Cass, and Raymond was my older brother. I want to thank everyone for coming today. Seeing so many people here, hearing you speak about Ray, knowing what he meant to you all, makes losing him a little bit easier."

These words are an absolute lie, but the crowd eats it up. Nothing makes losing him easier.

"Since Ray loved baseball, there's no better way to honor his memory than to play a couple innings in his name. Let's have a little fun today."

A round of applause begins, and I move to put the microphone down, but Mr. Alvarado swoops in out of nowhere to snatch it from my hand. "Thank you, Cass," he says and then sweeps his arm out in front of him, "and thank you all for coming. My name is Victor Alvarado, and I'm the principal of Edison Middle School. Go Leopards!"

That sparks a few woots and claps from the crowd, and I roll my neck to release the tension.

"RJ was a beloved teacher at Edison, and we were all devastated when we heard the news of his sudden passing."

I squeeze the bridge of my nose.

"His fellow teachers and some of his students are proud to be here to represent him on this beautiful day, and we cannot thank everyone enough for their generous participation in this event to raise money for our school."

With my hand on my temple, I turn to my left, where the news camera crew is filming all of this. Mr. Alvarado's big grin, the cheering crowd, the perfect blue sky, and I think it would make a feel-good ending to some movie, one where everyone learns to celebrate life or some bullshit.

I'm sick of Alvarado's self-congratulatory speech and search for an escape. I spot my parents not too far away and make my way to them, keeping Gracie close at my heels.

"Do you want to say anything?" I ask them. Might as well, since the speeches have already gone off the rails.

"No," Dad says.

Mom's voice squeaks from behind her fist still pressed to her lips. "I think, maybe, I'd like to."

"You would?" My eyes practically bug out of my head.

Dad is just as stunned. "Donna, really?" he admonishes.

"Well," she starts, dabbing at her eyes, "it's nice all these people came here for Raymond. It's so wonderful," she says, breaking down into more tears.

I rub her back, pleased for once she's acknowledging all of this—the fundraiser, the grief, the death of her son, accepting it, almost.

"For Christ's sake, you can't talk to people when you're a blubbering mess."

My father makes her cry even more, and I throw my arms out to the sides. "Really?"

He peers over my shoulder as if he's making sure my outburst isn't causing a scene. I don't care if I am. "I thought when Ray died, you'd find it in your heart to be a little nicer to everyone, but you can't even do that, can you? You're such a..." I pause, various derogatory names flashing in my mind, not sure if I can or should use them to describe my dad. Then again, the truth has to come out some time. "You're such a prick."

"Cassandra," my mom says through her tears. "Don't talk like that."

"What?" I tighten my hold on Gracie's leash and ground my feet under me. Guess the pressure of the tournament has pushed me to the brink, and there's no turning back now. "You might be okay with him treating you like this, but I'm not."

My father's face goes red. "First of all, lower your voice. Second—"

"Second, nothing," I say, pushing his finger out of my face. "I know I've never been your favorite. I wasn't easy like

Ray. I didn't fit into your picture-perfect idea of a speak-when-spoken-to little girl. I get it. But ever since he died, you act like your only child died. Thing is, I'm still here. I'm trying to show you *both* that I'm here. I've tried everything. I've tried to keep this family together, and I'm exhausted from carrying the weight for you. I did all of this," I say, motioning behind me. "And all you can do—" I point to my dad "—is be an asshole, and all you—" I point to my mom "—do is defend him. I'm done with it."

I spin around, blinking back the tears rapidly forming behind my eyelids and jog off, wanting a moment of quiet away from the circus, but a familiar figure stops me.

"Cassandra."

"Nell." My brother's girlfriend.

Zeus save me.

CHAPTER 20

$\mathcal{B}$ehind me, the first game has started, and somebody yells instructions about playing first base. In front of me, I wave uncomfortably. The last time I saw this woman was at Ray's funeral, and the time before that, we met in passing after I was sworn to secrecy by my brother.

"I don't know if you remember me," she says sheepishly.

"I do."

She shifts her weight, her hand restlessly combing through her shoulder-length hair. I can imagine why my brother liked her. She appears the opposite of Shayna, natural and shy. He probably basked in the spotlight she allowed him to have.

"I'm sorry we weren't able to get to know each other better."

I jerk my head back. "Why?"

"Well, I... RJ and I..."

"He was cheating on his wife with you," I state, and she visibly shrinks. I huff. She seems like a nice person. We might have even been friends if we'd met under different circumstances. But she was the other woman. Even though Shayna's not my favorite person, I can't get down with that. I fix my voice into a gentler tone. "I'm sorry, that was harsh."

But true.

We stare at each other for a few too-long seconds, and then she blurts, "I loved him. I loved him so much."

Gracie tugs at her leash to go, but this girl's sad eyes keep me in place.

"I miss him so much it hurts sometimes."

"Yeah, I know," I say, a familiar rock in my stomach forcing me to agree with her.

"I thought I would come today to be close with him somehow." She chews on her lip for a moment before saying, "Maybe we could hang out and talk or something."

"I'm really busy."

"I can help," she says a little too fast, with her hands reaching out to me. "I need to do something. I want to do something for him. For you."

I give in because I don't know if what they had was real, but I do know what it's like to want to rewind somehow, have a little piece of him back. "My aunt's at the registration table. She'll give you 50/50 tickets you can sell. Sound good?"

She wipes at her nose and straightens herself up. "Yes, great. And maybe afterward, we can hang out? Maybe finally get to know each other? I'd love to ask you some questions about RJ."

I offer her a fake smile and mumble a thanks before skirting her because, hell no, I don't want to get to know her. I don't want to be her stand-in for Ray or her crutch to lean on. I have enough of my own shit going on to take on hers too.

Gracie and I jog off behind the fence to a small patch of

grass by the parking lot, where I sit next to her. "Why does everyone think I can manage their grief?" I ask Gracie. "I can barely manage my own." She licks me. "It's not like I can bring him back from the dead."

I people watch, glaring at them as I'm overwhelmed with animosity toward everyone here at the park.

I know it's irrational, but ever since Ray died, I resent everyone for living their normal lives. Typically, my hatred's buried under the depression and anxiety, but it's out in full force today. I don't want them to be happy. I want them to suffer.

I want them to endure what I do. Live in the shadow of a ghost. Be responsible for every fucking person's memories. Rip open their rib cage in order to put their heart on display for the world.

I grind my teeth and growl.

What I wouldn't give for something to take the edge off right now. When I lived in the city, I had a friend, Marissa, who dealt weed. It was some real cheap stuff she upcharged rich college kids for, but she'd always let me have some for free. The rare times I had the night off, we'd spend it on her couch, under her weighted blanket, watching *Boy Meets World*. I'd usually conk out after one episode.

I thought my life was shit then.

Oh, how the mighty have fallen.

Gracie and I soak in some sunshine for a few more brief moments while I put myself back together. I've become quite adept at it since Raymond's death. I give in to the emotion only enough to relieve the pressure, a pinhole in a balloon, then slap on another Band-Aid to keep it all from draining out. After tying my hair up in a bun, I stand and stretch my back. For a moment, I consider actually opening that yoga app I have on my phone every once in a while, but who am I kidding?

Making my way back over to the field, I'm stopped by a man who introduces himself to me as a reporter for the local newspaper, and I paste on a grin. I'll be the person I need to be for now and figure out the rest later. The reporter questions me about my brother, and I offer bland answers I know everyone will want to read. We discuss how the tournament will help out the school before Mr. Alvarado intercepts us. This time, I don't actually mind. I've planned this event for months, I should enjoy this, but instead, I can't wait until it's over.

It's a long day, and Gracie stays by my side the whole time. Between counting money and restocking snacks, I stop to watch one of the games. Vince's team is playing. They're all old teammates, and it actually brings me a small amount of joy to see them laughing and clowning with one another. Some of them look familiar, most of them don't, but it wouldn't matter anyway as my eyes always find Vince. He's behind the plate, shouting directions, playing catcher. He's so at ease, a complete natural, even now, all these years after he stopped playing. I wonder if he regrets not taking that scholarship. I sort of regret it for him. It's clear he loves playing, and I want him to be happy.

At his next turn up to bat, he notices me and winks with a tip of his helmet. It's totally dorky and endlessly charming. Not to mention, the wave he throws me as he jogs to first base after his home run. I refrain from melting into a puddle and take Gracie to the shade under a few trees. I try to enjoy a pack of nuts, but more people keep coming over to talk to me. They want to tell me stories about Ray, and I laugh or frown on cue, but underneath, my patience wears thin. I suppose I should be comforted by all of their words, yet I'm not. They knew "RJ," some veneer of a person Raymond put on for them. He might've been the life of the party, but he was certainly no hero.

He was just your average guy. A guy who stole Nana's 80th birthday cake from the grocery store because he didn't want to wait in line to pay for it. A guy who'd split checks down to the cent over fifty-cent wings at our favorite pub. A guy who had good *and* bad qualities. But you wouldn't know it. To them, he's an angel, some kind of celebrity, a star in the middle of New Jersey.

To me, he was my big brother, and my love wasn't based on an idea of him. Rather, the real Raymond. I loved him for all of it, the good and the bad, the secrets and the loud parts. I love him so much it makes me hate other people for loving the version of him they thought they knew.

"He'd be so proud of you," someone tells me, and my skin goes hot. My fingers clench around Gracie's leash, and I give them a curt nod goodbye.

One more thing they don't know. Ray's not proud. He can't be anything. He's dead.

I ignore the calls for my attention, including Aunt Joanie beckoning me, and head straight for my car. I lock myself in, with only Gracie's shallow pants to keep me company as she sleeps with her head in my lap.

In the quiet, I let my head fall back and close my eyes.

Two soft taps on the doorframe wake me up, and I blink over to find Vince's face. The sun is almost set behind him, an orange halo around his dark hair. He motions for me to roll down the window, and I do.

"You're not supposed to lock dogs in the car in this kind of heat. It's how they die from dehydration and heat exhaustion." He squints. "Or was that your plan for the two of you?"

I know he's being facetious from his tone of voice, but he's doing the skeptical eyebrow raise that makes me think twice. "I'm depressed, not suicidal." I hold up the water Gracie and I had shared. "I had the windows cracked, and we were only in here for—" I check the time "—fifteen minutes."

His hazel eyes appraise me before he juts his chin toward the passenger seat. "Can I sit?"

I nod, and he makes his way around the front of the car. Sitting down, he leans against the door to face me and removes his baseball cap, his hair sweaty and sticking up every which way. Gracie settles herself in his lap.

"Tough day?" he asks, and I turn to the window.

"I thought it would be different doing this."

"Different, how?"

"Closure, I guess." When he puts his hand on my neck, I face him. "I thought it would be fun, but this sucks."

He bursts out in a big laugh.

It's contagious, and I laugh too. "Why are you laughing?"

"The way you said it," he says after a while. "You're the boss of this whole thing, and you hate it. It's funny."

"My misery is funny?"

"A little."

When I look back to the window, he keeps his hand on me, fingertips stroking up and down the side of my neck. My skin tingles under his touch, and I want it all over me. I should tell him to stop. I should push him away. A voice in the back of my head reminds me there is no room in my life for Vince and his open, giving heart. There's nothing I can give him in return. And yet, when his hand moves down, pressing in a soft massage, I smile at him.

And he smiles back.

And I shove that voice away, pretending I'm not broken. At least for now.

"I told your aunt I'd help find you," he says. "The last game just finished."

"Who won?" I ask.

He smirks his answer.

"Your team?"

"Of course."

"Well, I hope you enjoy your gift certificate to Big Al's Barbecue."

"Great." He tugs on a lock of my hair. "I can take you on a date."

I ignore the flip of my stomach and shake my head. "My tastes are more expensive. I'm more of a champagne and caviar gal."

"Okay," he says. "I'll remember that." He drops his hand to put Gracie's leash back on her. "We better get you back out there. You need to present me with my prize."

I roll my eyes but follow him out of the car, our arms brushing against each other as we walk. Juan is playing "Karma Chameleon" over the sound system, and Vince sings it softly. I stare at him until he grins. Then I grin.

And I'm fourteen again.

The moment is ruined when Aunt Joanie palms my shoulder. "Where the hell have you been?" She doesn't let me answer. "Alvarado's basically taken over. He's acting like he put this all together."

"Well, I—"

"Go over there and say something." She pushes me to where Juan is at the table with the sound system.

I hesitantly shuffle over to grab the microphone. I tap it twice to make sure it's on. "Hi...hello, everyone. It's me again, Cass. I wanted to once again thank you all for coming out. And present our winning team—" I motion to Aunt Joanie, and she hands me a basket filled with gift certificates and a couple bottles of alcohol, along with a paper of the teams "—with the prize."

"Our third-place team is the Blue Barracudas." A woman with short gray hair walks up to me to accept their fifty-dollar gift certificate and other prizes. "Second place are the Leopards." A group of teachers from the middle school jump and cheer as Mr. Alvarado accepts their gift certificates. He gives me a thumbs-up, and I pretend to be happy for him. "And to our champions, the Big Ballers…" I chuckle at the ridiculous name and the team's even more ridiculous celebration.

With the prizes awarded, Aunt Joanie hands me another piece of paper. "The winner of the 50/50 lottery will receive $246, and it goes to…" I glance down at the name and choke. "Victor Alvarado."

Mr. Alvarado strides up to me and leans in to the microphone. "I will, of course, give this money back to Cassandra to add it to the total."

A round of applause sounds, and I continue, "I hope everyone had fun today. With all of your help, we've raised over three thousand dollars to purchase new laptops for Edison."

The crowd whoops and hollers their praise, and I offer one final thank-you before they start dispersing. By the time I finish shaking hands and speaking to every person who stops me, the field is littered with garbage. I find a bag to clean up, noticing Mr. Alvarado has split the scene, literally taken his money and run, and it pisses me off. Also missing is Nell, not that I was looking forward to her company, but an extra pair of hands would be nice. My parents speak to a couple by the fence. Well, Mom cries and Dad has his arms folded.

"Hey," Vince says at my side. He's got a pair of Big Ballers behind him. "We're going to grab a couple drinks. Want to come with us?"

The men look friendly enough, but I don't want to be the sad, tagalong little sister. "No, thanks. I'm good."

"Come on." He bends slightly, lowering his mouth so I can smell the mint gum he's been chewing. "You need to get out."

"You guys go. I'm good, really."

"Sure?"

"Totally."

He eyes me for a second then turns over his shoulder to his friends. "I'll meet you there."

They nod, waving at us before it clicks in my head. He's staying with me. "You don't have to do this."

He takes the garbage bag out of my fingers. "You don't either."

"Well, I kind of do," I say with my arms up to demonstrate the almost-empty field.

"You really don't, Cass." When I shrug, he continues to throw trash into the bag. "You know when you fly in a plane and the attendants say to put on your oxygen mask before helping someone else do it?"

"Sure."

He stops with a paper plate in his hand to stare meaningfully at me. I don't understand, and he lets out a low sigh. "You've got to put on your own oxygen mask."

He's only trying to help. However, what he doesn't understand is that if the plane is going down, an oxygen mask isn't going to help. "I never knew you were so metaphorical."

"I'm being serious."

His words set me back, and I'm too embarrassed to look him in the eyes. Gracie rests a few feet away, and I focus on her instead. She doesn't make me confront things I'm not ready to. "I know you are. And I appreciate it."

"But...?" he intones, guessing correctly.

"But it's complicated."

"Then explain it to me."

I take a breath and pick up a few pieces of trash. "I didn't want to do this, but I didn't want anyone else but me doing it either."

"I don't get it," he says, tying up the bag and setting it aside so we can gather up all the leftover T-shirts and supplies.

"I guess..." I'm not sure I have the words to describe the devotion I have for my brother, and I search the sky until I find it. "I'm protective. Like, you can't make fun of my brother, only I can...except opposite. You can't properly talk about my brother or raise money in his name or bury him or..." I glance over to Vince with tears in my eyes.

He immediately puts down the pallet of water and gathers me up in his arms, whispering "sweetheart" against my temple.

I'm becoming dependent on Vince's soft words and comforting hugs, and I don't have the will to pull away from him. When I tip my chin up to him, a few inches separate us in height, but it's easy to rise up and kiss the corner of his mouth. Only a peck, nothing really.

Except, it's not. It's everything.

It's comfort and tenderness and everything sweet.

He blinks at me, as if to collect his bearings, then leans down for another kiss. I accept his mouth fully against mine, not hurried or pushing for more. We're simply together. There is nowhere else for us to go, nothing else for us to do. The tip of his tongue finds my bottom lip as his hands sink into my hair and twist into my T-shirt, pressing against my back. His feet bracket mine, every part of my body cradled by him.

When I open my mouth, accepting his searching tongue against mine, he lets out a barely audible groan, but it still sends goose bumps up my arms as I wrap them around his neck, forcing both of his hands to my waist, the tips of his fingers rounding over my backside, digging in ever so slightly. Like he holds on to my neck. Like he knows I need something to keep me moored to the earth. To him.

Because I do. I need it.

I need him.

And that's when I realize what I'm doing, instantly regretting it.

I can't act like this with him. I can't accept his kisses and touches when I know what he'll expect in return. Vince deserves someone who is whole and ready to offer him everything they have.

I am *not* that person.

I break away so quickly, stumbling back, my lungs seizing like he stole all the air from them. I press one hand to my breastbone, the other to my mouth, and he holds on to my elbow as I steady myself.

"Thanks for helping me," I eventually mumble then pivot around, finishing packing up. "I don't want to hold you up any longer. Go have fun with your friends."

He wraps his fingers around my forearm so I'll meet his gaze, and his eyes move back and forth between mine. His pupils are dilated, both attraction and confusion there. I try on a smile.

He doesn't respond with one. Instead, his hand drifts

down, his fingers finding mine for a too brief moment, and then he turns to walk away with Gracie lagging behind. "See you later, Cass."

My cheeks expand on a big exhale, and I load up my car as I replay those moments in my head. Vince is steady, an anchor in the storm, but I have to be able to stand on my own two feet. I don't want to rely on him. Or anyone, for that matter. I can't let my emotions run wild; it's not fair to him.

"You're the worst," I admonish myself.

"Talking to yourself?" Aunt Joanie snickers, coming up behind me. I force a laugh too and take the envelope she extends toward me. "It's all the cash from the concessions and fifty-fifty."

I open the envelope to count out a couple of twenties. "The school won't miss this," I say, raising my eyes to Aunt Joanie. "I figured I should give some of this to Shayna for the girls."

"Of course."

Mom and Dad approach us. Mom kisses my cheek, barely a whisper of a touch, while my dad swings his car keys in his hand. "Good job with this, Cassandra."

"Thank you."

He clears his throat, his eyes wandering around the field as if he's seeing something no one else is. His face goes pink, and he blinks rapidly before clearing his throat again then backs away toward the car. Mom follows dutifully. Aunt Joanie leaves after another hug.

Then it's only me and a couple bags of garbage. I haul it all to a bin at the other end of the parking lot before sitting in my car. As I put the key in the ignition, my breath is suddenly impossible to take in.

It's finally all over, and the relief I thought I'd feel is

nowhere to be found, while the loneliness is in abundance. My high hopes for this fundraiser to bring my family back together are dashed. My parents are more disconnected than before. Detached from me, from each other, from reality.

All day, all I wanted were moments by myself, and now that I have them, I'd like to give them back. The funny thing about going through all of this is when I think I have what I want, it's not any better. Day to day, moment to moment, it's a fight to get through, and right when I think I'm good, a wave knocks me back over and I have to start again.

And sitting in my car alone, I know I have to start paddling back to shore again. But it's hard, and I'm out of breath.

I squeeze my fingers around the steering wheel and jam my head back against the seat, closing my eyes to the tears. I try to imagine what Ray would say to me.

Why didn't you go for a drink, you loser?

Nell was only trying to help.

I can't believe you actually put this together. You had to talk to people, like, real live people. Did it hurt?

Maybe he'd be happy. Maybe he'd think I was being overly sensitive. "If you were still alive, I wouldn't have to wonder."

I open my eyes and drag my palm down my cheek before swiping my phone on. The deflated balloon hanging off the gatepost is a perfect metaphor for me, and I snap a picture of it, writing a post. Each movement of my thumbs stamps my anger and defeat into words.

Once it's posted, there are immediate interactions, likes, and comments.

"You should write a book about this," someone named

Harmony writes, and I laugh. If I were going to write a book, it'd be a historical romance with courting, kissing, and a devastatingly handsome dark-haired, hazel-eyed hero. Not a melodrama starring a jaded girl and a dead guy.

JUNE 22

Did you know you can WebMD grief? Some symptoms of grieving are: increased inflammation, lower immunity, high blood pressure, fatigue, dry mouth. This list goes on. But symptoms, to me, allude to a diagnosis, a problem that can be fixed with medicine. A pill. Or surgery. Or Jell-O and an IV bag.

But there is no cure for this.

I don't need a doctor to tell me I'm sick. I'm like Jessie in that episode of *Saved By The Bell*. You know the one. I'm her, minus the pills and singing group. When she's running around like, "There's no time! No time to study, no time for Stanford, no time to sing!" I'm like, I get it, girl. I get it.

There's no time. And all I want to do is sleep. Or cry. I'm on the edge of a breakdown, barely holding it together, one hug from Zack away from totally losing it.

Unlike Jessie, I'm not auditioning for a record label, I'm just tired. Tired of being angry. Tired of taking care of everything and everyone else. I'm tired of being tired.

I am defeated. Deflated. And not so good at accepting hugs from my own Zack Morris. Guess it's true what they say. TV will rot your brain.

#Grief #GriefSymptoms #RaymondStGeorge #JessiesSong #JessieSpano #SavedByTheBell

CHAPTER 21

It's the dead of summer, and without a distraction, the days slog on longer and longer. Admittedly, I didn't enjoy organizing the Raymond St. George Charity Baseball Tournament, but it was a reprieve of sorts. A mental vacation from my daily grievances. But I'm back on my bullshit.

Every day's more of the same. Work, unsuccessfully convincing Mom to get out of the house, work, wondering if Dad will come home, work, *Price is Right*! Which is why when Vince calls me on the Fourth of July to invite me to a picnic, I agree. At least, I tell myself it's a distraction and nothing more.

Not even when he smiles at me as I open the door to him.

His T-shirt matches his eyes, which are locked somewhere around my lips. I have my Russian Red on, and my body hums at his reaction. When his gaze finally finds mine, his mouth slants up. "You look beautiful, sweetheart."

"Thank you." I cross the long strap of my purse over my chest and shut the door behind me, unconsciously reaching for Vince's hand, almost like we're on a date or something. Halfway to his fingers, I stop, leaving my arm dangling inelegantly between us, and I force a giggle then stick both of my hands into the pockets of my black dress. It was too hot for anything else, and my legs look like hot dogs in shorts, so sundress it was.

He doesn't notice this awkward display. Or if he does, he doesn't act like it. What a gentleman.

"Are your parents home today?" he asks on the way to his car.

"I haven't seen my dad since the day before yesterday, and my mom's with my aunt."

He opens his car door, his eyebrows furrowed in question.

"Her condo has a pool, so I guess the way to pry her out of the house is the promise of a floaty and a Xanax."

"Sounds good to me." He laughs, and I open the passenger side door with a smile.

The last time I was in this car was after Ray's funeral, and I push that day out of my mind as I plug my phone into the stereo system to play Jack White.

"Help yourself," he deadpans.

Then it falls uncomfortably silent, and it's all my fault. I ruined it when I stupidly kissed him. It's been weeks since the fundraiser, but we've only texted a handful of times. I've shut down any type of flirtation to the point that he had stopped messaging me. That was, until yesterday.

I wasn't happy about giving him the silent treatment, but I wanted to be clear. That kiss was a bad idea, and I don't want to lead him on.

"How's the Underworld been treating you?" I ask to fill in the space between us.

"Well, everyone I work with is pretty quiet, so..."

"Terrible joke."

He glances at me with a shrug. "I don't have your natural wit."

"And charm," I add.

"And charm." He offers me a magnanimous head bow then taps my knee with the back of his hand. "How's everything with you? How's work?"

"All beers and boobs."

He huffs. "Why do you stay there?"

"Because they pay me."

"You hate it there."

I stare at the side of his face, waiting for him to turn to me. When he does, I raise my eyebrows. He's *not* going to lecture me.

"What?" he asks, as if I couldn't read the thoughts written on his face. The same ones everyone else has too.

I preempt him. "I have no skills suitable for this economy. No one wants to hire a graduate from Columbia who can talk at length about the feminism of Virginia Woolf but can't send a fax."

He bites back a smile. "That can't be true."

I lean my elbow on the door. "I don't even know why people send faxes anymore."

"Can't you be a teacher or something?"

"No, Mom, I can't." He throws me a sarcastic glare, but I continue. "It costs money to go back to school for any kind of degree, and I'm already drowning in debt. Plus, high school kids are rude."

"What do you want to do?"

Thinking, I watch the trees and telephone poles zoom by outside of my window. "When I was real little, I wanted to be a TV game show host, like on *Price is Right* or something. I wanted to hold one of those long microphones."

He lets out a squeaked, "Really?"

And I don't know whether I should be offended or not. "You don't think I'd be a good host?"

"Nah, I think you'd be a great host. You're really fun when you aren't trying to scare people away." At a red light, he shifts in his seat. "You have a lot more to offer than you think you do. You're smart." He pins me with an impatient raise of his brow, as if I should know this. "Like, really, really smart. You're able to speak about so many topics, have philosophical conversations."

I wave his words away. "You make me sound arrogant."

"Maybe you should be a little bit more arrogant. You don't see yourself clearly, and it's why you're working at a restaurant that forces you show your ass every time you serve a burger."

My skin heats at his chastising words, and it takes me a few seconds to recover from what feels like a physical blow. "Gee, thanks."

He parks the car in front of a brick and beige-sided home then unbuckles his seat belt and grasps my hand. "I'm sorry. I didn't mean it to sound like that, but I don't know why you sell yourself short. You could do anything you want to, but you put up these walls. You pretend like you can't do anything else, when I think you're just afraid of trying."

His eyes roam over me, and I don't like the way he's able to turn me inside out. I'm ashamed for what he's accusing me of, but I also want to be the best of what he thinks I am.

"What are you so afraid of people seeing?" he asks, his thumb smoothing over my knuckles.

What am I so afraid of? Isn't it obvious?

I'm afraid of this. Of someone looking deep into my eyes and seeing my heart. I'm afraid because when they do, they'll find a withered and bruised lump of clay that's been torn apart and mashed back together, kneaded and rolled to resemble a heart. Barely an imitation.

I'm afraid of *him*.

And he doesn't care. He pushes on. "I see a woman who's one of the strongest people I know, who cares deeply about her family, and who has been selfless at a time when she shouldn't have to be."

No.

He's wrong. I'm weak and selfish, overly sensitive and filled with rage. It's not pleasant to have this hurricane living inside me, and I don't know how Vince can possibly think these things about me.

He forces me to look up when he tugs on a strand of my hair. "I know you don't like being vulnerable, but you've been putting yourself out in the world through your posts. Do you read all the comments? Because I do. People love it. Imagine what you could do if you did it without a screen, if you really offered up everything you have."

I shake my head. The idea is outrageous. He wants me to, what? Be some kind of motivational speaker? Writing a few words on social media on my phone is a lot different from what he's suggesting. I'm not going to cut myself open to show the world how I bleed.

Nope. No thank you.

"Look, I don't care what you do," he says, letting go of my fingers. "I only want you to be happy."

"What about you?" I snap. "Why aren't you doing what really makes you happy?"

"What are you talking about?"

"Baseball. You had a scholarship. I saw you playing at the tournament. I can tell you love it. Anyone could. But you gave it up to be a funeral director?"

"Cass, you know—"

"I know. You gave it up to do what you had to for your family, right?" I tilt my head. What he did isn't all that different from me. We've both made sacrifices for our families. "Why don't you coach? You did a good job with me at the batting cages."

With his chin down toward his chest, his lips tip up. I assume he's thinking about that night. When I spent over an hour swinging a metal bat, sending my aggression into baseballs flying through the air.

"I never thought much about it." And my clumpy, withered heart shrinks even more. Until he meets my gaze again. "Coaching, I mean."

"Well, why don't you?"

If he wants me to be introspective, he's not getting off scot-free.

He nods and opens his door to step out of the car.

I wait a minute, brushing my hair aside, checking my makeup in the mirror, making sure my outward appearance isn't as messy as my insides. I mean, really, I thought I was going to drink beer and eat chips at a picnic, not receive a *Come to Jesus*.

"You mad at me?" he asks when I finally meet him at the front of the car.

"A little," I answer honestly. He's helped me through everything with my brother and is more or less my best friend—my only friend—but I hold on to that little bit of anger. It's easier than dealing with the other, more treacherous emotions. "You're not the first person to tell me I'm wasting my life."

His eyebrows shoot up. "Who said that? I didn't say it."

"My brother, my parents," I tell him. "You insinuated it."

He brings his head down closer to mine. "I'm sorry. I don't ever want to hurt you."

His voice is low and slow, his meaning something much deeper than I want to face. And I don't mean to, but when he kisses my temple, I lean into him. Keeping my hands at my sides is a fight as my pulse echoes all over my body.

He backs up a bit, gazing expectantly at me, yet I can't say anything. I know any words I may have are insufficient, so I give him a friendly elbow instead. "Okay."

His defeat is palpable, and it reminds me why I'm not fit for relationships. I can't give myself to others like he can. No matter how much I wish I could, I can't until I have my life sorted out. But I'm not sure how to do that right now.

The last cruel joke from my brother was him telling me to move out of Mom and Dad's house and get a new job. Then he went off and died.

Threw me in the deep end with no floaties.

I walk ahead, and Vince catches up to me as we reach the porch. Voices carry from inside the house and the backyard.

"Sounds like a lot of people," I note.

He nods, and I watch as his face morphs from sullen to the bright-eyed and easygoing smile I'm used to. "Hope you're hungry."

He opens the front door and ushers me in front of him. There are festive red, white, and blue steamers everywhere and a couple little kids lingering in the hall, giggling. When they see Vince, they scurry away out through the sliding door by the kitchen.

"Hey, Vinny!" A gray-haired man in a tank top and gold chain holds his arms open. "How are ya?"

Vince hugs him. "Hey, Uncle."

"Who's this?" his uncle asks as he opens the refrigerator.

"This is my friend, Cass. Cass, this is my uncle Dominic."

"Nice to meet you," I say.

"Here." He hands a twelve-pack of beer to me and piles wine bottles, cans of soda, and limes in Vince's arms. "Bring this outside. Your aunt needs her spritzer," he says with a roll of his eyes.

I follow Vince outside and laugh when I notice Uncle Dominic carrying nothing. Although, after showing us what coolers to put everything into, he pats my back and sticks a Corona in my hand.

"One of my mom's brothers," Vince whispers in my ear before accepting a hug from another woman, I assume the aunt with the spritzer. He receives a hug and a kiss from every person we pass. I meet them, trying to shake hands, but they mostly push my palm away for embraces.

"Cassandra." Mr. Mancini greets me with a light squeeze, his hand rubbing my back. "How are you?"

"I'm good, thanks."

"How're your parents doing?"

"They're okay," I lie.

"Good. You have a drink?"

I hold up my beer.

"Make sure you grab some food. My sister makes the best pasta salad, but—"

"Hello." A woman with a sleek two-tone pixie cut sidles up next to Mr. Mancini, and he introduces us.

"Cindy, this is Cassandra St. George. Cassandra, this is my wife."

"Oh, Cassandra." She presses her palms against my cheeks. "I'm so sorry for what you've been through. My heart aches for your parents."

I force a smile.

"I'm happy you're here," she goes on, gently patting my cheek.

Vince's attention is on a toddler showing him some kind of motorized plane with blinking lights. He's of no help to me.

"Cindy, let the girl breathe," Mr. Mancini says.

"Of course. I'm sorry." Cindy catches herself, pressing her hands to her chest. "Vinny's always yelling at me about personal space."

Vince butts in. "I'm what?"

"You always say I smother people," she says, running her hand down the side of his face. "But I can't help it, you know. It's how I show love. And I'm your mother, I can do whatever I want with you."

Vince rolls his eyes but presses his cheek into her hand, and I'm actually jealous of the exchange between them. There's so much love there.

"So, you've met my mom," Vince says to me as he wraps his arm around his mother's shoulders.

"Thank you for having me over."

"It's absolutely my pleasure. Make yourself at home." She waves her hand in an arc encompassing her whole house, and I use this moment to take my leave.

Vince follows me to the six-foot-long table covered with a flag tablecloth. "Sorry 'bout that."

I pick up a plate and scoop pasta salad onto it. "Don't worry about it."

"Mom's a hugger. I know you aren't."

I grab a cheeseburger. "She's not the only hugger around here."

He agrees and fills his plate high with food before we go to a table where his cousins Nick and Tony are. Since I'd met Nick at Sassie's, we all fall into easy conversation. Tony's pregnant wife, Annie, tells me stories about the hard time she's having. Normally, I'd be totally put-off by the baby topic, but it doesn't irk me so much now. I haven't been around many women—or people, for that matter—my age since I've moved home, and especially since Raymond died. I've cut myself off from the outside world completely. I've had my head buried in the sand, so I like being here.

I like talking with Annie and grow some secondhand excitement for her baby. I don't even mind when they ask me personal questions about my childhood with Ray and how I've been dealing with his death. I'm honest, for the most part. I tell them about the time Ray "accidentally" lit the carpet on fire in the basement and how his pyromaniac tendencies continued into adulthood with the time he put so many birthday candles on Lucy and Lara's cake last year, his kitchen curtains caught fire.

Vince brags about my growing social media and how I write "so eloquently" about my grief, and they all pull out their phones to follow me. It's oddly satisfying to watch them read through a few posts and witness their physical reactions to it in real time.

"It's beautiful and sad," Annie says. Nick and Tony agree, and Vince raises his eyebrow at me in a *See?* look.

"I'll think about it," I whisper to him, referring to that idea of his.

After a few hours of being cajoled by Uncle Dominic, I finally relent and allow him to teach me how to play gin rummy. And after a couple big glasses of cousin Margo's homemade wine, I really start to adore this huge, chaotic family. They're nothing like I'm used to but also kind of great. Everyone has their own drama and eccentricities, so it's easy to slip out of my own and into theirs. I cheer along as Mr. Mancini, who insists I call him Rob, sings "Mack the Knife" during karaoke, and I hold Aunt Jeanne's hand as she describes her botched foot surgery. Then I fetch her another Chardonnay.

When the sun sets, Vince finds me next to his mom, listening as she gossips with Margo, Stella, and Aunt Mary. He holds out his hand. "Come on."

I stare at his outstretched hand then meet his eyes. It's different, agreeing to come here with his family, to take his hand now, to make the decision to go with him.

It's weightier.

Meaningful.

Dangerous. For me, but especially him.

Except, when he smiles, I can't say no.

Behind me, Cindy pats my back, pushing me to go with him, the others grinning happily. Because they know too. What this all means.

And I should not take his hand. I should ask him to take me home.

But I don't.

Instead, I set my palm in his and let him wrap his fingers around mine.

CHAPTER 22

"*F*ireworks are starting soon." Vince informs me, and I stand up from the Adirondack chair with his help, and he tips his head toward the house. "Let's go to the roof."

"The roof?"

He indicates the flat part above the garage then to the higher portion next to it. "Used to climb out from my bedroom window."

"You snuck out a lot?" I ask, moving slowly from the wine.

He laces his fingers with mine and shrugs. "A few times. Sometimes, I'd sneak *in*. Until Mom caught me trying to get Amanda Bittmeir to climb up."

I tuck my face into his shoulder, buzzed enough not to be jealous of stupid Amanda Bittmeir.

"Haven't been on the roof for a while, though," he goes on, leading me inside the house and upstairs. "Thought you might like the view better from up here."

He opens the door to a bedroom at the end of the hall. With the navy walls and some memorabilia still around, it very clearly used to be his. I help myself to lounging on the bed as he opens the sliding closet doors to snag a thick quilt then leans over me for the pillows, his eyes roving over me. He smells of pine and the outdoors. I'm reminded of the time I was in gym class, sprawled out on the grass after "running" on the track. For some reason or another, Vince was speaking to the teacher and ended up flopping down next to me, our faces turned toward each other, his smile boyish, my heart leaping.

For a moment, I think he's going to lie next to me now, but he only crosses the room to the window, shoving it up and open with one hand before tipping his head for me to get up.

"Go foot first," he instructs. "The roof's still pitched here, so be careful."

When I make it out, he smiles. "Attagirl."

Then he tosses the pillows and quilt out, easily ducking his long frame through the window. With everything in hand once again, he helps me hop down to the flat roof of the garage, where he creates a makeshift bed for us.

Below us, sparklers flicker, tiki lights shine, and voices carry, but up here, it's muted, with the overhead sky nearly black. Like we're in another world.

"Here, come here," Vince says, opening his arm up to me so I'll sidle next to him. I don't hesitate.

Maybe because it is so dark on the roof, it doesn't feel real.

"I'm glad you agreed to come with me today."

"Me too." Our thighs rub against each other, and my pulse pounds everywhere. In my wrists. My throat. My chest. Between my legs.

He inches even closer, his breath hot on my bare shoulder. "And I'm really sorry I made you uncomfortable in the car earlier."

"You didn't make me uncomfortable. Took me by surprise, is all." He seems to accept my words and tilts his head back to gaze up at the sky, but I'm emboldened by the wine and the black of the night to give him more of an explanation. "You're really sweet, Vince. Too good for this world. Far too good for me."

"What?" His head snaps back to me. Only the whites of his eyes are visible in the dark, yet I shrink under the weight of his gaze.

"I know I'm tiring. I'm tired of me, so I can imagine someone else having to deal with me is exhausting. I'm closed-off and sarcastic. And you—"

He cuts me off by pushing me to my back, my head on a pillow, my wrists in his hands. With the skirt of my dress rucked up, he settles his hips against mine so he's hovering over me. "Stop."

"I—"

"You have to stop with this."

I feel his body heat even as the air around us is hot and humid, and my skin pricks with sweat. He leans down, resting his forehead to mine, his chest hard against me, his weight solid and comforting on top of me. I bend my knees, mechanically bringing him closer, slotting him into the pocket of my open legs, and I don't recall what I was even saying. What I have to stop.

Because I want him to keep going.

"I could never tire of you," he says, our breaths mingling as his lips graze mine.

There is no ounce of hesitation, no conscious thought, merely wild flowers smashing through the cement for light and air. I'm *alive* and want to be alive with him.

Need to be alive with him.

"Vince…"

He fits his mouth against mine, tasting faintly of beer and the strawberry dessert his aunt made. I sink one of my hands into his hair while letting the other skate down his back, finding his skin underneath his T-shirt. When I scratch my nails across the muscles on either side of his spine, he hisses his pleasure and drags his lips across my jaw, the stubble of his five-o'clock shadow scraping me in return.

I can't get enough of it.

Of his roaming hands and fingers on my waist, my breasts, my throat. Or the way he sucks on my pulse point and I arch my back, inviting him to take more. He does, leaning on his side to slide his fingertips along the inside of my thigh, taking the soft cotton I'm wearing with it, revealing my thin underwear.

And that's when the first firework is loosed, exploding over us, and I flinch involuntarily.

"You're okay," he reminds me, and I nod even though it wasn't a question. Because whenever I'm with him, I'm always okay.

Then he lowers his mouth to my ear so I can hear him breathing over the booms and pops above us, the bright blues and whites and greens lighting up the sky enough that I can see how the veins in his throat and arms stand out starkly in shadow. He's so strong and sure, and I want to be like him, give in to him. Ask him to make me whole again.

But I don't. Instead, I release a moan that only he can hear, our desires protected from the outside world by the celebrations above and below us.

But, Vince and I, we're celebrating life in a whole other way.

"I need to feel you," he says, nipping at the skin of my throat, and I place my hand over his, guiding it to slip underneath my damp panties. I inhale sharply at the first tender slide of his fingers against my sensitive flesh, and when I start to lift my hands to dig them into his shoulders, he shakes his head, catching one and then the other, raising them above my head. He holds my wrists in one hand then tugs slightly, pulling me taut like a bowstring. My nipples are tight, my breasts heavy, and he dips his head down, kissing the curve of them and then up my throat. "Let me take care of you."

He's been taking care of me for months now, and there is no better feeling in the world than giving in to him. So I do.

"Please," I whimper, and his hold on my wrists tightens as he sinks his other hand back below my underwear.

I'm wet, I can feel it, and he groans when he does too. "You don't know," he starts, his lips whispering against my collarbone as two thick fingers pet and prod me open. "You don't know how sweet you are."

"I'm not." I sigh when he strokes those fingers inside me. "I'm not sweet."

"You are." He shifts, raising his head over me, his eyes black pools, even with the bursting colors above us. "You're the sweetest girl I've ever known, delicate and soft. I've always known, always saw it in you, no matter how you try to hide it."

My eyes and nose burn, and I lift my head, closing the distance between us to kiss him, forcing him to stop talking with my teeth and tongue, but he smiles against my mouth and slowly drags his fingers in and out of my sex, torturing me until I'm writhing beneath him.

Only then does he tend to where I'm most sensitive as he nips my earlobe. I involuntarily clamp my knees tighter at the onslaught of sensation, and he sinks down farther, finally releasing my wrists. Although with the quick pinch of them against the rough shingles, I know he wants me to keep them there, so I do.

He rewards me by cupping my breast through my dress, sweeping his thumb back and forth over my peaked nipple. He licks and sucks across my throat, edging my legs back open with his elbow before pressing and circling harder against my clit. "You're sweet here too. Tight and hot, but you've got to let me in." He smooths his hand up my throat, over my jaw and cheek, curling his fingers into my hair, holding me. And thank Zeus because I think I might break into pieces.

He draws the tip of his nose down mine then kisses me again, prying soft sounds from the back of my throat. "Let me in, and I'll take care of you."

My body responds before my mind can, and I relax my legs, sink into his sure and steady hold, and he presses the advantage, dipping his fingers inside me, twisting until he finds the spot that has me moaning and my fingernails digging into my palms.

"I would wait for you forever, but I'm glad you're not making me," he says, and I can't register what he's telling me. Not when his stubble is raking over my skin and his lips are turning me to mush. "You feel it? You feel how much you want me?"

I can. I can feel my inner muscles working, convulsing around his fingers. I can feel my heart racing, my chest heaving with each breath. I feel everything. I feel it all.

And it's too much.

"It can be like this all the time," he murmurs against the shell of my ear. "Let me in, and I'll make sure it's like this all the time."

Then he bites the slope of my neck and shoulder, and he presses hard inside me at the same time he circles his thumb over my clit, and fireworks go off inside me too.

Above me, they pop and sizzle, like my heart when Vince smiles down at me as if everything is right in the world.

But it's not.

He tenderly removes his hand from inside me, slipping out of my ruined panties, and gently brushes my hair back from my sweat-slicked temple. Then he sticks his wet fingers in his mouth, ruining *me*.

And I blink, trying not to cry.

He rolls on top of me. "Don't, sweetheart. Please don't overthink this."

I shake my head and push against his chest, forcing him to give me room.

To breathe.

To think.

Because, yes, I am overthinking.

I sit up, mindlessly wiggling my fingers and arms, anxiety and alarm creeping into my bloodstream as his words finally hit me.

You're the sweetest girl I've ever known, delicate and soft. I've always known, always saw it in you, no matter how you try to hide it.

Let me in, and I'll make sure it's like this all the time.

I'll take care of you.

I would wait for you forever.

And it's not fair. It's not fair of me to make him wait and take care of me.

He shouldn't have to.

He shouldn't *want* to.

I'm broken beyond repair.

I fix the straps of my dress and settle the skirt over my thighs, telling him the first honest words that come to me. "I would drag you down."

He leans into my space, laughing like I'm kidding. I'm not.

"You think you could actually drag *me* down," he says, wrapping me up. "With these arms?"

Even now, I want to laugh. I want to cry. I want to stay in his perfect embrace, but I can't, and I wiggle out of his arms, meeting his amused gaze until he sees the truth in mine.

He drops his chin toward his chest for a moment, his shoulders rising and falling on a breath I can't hear over the fireworks. He nods a few times to himself before lifting his eyes to mine. The corner of his mouth hooks up sadly. "You won't accept it, will you?"

You won't accept me is what he's really asking. And I can't.

Because I'd ruin it.

Ruin him.

Ruin us.

"I'm sorry," I tell him, and when he doesn't respond, save for a tic in his jaw, I ask, "Can't we just be friends?"

I make sure to look him steadily in the eyes that I can see now as the fireworks light up the sky. Bright white, green, and pink explode, reflecting on Vince's face.

Boom.

Boom.

Sizzle.

Finally, Vince agrees with, "Yeah, okay. Friends."

But it feels like an ending. Like the fireworks. The sky quiets and darkens, and so do we.

JULY 14

It's been over two weeks since July 4th, but I swear I can still feel the thump of fireworks in my body. Growing up, I loved Independence Day, the picnics, sparklers, fireflies, endless days, and warm nights. It represented the best time of the year: summer. It was a marker to look forward to, but then it was over, and we began a different kind of countdown, one to the first day of school. That countdown was much less fun.

Raymond is gone five months today, and each day adds to the running total of how many days we're without him. For now, it's a small number, only 151. It seems big. It's a triple-digit number after all, but eventually, the number will grow to four digits, and then five. It will grow larger than 11,087, the number of days he walked on this giant rock. Eventually we will live without him longer than we lived with him. I am resigned to that fact. And completely gutted.

Sometimes I pick my phone up to text him. I still have things I want to tell him, like how he would really like this new song on the radio or that there was a two-for-one sale on those cheap grocery-store brownies he loves. But my fear is when I stop all that. When I stop thinking of him or can't remember what he smelled like or the way he cleared his throat before he told a story. What if I forget the sound of his voice or the exact ashy-gold color of his hair? Or the way he said my name, and how he loped when he walked, as if his arms were too long for his body. What if I forget all of this?

What then?

#Grief #Calendar #FinalCountdown

CHAPTER 23

"I'd like to register for a library card," I tell the small, cardigan-clad woman behind the desk. It's ninety degrees and rising outside, but the air conditioning works perfectly in the Plainfield Public Library.

"Sure," she says and hands me a few papers to fill out.

As her fingers clack away on the computer keyboard, the smell of all the books restores my weary soul, while the barely audible sounds—the padding of feet, the turning of papers, the slight crick of a book spine—are a lullaby. I haven't been to a library since I lived in Brooklyn, but being here feels a little bit like coming home.

I hand the woman the papers, and she hands me the card. "My name's Trisha, if you need anything."

"Thank you," I say, storing the card in my wallet before exploring the stacks.

I've been doing a lot of thinking this past month—about my brother, my parents, and Vince. It's been six months since Raymond died, and each of those days has been a surprise. Sometimes the grief is so bad, I sit on the shower floor crying. Other days, it's as if Raymond never existed; there is no piece of him left to remember, my day too busy to form a picture of him in my mind. Some days my mom does well; some days she doesn't. Some days my father comes home, and some he doesn't.

It's exhausting, living in a perpetual state of the unknown, and it's becoming more and more obvious to me that Vince was right. Of course.

I have to help myself before I can help anybody else, and that means I need to figure out what I want for myself.

So, I'm here, browsing for a book, something *I* want. Something I need.

When I can't decide between the historical fiction about Arthur and Guinevere, the thriller about the woman who takes revenge on her nasty husband, or the contemporary romance with the cartoon cover, I pile up all three under my arm and find a table to fulfill the next step in my plan. I've been out of college for six years, but I pull up my email to write Professor Christine Row. With my original dream of being some sort of entertainment journalist—writing snappy pieces on pop culture, reviewing music, or political satire—in the metaphorical shitter, I've been wondering if maybe I should write a book.

I haven't even fully fleshed out the idea, but I ask Professor Row what she thinks. We'd kept in touch for a year or so after I graduated because she always had great advice, and if there is one thing I need now, it's advice. I fill her in on my life and ask her if she'd be able to direct me in any direction of a job opening or internship. I'd always been opposed to something unpaid—because bills—but if I'm going to shoot my shot, it's got to be now. Unpaid or not.

Hitting send is gratifying. It's a relief to finally give in to the voice in the back of my head, the one that sounds a lot like Vince.

My heart sinks a little. We haven't spoken much since the Fourth of July. He said he's been working on his house a lot, and I have no reason to think he's lying. Besides, with the summer winding down, I'm trying to get in as many shifts at Sassie's as I can before patrons start burrowing away again for the winter. We agreed to be friends, at my request, so that has to be that.

And it's fine.

I'm fine.

Even as my hand reflexively reaches for my phone to text him.

But I'm fine, so I stop myself.

It's not fair to him to keep him on the hook when I know I'll never be enough for him. What I have to offer is nothing in comparison to what he gives me.

I have to focus on me, figure my life out first. Then maybe, down the road, I'll be the type of woman who'll be able to take care of him the way he has taken care of me.

I spend the rest of the hour researching writing groups and resources until I need to leave to pick up my mom and grandparents. It's Lucy and Lara's fifth birthday, and Shayna's throwing a big party at their house. I'm really not looking forward to it, for a bunch of reasons, not the least of which is my brother won't be there.

The stifling heat of August invades my car. I check on Nana and Pop in the rearview mirror to make sure they're all right, then hit the dash twice. Cool air spits through the vents in stops and starts. Normally, I wouldn't care that my jalopy of a car originally belonged to Fred Flintstone, but with my mom and grandparents in it, I worry somebody will pass out from heat exhaustion. "Everybody good?"

My grandparents don't drive much anymore, and my brother was always their chauffeur. Now, it's up to me since Aunt Joanie can't make it to the party today. So far, the car ride has been silent.

"Huh?" Pop yells behind me.

"Are you too hot?" I ask loudly, eyeing him in the rearview.

"No, I'm not hungry," he says, and I hide my smile, pressing on the gas harder.

"Dad," my mom says, shifting in the passenger seat. "Are you hot? Hot?" She nearly screams the word.

Mom has been in a relatively good mood lately. I think it's because of the sun. I took the curtains down in her bedroom and never put them back up, crafting a story about accidentally bleaching them in the wash. She only told me to be more careful next time and never brought it up again.

"Hot?" Pop says, his hand cupped around his ear. "Yeah, I'm hot."

Mom uselessly flicks at the vent in front of her. "You need a new car."

"That would be nice," I say.

"Is your father coming today?"

I find it odd she's asking me this question, as if I talk to him more than she does. "I guess so. I told him about it."

She stares down at the two pink envelopes in her hands. "I can't believe Raymond isn't here for their birthday."

"I know," I mumble, the two words insufficient for the dark cloud hanging over what should be a happy time. I can already picture their pouts and big eyes because their daddy isn't there to sing to them.

When we arrive at Shayna's—and Raymond's—house, I park in the driveway, the same spot where Ray would park his big SUV, and help Pop and then Nana out of the back seat to lead them up to the front door. Pink and silver Mylar balloons are tied on the railing, and I have to knock them out of the way to open the front door, allowing my grandparents and Mom ahead of me.

Before I'm even inside, the decibel of screeching makes me wince, and I leap out of the way of three little girls in costumes running in a circle around the house. There's a princess, a firefighter, and an alligator, I think. I don't recognize any of them.

Shayna's in the kitchen with two women when we walk back there, and she hugs my mom and grandparents, then gestures to the twins in the backyard, where they're jumping on a trampoline. They all coo at the adorableness of their matching outfits and bouncing curls before heading outside to the pandemonium. None of it looks fun to me. Kids zooming in all directions, pink decorations covering every inch of the place, and the sounds? Even Pop can hear them.

"Got anything to drink?" I ask.

"Soda." Shayna motions to an open liter bottle of Diet Coke.

I'd rather alcohol to dull my senses but settle for the soda and fill up a pink paper cup. "How are you?"

"Great," she says, and I don't know whether to be concerned or impressed by her answer. I'd thought she might be having a hard time today, being without Ray and all, yet she's her usual self, hair and nails done, dressed like she runs a pyramid clothing scheme. She angles her shoulder away from me, toward the women next to her. "This is Cassandra, RJ's sister."

The two women smile at me but neither introduces themself, and Shayna evidently has no intention of doing it either. It's clear I'm unwanted in their circle and move to the door, but a man with a trim beard opens it to stick his head in. "Babe, the princesses are here."

"Perfect," Shayna says, and my brain actually sputters as I make the connection that this man called Shayna *babe* and she answered. "Want to bring them in, and I'll round everybody up?"

"Sure," he says with a grin and spins around to bring the princesses in.

I steady myself with a hand on the counter. They know each other really well, apparently. Enough to bring the goddamn princesses in the back.

"Who's he?"

"Todd," she says like it's no big thing and steps outside with her two friends.

"Todd," I grumble. "Fucking Todd."

I don't know why I'm so upset. The fact that she's in a relationship with someone who isn't my brother. Or that she's happy and I'm not. Or that my brother isn't here, period. I don't know. Probably all of it.

She'd told me she was moving on. I understood it then, but seeing it in real life is totally different.

"Come on, everybody!" Shayna waves her arms outside, gathering everyone close. "We have some very special guests here for the birthday girls!"

Todd offers me a bland, closed-lip smile that someone would give any stranger as he makes his way into the kitchen with two young women made up to look like vaguely familiar Disney princesses. They both tilt their heads and give me a practiced wave. I raise my cup to them in a salute.

As the princesses elegantly stride outside, screams erupt, and I plop down on one of the high-backed stools at the eat-in counter. If Ray were here, then he'd probably be dressed up as a prince to match, singing and dancing to his daughters' delight. I close my eyes to imagine it.

If Ray were here, then I wouldn't have had to drive my family to this party or be ashamed of the car I bought with my own money.

If Ray were here, then I'd probably try to duck out early, though he'd guilt me into staying, and then further guilt me into taking part in the festivities. But he's gone, and I have to force myself to do the things he'd want me to.

If Ray were here, then I wouldn't have to think of these if/then statements.

I inhale a deep breath and make my way outside to snap some pictures of the girls as they twirl with the princesses. My grandparents clap along, and I take a picture of that too. I don't know what I'll do with these pictures, but Ray would have played photographer, so...

Trying to busy myself, or at least look like I'm busy, I clear away some garbage and exchange a few pleasantries with Shayna's parents. I have nothing in common with the other people here and mainly float around the pairs and trios gabbing away about their favorite rosé and vegan lasagna recipes. I watch the princess show in a daze until they finish to a wild round of applause, and I clap on cue.

"Who's ready for cake?" Shayna asks.

Every hand of every child extends into the air, and she hauls out a big sheet cake. I film a video of Lucy and Lara blowing out their candles. Shayna's behind them with one arm around the twins and the other around Todd's waist. For his part, he has one arm around Shayna's shoulders and one hand on the head of a girl with pigtails, who I assume is his daughter. They're like a little family.

I want to puke.

Todd picks up a knife to cut the cake, and the three girls dance impatiently.

"I want the purple flower, Daddy!"

I freeze at the term of endearment from Lucy. She called Todd *Daddy*, and I know my mother's heard it too because the color has drained from her face.

Fucking Todd.

As my brother's life erases before my very eyes, I catch Shayna's attention, and she has the decency to appear a little sheepish, but then her focus darts away from me and back on to the girls. The heat of this weather has nothing on the fire raging inside me. If I could, I'd mold it in my hands and destroy this whole party. But I'll settle for Shayna.

I rub my mom's back as she wipes tears from her eyes. Nana shakes her head, muttering things under her breath. Pop's unaware of everything as he eats cake and ice cream, his hearing aid most likely turned off on purpose. What I wouldn't give to be him, to be able to avoid the drama. I can't, so I face it head on and corner Shayna in her living room.

"What the hell?" I blurt out.

"What?"

"What the hell is up with the girls calling Todd Daddy? I mean, Jesus, Ray isn't even gone a year. Barely even six months!"

She lifts her hands in defense. "Look, I know it's probably hard for you to—"

"You are *not* about to lecture me," I say, measuring my words. "What's wrong with you? Raymond is those girls' daddy. Not Todd!"

Shayna strides close to me, her eyes narrowing, sticking one perfectly trimmed white-and-glitter nail in my face. "First of all, do not yell at me. You are a guest in my house.

Second of all, you have no idea what it's been like for me since your brother died. Those girls need a father figure. If they want to call Todd Daddy because it makes them feel good, I'm not going to stop them."

"He's not their father!"

She folds her arms. "I know he isn't, but I'm not arguing with you about this. Lucy and Lara need a man in their lives, and Todd is a good man. I'm sorry if it makes you upset, but I'm not going to stop the girls from expressing themselves."

"So, that's it? You're going to pretend Ray didn't exist?"

"Of course not." She sneers at me. "I'm not the heartless bitch you think I am. I have framed pictures of him. I talk about him all the time, but the girls are little, they don't understand. All they know is their daddy went to heaven, and Todd is here."

My face hurts from trying to keep it in place, refusing to give away how much this not only hurts me, but everyone in my family.

"Todd isn't taking Raymond's place, but I can't do this on my own." Her voice cracks with emotion, and for a moment, I'm contrite about being so angry with her. It has to be difficult raising two little kids on her own. When I don't put up any further arguments, she wipes at the corner of her eye, then fixes her hair and weaves around me, leaving me alone to wallow.

A little while later, my grandparents shuffle inside with my mom between them. Wordlessly, I grab my purse and we pile in the car. As soon as I pull away, Mom breaks down. The squeak of my brakes and her sniffles are the only sounds to keep us company on the ride home. By the time I drop my grandparents off, Mom's mascara is zigzagged down her cheek, and when I open the front door at home, she rushes upstairs, right past Dad passed out in his chair.

I've seen it so many times, I have no energy left to be disappointed in him. I should've guessed this was how he would end up, even if his grandchildren had a birthday.

Downstairs, I throw myself onto my bed, thoroughly drained.

Two steps forward, one step back.

AUGUST 15

Welp. August sucks. I'm ready for summer to be over. It's hot. And no, those aren't tears on my face, that's my sweat. But yes, six months and it's not any easier. Grieving is supposed to get easier, isn't it? Someone told me that.

#Grief #Summer #Sweat #Lies

CHAPTER 24

*E*ver since the *Daddy* debacle, Mom's been spending a lot of time in bed, so I'm back to doing the grocery shopping, cooking, and cleaning. Not that she eats or moves all that much when she's in her downswings.

Professor Row emailed me back, but I've been too busy to open it. Although, if I'm honest, I'm afraid to open it because she might have something wonderful to say. And even if she has something wonderful to say, I know I won't follow through.

I can't. Not now when Mom is so depressed.

I couldn't possibly leave her.

Pushing those thoughts away, I press play on another true crime podcast before folding my clothes then sorting through my parents' clothes. I stop when I see it, a smear of pink that can only be lipstick on the collar of one of my dad's shirts.

I rub my thumb over the stain, thinking about all the nights I hoped what I feared wasn't true. He wouldn't betray my mother. Not after everything we've all been through.

But the evidence is right in front of me.

Setting aside the tainted Brooks Brothers shirt, I finish the rest of the laundry, planning what I'm going to say to him.

How dare you?

Are you deliberately trying to destroy our family?

Instead of coming home, you're spending your nights with another woman or women?

You're selfish and insensitive.

You only care about yourself.

I repeat those sentences and more in my head, hyping myself up for the confrontation, but I don't get the chance.

Three, four, five, six days go by. Then it's a full two weeks before my father finally comes home.

It's a Saturday in September, the kind of perfectly clear, mildly cool day that hints at the months to come. It's the kind of day I might want to find a perfect photo of some fall foliage, yellowing trees, apples, or some other stereotypical thing to post along with #Unbeleafable and #Sweater-Weather.

But I don't do that. Instead, I write a very different post about my brother, along with an old picture of us when we were little, two and five, maybe. My arms are wrapped around his middle like I'm squeezing really hard while he's shoving me away.

It's Ray's birthday. He's thirty-one years old today. I write about some of the birthdays I remember and grieve all the birthdays he won't have.

This is the day my dad decides to return home.

His face is blotchy and red. His work clothes are wrinkled and untucked like he's been in them since yesterday. He smells like he's been dowsed in alcohol. "Hey," he says, keeping his balance with a hand on the wall as he takes his shoes off at the door. "Taking care of your mother?"

I grit my teeth. "Yes, I'm taking care of her."

"Good. Very good." He sinks down into his chair, eyes closed. This is my chance to get it all off my chest, tell him how he's completely abandoned Mom and me since Ray died. I want to tell him that we deserve better. That I want us to be a family again. But all of my preplanned material leaves my brain.

All I can stutter out is, "H-how could you?"

He opens one eye. "How could I what?"

"You're having an affair."

He makes a face like I'm crazy.

"There was lipstick on one of your shirts."

He picks up the remote to turn on the television.

"Dad."

He ignores me.

"Dad," I say, moving closer to him. "Why? After everything that's happened, why would you cheat on Mom?"

He rubs his hand over his face but doesn't answer.

"Dad!"

His eyes slant to me, sharp and alert. "Don't shout at me."

"You don't get to tell me what to do anymore. I'm not a child."

"Then stop acting like one."

I lose it. Absolutely lose it. "You can't be gone for weeks at a time and then come back pretending to be my father! You have no right to do that! Not after how you've left us. And now you're cheating on Mom. What's wrong with you?"

He shoots up like a raging bull. "Your mother," he sneers at me, "is a zombie, a shell of a person. Don't talk to me about your mother." He waves his arms back and forth in front of me. "You have no idea what it's like for me. I have to work to keep this family afloat to come home to a wife who's dead in the eyes and an ungrateful daughter."

Somewhere in the back of my mind, I think his words should hurt me, but they don't. I'm numb to them, to him.

"You don't know what it's like when your child dies." His voice quivers. "Your boy...you don't know..."

He crumples in half, heaving giant breaths in and out, weeping. I've never seen him like this before. I don't know how to comfort my father or if I even want to. I simply watch him melt into a puddle on the floor. "My baby boy," he cries over and over.

I slump on the couch, dejected, apparently incapable of even leaving my asshole father alone while he's like this, and I stay with him until he falls asleep, his shirt soaked with tears. I don't realize what time it is until it's too late and hurry to change for work. Gary didn't send me any passive-aggressive texts or phone calls, so I hope he doesn't notice I'm almost an hour late for my shift as I sneak in before the dinner rush. It's raucous today with a huge bachelor party. They look like they've already tied one on during their golf outing with their polos, hats, and booming laughter. Plus, there's a large table in the back for a 50th birthday party.

It's another reminder of Ray.

Last year for his birthday, I'd begged him to go out and have a couple drinks with me, but he refused. He ended up taking the twins to a movie and then texting me a picture of his drink, a frozen blue Icee. I blink away the memory and the sting in my eyes.

The cloud of my brother and father looms large above me as I work, trying to ignore the stupid jokes from the bachelor party. They aren't even my table and yet insist on being completely disgusting to every server who passes.

"Hey, girlie..."

I spin toward the guy with the backward Puma cap. "What?"

"You'd be prettier if you smiled more."

The men behind him snicker, and I dream of stabbing him with a dull knife. I settle for a snarl instead.

"Bet she's an animal in bed," one of them says as I stomp away.

I'm about to pivot around to say something, but Celia, their server, snags my wrist. "It's not worth it," she says and nudges me to the back. I lean against the register stand and take a minute to peek at my phone. There's a message from Vince.

How are you today?

He's checking on me because he knows it's my brother's birthday. I guess he's probably seen my post. God, I miss him.

I'm okay, I type back and ask **How are you?** Because even though they seemed to have grown apart in recent years, he was Ray's best friend at one time. Like brothers.

A few seconds later, the bubble pops up that he's replying, but as the message appears, a purposeful throat clears behind me.

"Cass."

I recognize Gary's voice and hide my phone like a kid caught with candy. "What's up?"

"I was going to talk to you after your shift, but let's do it now." I follow him back to the small office. He sets his feet wide and crosses his arms. "I've given you a lot of room after what happened with your brother, but you've continually broken the rules here—"

"I don't—"

"I'm talking," he says. His face is the most serious I've ever seen it, and I'm taken aback, immediately quieting, a queasy feeling settling in my stomach. He shakes his head at me. "Quite frankly, I don't think you need or deserve an explanation, but you've been late on multiple occasions, you have a bad attitude, and you're always on your phone, so I'm letting you go."

"You're firing me?" I'm stunned. I've never been fired before, not that I've worked many jobs, but still.

"I can't believe you're so shocked. Honestly, do you even care?"

"Yeah, I work here. I need to work here."

"Well, you don't act like it," he says, leaning against a small shelf. "You think you can go through life half-assing it?"

I want to argue, although I can't come up with anything to fire back at him. This job sucks, but I need the paycheck. "Come on, please. I'm having a really hard time right now."

He's unmoved. "I've given you countless warnings. I know you're going through some things, but so are a lot of people." He vaguely motions over my shoulder. "You don't need to finish your shift. I'll get your tables covered, so you can head out now. I'll send your check home. Leave your apron in the locker."

I back out of the room, trying to be tough about this, but I can't. I take my bag and leave my apron before heading out the front door, too embarrassed to even say goodbye to anyone. Gary didn't lie when he said I half-assed this job. It's true I need the money, but I despised working at Sassie's. But with no job, I have nothing really holding my life together. The only bright side is that my parents won't care. They won't even notice.

Sitting behind the wheel of my car, I open my text thread with Vince to read his last message. **I'm all right. But**

I'm thinking of you today. All days, but especially today. I hope you're blasting some Bruce.

I sniffle and drop my hand to the steering wheel. Why does he have to be so perfect?

Especially when I'm not.

After a minute, I text him. **Not right now. I got fired.**

What?!?!

Your punctuation is totally unnecessary because the rhetorical question intonates your surprise.

What?!?!

I am unemployed.

Are you okay?

No. I type my answer without thinking, but I suppose the time for pretending I'm fine is over now. **Can I come over?**

The typing bubble doesn't immediately pop up. In fact, it doesn't show up until after I've counted twelve Mississippis.

Sure.

CHAPTER 25

As Vince opens the front door to me, Gracie dances on her hind legs behind him. He nudges her away then looks at me. And I fall into him. I don't even wait for him to bring his arms up. Pressing my cheek against his shoulder, I snake my arms around his torso, basking in his warmth and clean pine scent.

It takes a few seconds, but then his arms are around me, one hand at the back of my head, the other rubbing up and down my back. "You're okay."

And for *this* moment, I am okay.

I try on the truth. "I missed you."

He doesn't say it back, only hugs me a little tighter, kisses my temple. "What happened with your job?"

"I don't want to talk about it."

He slowly pulls away, nudging my chin up to meet his gaze. "What do you want to talk about?"

That's the thing; I don't want to talk. I don't want to think or be responsible. I want to be reckless, throw myself into things I know I shouldn't. I want to kiss him.

So, I do.

When I pull him down to me, he's taken by surprise, his gold-green eyes wide and confused, but when I press my lips against his, he closes his eyes and I close mine. His hands find the dip at my waist, mine wind in his hair. His lips are familiar in a way they shouldn't be, his soft grunts my favorite sounds. If I never heard or felt or tasted anyone else for the rest of my life, I would be satisfied.

Together, we take blind steps until we stumble against the staircase, which forces us to break apart, and I grasp his hand, leading him upstairs to his bedroom. He sits on the bed, slow to catch on as I toss my clothes aside until I'm in front of him in only my bra and underwear.

He blinks.

Blinks again.

Then he's up, clumsily stripping off his shirt and pants. His throat bobs on a swallow, his eyes drinking me in, and I become the most confident version of myself under his rapt attention.

He seems a little nervous, but his earnestness only proves how special he is, and how special he thinks I am that he continually chooses me.

I truly don't deserve him.

I take him in, from his bare toes to the top of his hair in need of a trim. His legs are covered in dark brown hair, his thighs like tree trunks, and I place my hands on them as I sink to my knees. He meets my gaze over the plane of his long torso, slightly muscled and fuzzed with hair that narrows down toward his belly button and his thick cock that hardens with every second we stare at each other.

I curl my fingers around the elastic of his light-blue boxer briefs, peeling them down his legs so he can step out of them as his erection extends out toward me. Before I can lean in to kiss it, he stops me with his fingers in my hair.

"Are you sure?" he asks even as his hips move forward, tapping the wide head on my lower lip. But with how his mouth opens on a sharp breath, I don't think he meant to.

I wrap one hand around the base and curve my other around his hip, and even though I know it won't fit, I pretend my stomach isn't flip-flopping at the thought and answer, "I'm sure."

He doesn't remove his fingers from my hair, but he does curl them tighter as he guides my head toward him, groaning quietly when I open my mouth to him. I suck the salty flavor off him, lick his velvety length, all the while, we never break eye contact.

He doesn't force me any further than I want to go, merely cups the back of my head, tells me that he's fantasized about this often. About having my sweet mouth on him.

I can't believe it. That this is happening, and that he's the one who's confessing how long he's dreamed of *me*.

"That first year you were in college, when you came home for winter break, you came to a party with RJ and me," he says, dragging his thumb around the corner of my mouth as I lave him with my tongue. "I hadn't seen you for a long time, and even though I always thought you were cute, I saw you that night, and..." He blows out a breath, his abs clenching, his fingers tightening in my hair when I lick the bead of his desire. "Shit, Cass, I thought you were the most beautiful girl I'd ever seen. I wanted to talk to you..." He grunts when I work my fist over him, sucking at the tip. "I wanted to take you to a quiet corner, tell you how I'd always had a thing for you, always thought you were stronger and smarter and more beautiful than you ever believed you were. But when we got there, some douchebag got your attention first."

My eyes tear at his confession, and I want to please him, give him something in return, but he doesn't let me. Instead, he bends and pulls me up off the floor, kissing my already-swollen lips until I'm out of breath.

He palms my backside, squeezing hard enough to earn a gasp, and tows me right up against him, all my soft along all his hard.

"I remember that night," I admit, thinking of the party in the basement of Joe Kieffer's house, a guy Vince and RJ graduated high school with. "That guy was Patch. We ended up making out."

"*Patch*?"

"I'm not sure where the nickname came from, but he was Keiffer's younger brother."

"Stupid name," Vince grumbles.

"You jealous?" The idea makes me giddy, and I trace the line of his shoulder, giggling. I think this is the happiest I've been in a good long time.

"Back then, yes." He slips his arm around my waist and hoists me up to toss me onto the bed. "But you're with me now."

I ignore how those words wrap around my clay heart, shaping it into something a little more usable. Something a little more valuable.

"I only did it because I didn't want to see girls hanging all over you," I explain, and he crawls over me with a playful grin then nips at my ear and shoulder like it's payback.

"You were the only one I wanted. And you broke my heart with *Patch*."

I laugh, toying with the small pendant on his gold necklace hanging between us. "I didn't break your heart."

"No," he agrees, "but you can."

It takes my breath away, this simple revelation.

I could break his heart.

"Now," he starts, skating his hand down my side, "you can make up for that night and all the others you owe me."

"Yeah?" I help him remove my bra and lift my hips when he tugs my underwear down and off. "There are a lot of nights?"

He nods and presses a kiss between my breasts. "You have no idea, sweetheart."

I guess I don't. Because the heat of his gaze on my bare skin is more than I expect. Like he's been waiting not only nights, but *years*. Those hazel eyes of his flutter like he can't believe what he's looking at, even though I've never felt all that special. Slim with big hips, long legs with dimpled thighs, and a bust size that's nothing to write home about.

Yet he stares at me as if I'm flawless.

He tows me to the edge of the mattress, places my legs over his shoulders, and then with only a tiny smile my way as a forewarning, his mouth is on me. His licks are perfect, languorous like I'm a dessert he wants to savor, and maybe I am, if his satisfied moans are any indication. When I sink my fingers into his hair, he mumbles a quiet, "That's it," then loops one arm around my hip to press his palm above my pubic bone at the same time he slides two fingers inside me, pushing me closer and closer to climax.

"Never in my wildest dreams as a fourteen-year-old did I think I'd be here with you while you do this," I pant, and he tips his head up to laugh, his mouth shiny with the evidence of just how well he knows my body.

"Never?" he teases as he lazily plays with my clit.

I shake my head, tugging his head back between my legs.

"So demanding."

"Please, Vince," I whine, and he holds my gaze as he licks up the length of me.

"Whatever you want. I'll give you anything." He kisses both of my thighs. "Everything."

Then he returns to my pleasure as if he didn't just split me in half with his promise.

Like he means it.

Like I'm worth it.

Like he hasn't merely kick-started my heart into working order but sent it careening off a cliff.

With a cry that's half agony, half bliss, I orgasm, and he praises me with quiet words as he levers himself over me, his erection hard against my stomach, and I wrap my legs around his waist, holding him close while I recover.

"Since neither one of us really planned this, I assume you didn't bring condoms, and I don't have any either," he tells me, taking time to suck on each of my nipples so what he says doesn't quite register at first. "But it's been a while since I had sex, and I was tested after I broke up with Sandi."

That registers, and I roll my eyes.

He smirks against the underside of my breast. "You jealous?"

I'm unrepentant. "Yes."

His eyes flare a possession that makes my skin erupt with goose bumps, and he settles his hands on either side of my head. "What're you gonna do about it?"

Taking his cock in hand, I rub the head over my wet entrance. "Tell you that I'm on birth control, but it's been a really long time for me. Like, so long, I'm a little worried it'll hurt."

Vince's brows furrow. "I'd rather cut off my own dick than hurt you." He ducks his head, leaving an openmouthed kiss on the slope of my shoulder then another under my ear. "Guide me in. We'll go slow, and you'll tell me if it's too much, yeah?"

He kisses me, plying me to relax, before winding his arm under my leg, positioning me when I notch him inside. With a crooked and reassuring smile, he gently pushes in farther then retreats, waiting after each stroke for me to adjust.

He fills me so deliciously full that I can hardly breathe, and he must know because he presses his forehead to mine. "Breathe, sweetheart." And I do, allowing him to completely seat himself in me. "How's it feel?"

I fist the comforter below, starting to swivel my hips. "Good," I tell him. "So good."

He rests on his forearms, bringing us chest to chest, belly to belly, using shallow thrusts as he still holds my leg up. To help, I fit my hand between us, stroking my swollen clit, feel how slippery we are together, how desperate I am for him.

He practically growls, proud of me. "Attagirl."

Then he really takes off, hitting me exactly right, his muscles tensing with effort, his skin sweating from work. It's so fucking sexy, the way he's breathing and arching his back. He's doing this for me. Making it good for me. Taking care of me.

"Oh god," I whimper. "Never. It's never been like this." I squeeze my eyes shut. "Feels like..." I lick my lips, not quite able to put it into words. "*I'm dying.*"

He agrees with a ragged hum, occasionally licking and

sucking at my throat and the tops of my breasts. "You were worth the wait," he murmurs into my shoulder, almost like he didn't mean to say that out loud. But then he traces the shell of my ear with the tip of his tongue. "When you come, I want you to open your eyes and look at me. You understand?"

I do, and I nod.

"I want to see everything inside you. I want all of you."

I don't know how he does it. Makes me feel like I'm enough, and I blink my eyes to him, so that he can *see* me.

I want him to see me. All the good and bad, even the macerated thing currently working hard to survive inside my chest.

Vince reminds me of what I've been missing. It's been a long time since I've been with a man, and I need not only this release, but I need *him*.

It's with that thought that I fall off the edge, making sure to keep my eyes open, letting him in.

"That's it," he rasps, "give it all to me. Give everything to me, and I'll take care of you."

With one last thrust, he stills and lowers his weight on top of me, before rolling us so I'm on top of him. I don't hesitate to bury my head in his throat, and he tightens his hold on me, pecking kisses over my hair, ear, and shoulder.

After a minute, we disentangle from each other, and I help myself to his bathroom, cleaning up. By the time I return, he's back in his boxer briefs, and drinks and snacks are on the bed: two bottles of water along with a banana and a protein bar.

"Gotta replenish our energy," he says, and I can't quite swallow my laugh. "Come on." He tips his head to his bed, but before I hop on the mattress, I open one of his drawers. "What are you looking for?"

"T-shirt."

"Second drawer."

I find one and slip it over my head. It barely covers my bits, though Vince's grin is downright lascivious.

After we split the banana and protein bar, he tucks me into his side, and I drape my arm around his waist, laying my head on his chest. His heartbeat is strong under my ear.

I briefly wonder how I could get it on audio, make it my ringtone, maybe download it to my Spotify. I think I need proof of life now.

"I, uh...didn't expect that," he says after a while, and I huff out a laugh. He kisses the top of my head. "Do you want to talk about it now?"

"Talk about what? Me getting fired?"

"Yeah."

I sigh and toy with the gold pendant, bringing it closer to me so I spot the outline of a person on it. "Who's this?"

"Saint Vincent. My grandfather gave it to me for my eighth-grade confirmation."

"Saint Vincent," I repeat. "Patron saint of...?"

"Charities."

"Charities," I deadpan with an arched brow, the irony not escaping me. The half-naked saint Vincent currently keeping me warm has basically been running a charity with me being the only recipient since February 14th.

He shakes his head in amusement as if he can read my mind. "Never mind that. Tell me what happened."

There's nothing else to lose, so I give in. But I trail my hand over his chest as I do it.

"Gary basically said I didn't care enough about the job, which isn't entirely untrue."

"What're you going to do now?"

I purse my lips. "Get another job, I guess."

"Better learn to send a fax," he jokes, and I pinch him before shifting away. He rolls to his side, propping his head in his hand. "Do you want me to say some clichéd thing about how this is a door closing but a window will open?"

I snort then pull the covers up to my shoulders. "No. Sassie's sucked, but it paid better than some random entry-level job. This isn't a window opening. It's a wrong turn through this horrible maze." I raise one eyebrow at him. "Maybe I'll become a funeral director."

"Queen of the Underworld."

I fake a shiver. I may be in dire straits, but there's no way I'd ever want to do that.

"We haven't talked in a while," he says, the insinuation of my *let's be friends* talk hanging between us after what we just did. I see a yearning in his eyes to understand what's going on, although I can't tell him because I don't fully understand it either. All I know is that I need him. I don't want to need him, but I do. And I'm not sure how to feel about that.

"What's up?" he asks like he's not constantly picking me up off the floor from an emotional breakdown.

"I think my dad's having an affair."

He sits straight up, mouth open. "Your dad *what*?"

"I was doing laundry a while ago, and one of his shirts had lipstick on it. Like a scene from a soap opera."

"What'd you do?" His gaze is filled with pity, and even though I have nothing to be ashamed of, I'm humiliated. My life's become one big melodrama.

"When I confronted him, he didn't deny it."

"Jesus," he mutters, curving his hand around my shoulder. "I'm sorry."

"We started yelling at each other, and then he completely broke down," I continue. "It was like... You never expect to see your parents like that, especially him, you know? He's curt and gruff, and he's...not the best dad, but he's the only one I have. And this morning, the way his whole body crumpled to the floor. I actually felt bad for him. I could see the physical pain he had, in his face, his hands."

My eyes water, threatening to spill over, and I bat at the traitorous tears. I don't want to sympathize with my father, not after what he's done. "It's not fair," I say, dropping my chin toward my chest. Even though Vince is the one person I can talk to about all this, it scares me to say some of these words out loud. "I'm totally unequipped to handle this. It's not fair my brother died, and now..." I sniffle. "Now, I have to deal with my parents. My father's a drunk, doing god-knows-what every day, while my mother's wasting away. It's too much."

Vince tugs me to him with an arm around my shoulders, my back to his chest, and he leans his head against mine. "You're doing the best you can. That's enough."

"You keep saying that to me, but it's not true." I yank myself away from him. "Nothing I do is helping. I don't even know why I try."

"You're trying because even though everything's a wreck, you still love your parents. They're still your family. And you're still you." He slants closer to me and lowers his voice. "Your parents might be lost, and you might be too. It's normal to try to find a way back. Give yourself credit for trying, for wanting to. I've seen some people never recover after something like what you guys are going through."

I snort. "Might as well put us in that category."

He tucks a hank of my hair behind my ear. "You're okay, Cass."

Those words and his kind yet mischievous smile do me

in. I follow when he pulls me to him, and he kisses me like he can't get enough. He moves his fingers over my body like he already knows it.

And I like it, him knowing me. Me knowing him.

I really like it.

Might even love it.

SEPTEMBER 23

I thought I knew what rock bottom was, buried six feet in the ground in a dark oak coffin at Cedar Hill Cemetery. Turns out, there was further to go. Weirdly, it doesn't feel like I assumed it would. But maybe I've been living within a storm of emotion these last few months, so when a hurricane hits, it's not all that different. Just another thing. Except this time, my house was carried away.

Who needs a house, though? Not I. Not when I have a friend with a home. A very good friend, with a very nice home, who makes me believe that maybe the house I had wasn't so great anyway. A friend who doesn't mind my mess in their home.

Everyone should have a friend like mine, to help you up from the bottom and who shares an umbrella in the storm.

#Grief #RockBottom #Family #Pain #FriendLikeMine #EasyLikeSundayMorning

CHAPTER 26

'Ve been spending some nights at Vince's house. He makes me laugh with stupid jokes, and Gracie and I have become attached at the hip. The other day when I left, he said she paced by the front door for an hour. We cuddle all the time, and I think it makes Vince jealous—and also sort of happy. I caught him staring at us one lazy Sunday, with my head butted up against Gracie's belly as I read the latest Nora Roberts Vince had bought for me. He'd merely grinned and then gone back to watching the football game on TV.

I spend one hour every day searching for jobs and exploring different paths I could take, but I'm not particularly interested in selling Avon, teaching kids in Asia how to speak English, or working in another restaurant. I applied to a part-time job at the library, which I didn't get, and also put my application in at a gym, for shits and giggles. Understandably didn't get that one either. I sent my résumé off to a marketing firm even though I don't have all of the qualifications they're looking for. I figure if most men apply for jobs with half the qualifications required, I should too.

I continue to write grief posts, and they've earned me a few follows by a couple low-level celebrities, and I'm close to fifteen thousand total now. And if I'm really desperate—and by desperate, I mean I want to see Vince's face—I hang out at the funeral home for a few hours, but mostly, I spend my days walking.

It clears my head, quiets my thoughts, and has done some really terrific things for my butt. Sometimes I get cocky and challenge Vince to a race when he joins me, but the guy's like the Energizer Bunny. He goes and goes. My lung capacity can't seem to make it past the pace of a third grader, but nevertheless, I love it. My shoes, on the other hand, don't.

Without a job, I've severely cut back my spending. But I need new sneakers, and this is my first purchase outside of necessities in weeks. Buying a pair of HOKAs isn't exactly the same as a Sephora spending spree, but it is oddly satisfying. And I wonder if this is what it's like to grow older. Finding immense joy in appropriate footwear?

It's not half bad.

I dig out my debit card at the register, ready to pay, when the kid behind the counter tilts his head at me. "Hey, I know you."

I raise one eyebrow.

"You're Coach George's sister."

Coach George, the moniker hits me like a wave. I hold on to the edge of the counter, treading water. I haven't had an episode like this in a while, and I've almost forgotten what it's like to drown in grief.

"Yeah, I'm his sister," I say after I can breathe again.

He rings up my sneakers. "I played outfield. Man, I really miss him," he says nonchalantly. "He was the best."

"The best," I agree, putting my card into the machine to

pay. He hands me the receipt and bag, a wobbly smile on his face. It connects to something inside me, a shared experience, even though we don't know each other.

"How are you?" I ask, my heart taking another punch.

His cheeks pink as he casts his eyes down. "I'm good. The team didn't do very well last season."

I assume he's probably ashamed, but I'm no athlete, definitely no coach, and have no advice. "Well...I'm sure it's hard for you guys without..."

He swipes at one of his eyes with the back of his hand before meeting my gaze again. "Coach Fetterman took over, and none of us like him. He's kind of a dick."

Of course he is. I don't know Coach Fetterman, but he's not my brother, so...

I think of Vince. Of how much he loves baseball, how he gave up his scholarship, and how he would be a great coach. I tuck that idea away for later.

"Well, good luck."

When I start to leave, he raises his hand to stop me. "You should come to one of our games."

The invitation has me rocking back on my heels. I can't imagine it would matter if I'm there, but the sweet sentiment makes my eyes water. I can't say no to the kid, so I only smile.

It's amazing to me how I can go from being *fine* with my brother being dead one minute to eating a giant cinnamon roll in my car by myself the next. Intellectually, I know there's no right way to grieve—I read that in a pamphlet— but this is extra pitiful. I imagine how I might look from the outside, smeared eyeliner, hair in my face, and icing on my chin.

A mess.

I've been listening to Bruce Springsteen more and more

lately, finding the *soul* in the music Ray always went on about, and I fire up "Tougher Than the Rest." With the windows down, I take the long way home as The Boss keeps me company. I sing along to "Downbound Train" and then scream into the wind "Born to Run."

It releases the tension in my body. I don't care the guy in the car next to me gives me a funny look; I keep it up. Ray used to do the same thing, and I found it endlessly embarrassing, but he'd chuckle and sing-yell even louder. Doing it now helps. Like the lyrics of the song, I am wild and free, and maybe that's why my brother liked to do it.

It's a call to life.

And it grants me a little bit of peace, a way to be closer to my brother, who no longer exists on this plane.

Maybe we can find each other again in some in-between place, where only music lives.

That thought makes me smile, but as I pull into my parents' driveway, the same peace that filled me up with tranquility seeps out, steam rising on a cold day.

Dad's car is parked out front. It's odd because it's a weekday, and I haven't seen him in over a month. I open the front door, dropping my overnight bag in the entry. I'd planned to repack some clothes to take to Vince's, but I can't shake the foreboding pit in my belly.

Stalking toward the kitchen, I backtrack, noticing an unfamiliar figure in a uniform out of the corner of my eye in the dining room. I choke on a breath, flashbacks of *that* night flipping through my memory. My skin prickles with fear as I lean against the wall, out of sight. The officer in the sheriff's uniform says something quietly to my mother, who's sitting at the table, eyes distant, then passes me with a terse nod to leave.

"I'm sorry," Dad says, from somewhere I can't see. I tilt

my head around the wall, and there he is, in the corner with wrinkled clothes and familiar red face. He doesn't look drunk, though.

Mom fingers the edge of a thin packet of papers, unresponsive to my father.

"You can't be surprised."

She doesn't respond.

"It's like you're living in a different world, and I'm unhappy."

My heart rate spikes as I connect the dots.

"I—we don't have to live like this anymore. I won't even fight over the house or—"

"What's going on?" I ask, stepping forward, even though I already know.

Dad spins toward me, his face going slack. "Hi, Cassandra." He rubs his hands on his work pants, and I don't know if I've ever seen him so nervous. "I... Uh..."

"You're divorcing Mom?"

She still hasn't acknowledged anything else but the papers under her hand.

"Listen, I—"

"You thought it was necessary to have the sheriff bring the papers?" I interject, disgusted.

"Cassandra," he starts in the patronizing tone I'm used to. "You don't understand what—"

"Don't tell me I don't understand!"

"Cassandra," my mom says in nothing more than a whisper, "please keep your voice down."

Her dead eyes set me off again, this time at her.

"That's it? That's all you have to say? *Cassandra, keep your voice down*? He wants to divorce you, but *I* have to keep *my* voice down?"

She wipes at her eyes before aiming her head toward the wall, away from my father and me.

"Don't yell at your mother," Dad says.

"Oh, fuck off. You don't give a shit about her or me. You don't care about anyone but yourself." He crosses his arms but doesn't argue, so I keep going. "If you cared about Mom, you'd try to help her, not divorce her. But what did you call her?" I press my finger against my temple in mock thought. "That's right, you called her a zombie. You hear that, Mom? You're a zombie!"

She can hear me fine, yet I still shout. Everything is falling apart around me, and like Samson, I want to be the one to wrench the final pillars.

"So, what now, Dad?" I ask, waving my arm at him. "You going to find some twenty-year-old to fuck while Mom slowly kills herself?" I spin toward my mother, marching around the table to bend down to her level, making sure I have her eyes when I say, "What about you? You going to waste away to nothing, become a bag of bones like Ray?"

Her eyes focus on me then, fire behind them, and she strikes me, fast and sharp across the cheek.

I rear back, placing my palm there, more in shock than pain. Whether I deserved the slap or not, my eyes fill with tears.

And that's it, the last straw. The final tug of the delicate string holding my family together has unraveled, and I'm shattered.

Dad's abandoning ship.

Mom doesn't care. About anything.

Which leaves nothing for me.

I scrub at my eyes, wiping the tears to clear my vision as I grab my bag by the door and press the tip of my car keys into my palm. Mom cries behind me as I sprint out of the house without another word.

The family I knew doesn't exist anymore. I've spent so much time and energy fixing something that, in the end, is unfixable.

I jump in my car with no particular destination in mind and drive. Memories of my family inundate me, rushing into my veins, clouding my eyes, filling my ears. I'm flooded with my brother's voice cheering me on when I finally skateboarded down the street without falling. My mother laughing as my father knocks into her bumper car at the fair. The embrace of my brother's arms around my shoulders when Jimmy Lei broke my heart in eighth grade. My parents holding hands as they walked in front of me through a park. My father twirling me around during the daddy-daughter number at my kindergarten dance recital. These memories are few and far between, but they're embedded deep inside me, and they're all that surrounds me.

They're all that is left among the ash. Only memories.

And I know I need to leave.

I can't stay.

CHAPTER 27

"*Cass?*"

I lift my head to a faded orange and purple sky, realizing I must've cried myself to sleep. After driving aimlessly, tempted to hop off the exit to the city, I turned around and headed to the only place that feels like home anymore. But Vince wasn't here, so I sat on his stoop, even as Gracie barked from somewhere inside. That was hours ago.

Now, I swipe at my eyes and notice he's wearing the socks I bought him for his birthday last week. We had cake and ice cream at his mother's house, and he hugged me when he opened the package of socks with the faces of famous people on them. He's got George Washington on, peeking out from under his pant leg as he sets down bags of groceries. His eyes search over my body as if to make sure I'm physically unhurt, then he hoists me up off the step to embrace me. "What happened?"

"Everything," I say into his shoulder.

He squeezes me tighter and drops quick, comforting kisses all over, the top of my head, my temple, the crook of my neck, and then he waits for me to let go. I breathe in the sterilized scent he always brings home from work that doesn't come off until he showers and changes into the paint-stained sweats he usually puts on.

When I finally back away, he unlocks the front door and ushers me inside, one hand on the back of my neck, the other carrying all the grocery bags. We settle into our normal routine without speaking. Since I always complain how cold his house is, he bought me a ridiculous pair of sloth slippers, and I slide them on as he slinks upstairs. I put away the groceries, packs of meat, veggies, my favorite cereal, dog treats, and more of his shampoo.

I toss Gracie a treat before bringing the shampoo upstairs. I open the shower curtain without asking. "You need this?"

Normally in this situation, he'd make a lewd comment, but he only accepts the bottle with a single, "Thanks."

Heading down the hall to the bedroom, I flop onto the unmade bed and throw the comforter over me. All the should haves, could haves, and would haves filter through my brain, and I wonder about the different possibilities of my life, if and what would be different if Ray hadn't died. In the end, though, I think no matter what I might've done, I would've wound up here *because* my brother died.

Here, meaning, this fucking upside-down my life has become and not Vince's house.

Because I never could have expected him and his quiet confessions about how long he's waited for me in a million lifetimes.

He pads into the room with a towel wrapped around his waist, his shoulders still glistening with water droplets. The gold of the Saint Vincent medal around his neck glints at me from the nest of chest hair that's soft under my cheek when I lay my head on it.

He lounges on the edge of the bed and snakes his hand under the comforter to find my ankle, wrapping his fingers around it. "You going into hibernation?"

"Yes."

He frowns at me before wiping his thumb beneath my right eye. "What happened?"

"What hasn't happened?" I say, catching myself leaning into him. The response we have to each other is automatic and effortless, and it's so easy to be with him, it feels out of place. When the rest of my life has gone to the dogs, *this* hasn't, and I don't know how to handle it, not when I'm in the mood to smash everything.

Antagonism rises up through the cracks in the cement, where green grass and flowers had been growing. Now, they're withered and wilted, leaving more than enough room for resentment to spread. I roll my shoulder away when Vince tries to massage it. "Don't."

He straightens up. "Why do you have the whole scared-cat thing going on again?"

I toss the covers away from me and, in my rush to stand up, get my legs all tangled. I kick at them. "Goddamn it."

"Cass."

"*What*?" I shoot my eyes to his after I'm standing.

"What's wrong?" He's patient with me, his face giving nothing away. And this is why I hate him. He knows me so well, he knows eventually I'll give in to him, spill all my secrets, and I hate that. I really fucking hate that. And if he's going to force me to bare my soul, I need him to put some clothes on at least.

"Can you put a shirt on or something?"

"What?" He grins, playfully flexing. "Can't handle this?"

I roll my eyes, and he thankfully snatches a T-shirt and sweats from the bureau. I don't watch him change. The act of him getting naked in front of me is intimate, and I don't want to feel close to him—or anyone—right now.

Dressed, he holds his arms out at his sides. "Good? Talk to me now."

I pull my cell phone out of my back pocket and flip it in my hand. "My parents are getting divorced."

He cringes. "Oh god, sweetheart, I'm so sorry." I wave off his words, but he continues. "That really sucks, but it's not unusual for parents to divorce after the death of a child."

I huff.

"I mean... It's not helpful to you, but I can empathize with them."

My hands fist at my sides. He's always so goddamn logical and agreeable. "You can empathize, huh?"

He shrugs. "People grieve differently, and when couples move to the extremes of the spectrum, it's probably really difficult to—"

"Could you not be so understanding right now? I'm pissed. I want you to be pissed too."

"I'm not sure what you want me to say here," he says then pats the place on the bed next to him for me to sit down, but I can't. The dam has broken. He wanted me to talk, so I'm going to.

"Nothing! I don't want you to say anything. I'm not asking for you to problem-solve right now. I want you just to be my—"

I stop short of the word *boyfriend*. Any other day, I probably would have said it, but now, the idea of having a boyfriend makes me want to cry. I've already decided I need to leave. I can't stay here with my brother living in a cemetery and my parents splitting up. What's the point?

I sniffle. "I don't need you to fix this or fix my parents or...or...or fix me. I only need you to listen to me!"

He stands up with his hands out to me, slowly closing the distance between us. "I know."

"No, you don't know. Your family's perfect, your parents still flirt with each other, your brother isn't dead."

"I get it," he says, reaching out to me, and I slap his hands away.

"Stop!" In my head, it sounds like I'm shrieking, but I have to get the words out louder than the swirling in my mind. "My brother is *dead*. His bones are in the ground. And my parents hate each other. They hate me. And you don't get it. You *can't* get it."

I inhale a ragged breath, feeling the walls closing in on me. I'm itchy and hot and need...

I don't know what I need, but Vince has to stop looking at me like that. Like he can fix me.

He can't.

"Don't touch me," I say, backing away when he tries. His mouth forms a straight line, and underneath my bitterness, I'm remorseful, but I can't reach it, not with the fury growing like ivy through my body. It wraps around my heart, my throat, my hands, and it's swift, cutting me off from anyone or anything else.

"I have no job, no family, nothing. I have nothing left."

"You have me," he offers, his voice quiet and even.

"Oh, please," I snap, and the wrath that had been filling my lungs sours at his suddenly pale face. I know I'm hurting him, but I have no other choice.

I have to leave.

"You have me, Cass, right here. I'll be here for you always. I love you."

It's an arrow to my heart.

He can't love me. I am unlovable. Everything in my life breaks, and I refuse to bring him down with me.

He takes a cautious step toward me, a wry curl to his lips. "What do you think we've been doing all this time? Playing house?"

I hold up my hand to stop him, but he keeps coming toward me until my fingers press against his stomach, and I stare at the floor, willing the tears away.

When I finally have myself under control, I make sure to look him in the eye so he understands. "There is nothing left for me here. I have no job, no house, nothing. I'm moving away."

He grips my hands, holding them against his heart. I feel its steady beat. I think it's so loud, I can hear it.

I know it'll haunt me for the rest of my life.

"You can't move away."

"Yes, I can." I wrench away from him and rush out of the room.

"Don't leave."

I ignore him and almost fall in my hasty escape down the stairs. My shoes give me trouble when I try to put them on, allowing Vince time to catch up.

"If I'm nothing to you, then what have you been doing here with me?"

That's the thing I've been trying to avoid facing.

I knew I couldn't give him what he deserves, and yet I threw reason aside because Vince made me feel good. In return, I can only offer him heartbreak. That's all I have. That's all I am.

"I've been by your side through everything, and I didn't mind. I wanted to do it. I wanted to help you, be with you, and—look at me."

I don't.

"Cass, look at me."

After I sling my purse over my shoulder, I finally meet his gaze.

"You can't tell me it meant nothing to you. This—" he waves between the two of us "—means nothing."

When I don't answer, his eyes go dark and angry. I jut my chin out, refusing to give in. "I'm leaving," I say, opening the door. "I'm not staying in this godforsaken town. I'm not going to be some pathetic mascot to be propped up for my brother, and I'm not going to watch my parents drive themselves into the ground. If they don't care, I don't either."

He follows me outside. "Yeah, you don't care, huh? Guess it means you don't care about me. You've been using me."

I gasp audibly as my hand clutches at my chest. He's right. I've been using him this whole time. "I'm sorry," I say quietly over my shoulder. "I told you, I'm no good for you."

He pulls up short in his tracks, giving me the space I said I wanted. "Fine! Run away! That's one thing you're good at!"

It's true. I'm a coward and deserve every bit of the physical ache between my ribs, but it's better this way.

CHAPTER 28

After a sleepless night, I escape to the city that never sleeps. Vince accused me of running away, but he's only half right. I'm running away from him, from my family, but toward my old life. It may not have been perfect, but it wasn't shrouded in pain, and that's all I want. A moment, a place, that's *mine*.

The brakes of the train hiss, and I follow the morning New Jersey Transit crowd out the doors to the platform in Penn Station. I fire off a few *I'm in town, what are you up to?* texts to some of my old friends. No one but Alma responds, my roommate from Columbia. **I'm working late tonight.**

Call out, I message back, to which she replies with the side-eye emoji.

Come on, I could always count on you for day drinking, I text before purchasing a new Metro card since I lost mine ages ago. While I wait for the downtown line, I use social media to check in on people I used to hang out with. Unfortunately, unlike the gross, humid underground air, a lot has changed. Geoff moved to Los Angeles to work for Jay-

Z's music service. He even got to meet Beyoncé. Tasha married her boyfriend, got pregnant, and is living in Syracuse. And Alma, the ultimate commitment-phobe, apparently has a live-in girlfriend.

Sorry, Alma finally texts back. A sweating face and champagne bottle follow. **Maybe we can catch up another day! Have fun!**

I'd been hoping I'd be able to rediscover my old life, footloose and fancy free, broke and bone-weary. Even though it wasn't much different from my current life, at least I was living in the greatest city in the world.

I could try again, move back here. I have a little bit of money saved. I could find a job, hopefully not in the service industry. I could…

I sigh. The thought of getting my life together is daunting. Months ago, I thought I had a chance. I had a plan, sort of, but that burned up with the embers of my family.

So, with nothing to lose now, I open my phone, finally reading the message from Professor Row.

Cassandra,

I'm happy to hear from you but so sorry you're going through such a difficult time. I find that when the world seems to be out of control, I focus on my work. It rights me, gives me a purpose, a sense of self. It sounds the same for you as well.

Regarding your idea for a manuscript, it is intriguing. I'd love to hear more about it. I have always adored your voice, and it would be my pleasure to read more of it.

As you know, job openings in journalism are few and far between, and I don't know of any internships right now. Of course, I will keep my ears open for anything. In the meantime, work on your book. It seems to me that is what is in your heart.

Please keep me updated on it!

The tiny bit of hope I held is extinguished, and I breathe

out a curse, deleting the email thread. I can't think about the book right now or how my one talent is almost impossible to make any money from.

So much for moving to New York.

I need a new place, a cheap place like Nebraska or a tiny boat on the ocean. But more immediately, I need to drown my sorrows at my favorite bar.

After hopping onto the train car, I catch some guy staring at me and scowl at him before moving closer to the door, but it's a long ride to Brooklyn, and I eventually bite the bullet, taking a seat opposite him. He continues to leer at me. How easily I forgot about the subway creeps when I didn't have to deal with them every day.

When the train stops at Grand Avenue, I hop off, almost smiling to myself at the familiarity of it. The smell—that weird smell you can only find in the city, as if the concrete is sweating. The whir of bicyclists as they pass, the voices of people all around, the honks and beeps of cars, it's all the same. But Bushwick looks quite a bit different. It's gentrified, more than when I left. I pass my old apartment building, which is cleaned up, new windows, a tiny garden where the patch of dirt used to be, and no Dominican flag hanging out of the third-floor window.

I hum disappointedly to myself as I resume the walk to my old haunt, a dive bar where Marissa and I always hung out. Marissa's brother owned the bar where you could order a shot of cheap tequila and a beer for five bucks and the jukebox in the corner only played Gloria Estefan. Marissa was an artist, made a small living from selling abstract art to rich, *hip* couples in Tribeca, but she also dealt on the side, and if there was ever a time I needed a smoke, it is now. I turn the corner off Knickerbocker to where Mis Tíos used to be.

My mouth gapes open at the storefront in its place. The sign reads *Branch* in big wooden letters above a smaller plank that declares it's an olive oil and vinegar shop. I reach for the long bronze handle and open the thick glass doors. The scents of fresh bread and herbs waft over me.

A petite blonde with pale skin smiles at me from behind the counter. "Hi, how can I help you?"

"How long has this place been open?" I ask, pointing to the floor.

She squints in thought. "Um, a little over a year. This your first time here? Can I interest you in a sample of anything?"

"No," I say as she hurries around the counter with her arm out as if to escort me over to the large glass apothecary jars of dark vinegar. My tone stops her. "Do you know what happened to Felix? The guy who used to own the bar here?"

"Sorry, no." She sweeps her hand over to a bottle of olive oil. "But we have a new blood-orange-infused oil, if you're interested."

I roll my eyes. "I don't want any fucking artisanal olive oil."

I pivot around and head back out the door to the girl wishing me a nice day. I don't even have Marissa's number to text her. We always connected in person, and for the first time since I moved away, I understand *acutely* how alone I am.

When I lived here, I had social media, but I also had friends who I didn't need to meet through a screen. I had honest-to-goodness relationships. When I moved home, I shut down, shut off.

My brother was right.

I didn't even try.

I was disillusioned and gave up. It was easier that way, to

live behind a screen and avoid sharing my failure every time I had to explain my situation to someone new.

After not sleeping last night, I'm completely strung out, and it suddenly hits me. I need to sit down. There's a place called VINO around the corner, and I take a seat at the bar, ordering a glass of red wine. The bartender talks to me about the vineyard it's from in California, but I don't really listen. I can only repeat "uh-huh" over and over as I contemplate the disaster that is my life.

"Are you okay?" he asks mid-Cabernet ramble. "You look..." He frowns, shaking his head like a bobblehead. "Knackered."

He's not far off. "I am most certainly not okay."

"You need a chat?"

I eye him. "Don't you have other customers to wait on?"

He laughs. I like the way his dark brown skin crinkles in the corners of his eyes. And I really like his English accent. "We just opened, it's barely noon. The only other people here are the yoga birds in the corner."

I turn to follow where he gestures. There's a trio of women, all in overly expensive athleisure wear.

"So," he says when I face him again. "Let's have a chat."

I down the rest of my wine in a few unladylike gulps and begin to describe the whole sad, sordid tale. I tell him how I used to live here, a few blocks away, and that I couldn't find a job, so I became the NDA's assistant. I explain how I eventually ran out of money and moved home to my parents' basement and took a crappy job. I unleash everything about my brother and how my parents are divorcing, and how I hurt the one guy I actually loved.

And I drink three more glasses of wine.

He hands me tissue after tissue.

I've eaten almost every appetizer on the food menu and

run up quite a tab by the time Cole, handsome English bartender guy, hands me a glass of water and tells me I should sober up and head home.

"I can't go home," I say.

"You can always go home."

Like it's so easy. He points to the water, and I down it, only to ask, "Can I try a glass of the 2006 Merlot?"

"Absolutely not," he says sternly but then laughs in spite of himself. I really like his laugh and wonder if he'll let me stay with him. I open my mouth to ask, but he shakes his head. "I'm cutting you off."

"Hey." I sway in my seat. "I thought we had a good thing going here."

He holds on to my hand. "We do, love, which is why I need to tell you, you're pissed, go home."

"Pissed," I repeat in an English accent, giggling.

I pucker my lips, trying to look cute, but he rejects me with a stiff, "No," then hands me the receipt to sign. My signature is chicken scratch. Cole takes the thin paper back, watching me as I cross the strap of my purse over my body. "You don't want to move away from home. That's why you're so upset, because you think you have to now. But nobody's got a perfect life. Go home and get sorted. You'll be good."

His advice floats through my brain like a feather and lands somewhere in the back, right at the top of my spine. Where Vince often held me.

I aim two finger guns at him. "It's been real, mate."

He nods at me. "Take care."

I plan on following his instructions and going home, but I make a quick pit stop at a liquor store and buy a small bottle of wine by the checkout. They stick it in a paper bag, and I drink out of it, like a true city caricature.

I slouch into a seat in the last subway car, raising the

bottle above me as a woman sings a Whitney Houston song in the corner, hitting all the high notes. I flip the light on my cell phone and hold it in the air. It's like our own personal subway concert, and I don't know why no one else is enjoying it. She finishes, and I applaud her. The woman cuts me a nasty look. I smile at her. She rolls her eyes.

At Penn Station, I traipse off the platform, my legs like rubber. I stop for a slice of pizza and a can of beer. Drinking wine makes me thirsty.

Once I finish everything, I go to the bathroom, pinballing off the wall on my way. I laugh when I knock my head on the sink as I try to pull my pants up, but I stop when I notice the red mark on my forehead.

"What are you? Drunk or something?" I ask my reflection in the mirror, but there are marbles in my mouth. I don't bother drying my hands and wipe the water off on my jeans. Out in the corridor, my vision blurs as I study the digital board for my track number. Someone in a rush bumps into me and says, "Watch it."

I stumble, throwing them the finger.

The walk takes forever, and I slump against the wall to take a few breaks before I get to where I'm going. I move to the end of the platform as the train pulls up, and I bend sideways to a short woman in a pantsuit. "This is going to Middletown, right?"

She rears back and cringes at me. "Uh...yeah."

I follow her to board the train and collapse into the first open seat I can find. I bumble around for my phone and blink at the time. It's blurry. I get up to ask the person behind me for the time.

"Quarter to six," the man answers, his head down over a book, his sandy hair artfully ruffled in waves. I tilt my own head, something familiar about him.

"Excuse me," an older woman says to my left. She wants to sit in the seat next to me, so I spin around to make room for her. She scoots in and places shopping bags at her feet. I can't help but sit up tall, craning my neck back to study the man behind me, but the train wrenches forward, and I rock in my seat.

"Sorry," I apologize to the woman when I accidentally knock into her shoulder. She doesn't respond, and I twist fully around. The man has on reading glasses like the ones my brother used to wear. He's got on a big, clunky watch, his suit jacket in his lap and his sleeves rolled up enough to display muscular forearms. Everything about him is so familiar.

I shake my head to clear my eyes but it throws my body off-balance, and I bump into the older woman next to me again. "I'm sorry."

"Be careful," she snips.

I'm surrounded by mud, my limbs can't trudge through it, my mind slogs along in it, my words and breath slowed down by it. "Ray?"

He doesn't look up.

I lean over the back of the seat and touch his shoulder. "Raymond."

The man looks up, his thin eyebrows angled down. His light-colored eyes obviously annoyed. "What?"

"You're..." I immediately start to cry. I can't help it.

I knew it wasn't him. I knew it.

But I hoped.

"You're not..." I choke, and the woman next to me says something I don't understand. Tears stream down my face, and I can't breathe. I need help, but I can't force the words out to ask for it. I reach for the man.

I need help.

I can't breathe.

I'm going to be sick.

He's talking, I can see his mouth moving, but my ears are filled with a buzzing sound. I gag, my throat constricting again and again until I throw up.

It's static in my brain. It crackles in my ears, louder and louder, until I force my eyes open. The bright light hurts, and I shut them again, throwing my hand over my face.

"She lives." The female voice sounds far away, but I can tell it's filled with laughter.

I blink my eyes open and peer between my fingers, slowly gathering it all together as my body comes back to life. There's a pain in my hip, and my head pounds like someone hit it with a bat. My shoulder's against something hard and cold. I lower my hand and arm with quite a bit of effort and move to my back so I am staring up at square ceiling tiles.

"I worried there for a bit," a different, male voice says, this time closer as something clanks. I blink over, barely lifting my head enough to view the bars of a jail cell open. I groan and let my head fall back down.

A moment later, something hard taps my leg, and I'm forced to lift my head up again, taking inventory of my body. Everything hurts.

"Need help?" the voice says again. I turn toward it. It's a big, bald police officer. He's scowling at me. He bends down and extends his hand to me. When I take it, he roughly pulls me to stand and doesn't let go. "All right?"

He waits until I nod to step away.

"I've got to be honest, I'm surprised you aren't worse off right now," he says like he knows me.

I can't pick apart the jumble of words through the fog in my head. "What...how...um..." I smooth a hand down my face and glance around at the empty jail cell, the door open, to where a female officer sits behind a counter a few yards away. She's staring at me with a mixture of disdain and humor.

"Was...was I arrested?" I ask to no one in particular.

The bald officer eyes me carefully. "Close, but no. We put you in here to dry out."

"Oh." I'm relieved but still overcome with shame and follow him out of the cell, where he stops by the woman at the counter so she can hand me my bag.

Lifting a cup of coffee to his lips, the cop says, "You remember me, Cassandra?"

Everything about this situation confuses me, and I'm rendered mute.

"I'm Officer Stone. I had the unfortunate job of delivering the news of your brother the night he died."

It all comes rushing back, and I collapse all of my weight against the counter. It's hazy, but I think he looks a little familiar.

"We got a call last night about a disturbance at the train station." He pauses for unnecessary dramatic effect because I know what he's about to say. "The disturbance was you."

I rub my temple. "What happened?"

"You apparently got hysterical on the train."

"Jesus," I wheeze, the bits and pieces of yesterday starting to come back into focus.

"You got sick, knocked over an elderly passenger, and wouldn't let go of another one."

"Wouldn't let go?"

"Physically," he says after a sip of coffee. "You wouldn't let go of him. That's when they called us. Lucky for you, I was the one who arrived on the scene."

"Jesus," I say again.

I run my hands through my hair. It's all tangled. The skin on my face is dry, and when I rub a finger under my eye, black makeup is left on my fingertip. "How'd I end up here?"

He shrugs. "Once you calmed down, you passed out, so I brought you in here to sleep it off."

I stare at my shoes, my cheeks heating. If I weren't so hungover, I might be able to cobble together some excuse or apology, but it's no use. I soak in my humiliation.

"I don't presume to know you at all, but I do remember *that* night," he says. "I've seen other people react the same way when they receive bad news. Something clicks, you can see it in their eyes, and it's almost like they go into overdrive. They overcompensate." When I don't make any move to respond, he goes on. "I could tell that was happening with you. Watching how your parents reacted to the news was difficult, knowing you would be left holding it all together."

He waits until I look up at him. He's so tall and muscular; it's an odd juxtaposition against his soft tone of voice. "It's obvious you're going through some tough stuff, but what happened yesterday isn't the way to handle it. There are people and places to help you, you know that, right?"

I nod. I have the pamphlets.

He finishes off his coffee and throws the cup in the trash can next to me.

"You've been dealt a bad hand," he says. "Make peace with it however you can, but next time I get a call about you, I will arrest you."

"Right. Got it," I say and shuffle out of the police station, only to realize my phone's out of battery, so I can't call anyone for a ride and have to walk the five miles back to the train station to pick up my car.

It takes me nearly two hours, and when I am finally behind the wheel, I take account of my wrinkled clothes, clown-like makeup, and hungover breath. The last twenty-four hours have been hell, and I've seen enough cops in the past year to last a lifetime, but it is a wake-up call.

Even though my compass might be a little off, I've made it through a storm. I've kept my head above water this long; there's no reason to drown now.

I start my car and drive straight to the one person I need to talk to. I park down a narrow lane in the cemetery, near the spot where my brother is, under a tree that provides some shade. I fold my arms over my chest to keep the cold away as I carefully tread across the browning grass crunching under my boots.

The seasons have changed. Persephone has gone back to the Underworld.

I don't like the idea of having a spot where people—or, more accurately, former people—are buried under the ground. I'd much rather be lit on fire and set out to sea like a Viking. Nevertheless, if society wants my brother's bones resting here...I guess there could be worse places.

Two headstones bracket Ray's, which are already carved with my parents' names, and there's absolutely nothing more bizarre than staring into the future. A chill rolls down my spine, and I curl my fingers into a fists so my nails pinch into my skin. The small bit of pain affixes me to the earth, and I remember I'm still alive, even in the face of death.

"Hey, bro," I say, assuming I should talk instead of just standing here, kicking at the grass around my feet. "Got some nice little pictures here."

There are a few scribbled pictures on colorful construction paper, held down by a rock in front of his birth date. I notice how clean it looks around the headstone, no weeds or anything, unlike some other burial plots near him. "You mowing the lawn 'round here or what?"

A bird chirps.

"Looks good. I guess."

Cars pass in the distance.

"I don't know what I'm supposed to do. Pray or something?" I glance around behind me. A gray-haired woman is bent over a grave, her head down. Peeking in the other direction, I notice the American flags, flowers, or other little decorations people have brought to their loved ones. I'm empty-handed.

"What are *you* gonna do with any of that shit anyway, right?" I say to Ray. I unfold my arms and stand taller, lift my chin like I used to do when I wanted to appear bigger as I argued with him. "Listen, I came here because...because I woke up in a police station this morning. I know you'd probably laugh at me and extort this information for money in exchange for not telling Mom and Dad, but it was awful. Like...everything is really awful. I went to the city yesterday and got bombed because, I guess, I'm so fucking depressed, and I'm... I'm tired of everything being so fucking awful."

It's liberating to speak my truth to and about the one person whom I both intensely miss and blame. My words come out faster and louder as I unload everything I've been holding in.

"You know, when you were here, it was so much easier for me to be the fuckup because no one cared about me. No one cared about what I did, if I was doing well or not, but now you went and died, and all of a sudden, it matters. I'm trying to keep it together, but how can I when I have to deal with all of this and, and..." I swing my arms around in a circle. "You left me!"

A small part of my brain warns me not to yell in a cemetery, but I don't care. Ray deserves to hear all of this, and I deserve to say it.

"You died, and Mom and Dad lost their brains. You know how difficult it's been for me, trying to keep Mom from digging herself a hole next to you? And Dad, he's a real asshole. I always knew it, but he's become worse. He's mean, so fucking mean. And Shayna, she's going out with some guy named Todd. Todd! Can you believe that? Shayna, who lives in a Pinterest-colored world, has a boyfriend with a generic name like Todd. And the girls are calling him Daddy. I had to defend your honor to her, and all I want to do is hate her, but I come to see you and find out she apparently comes here too because who else would decorate your goddamn final resting place with these ridiculous pink-and-green pinwheels."

I sniffle and wipe at my eyes, but it's no use. The flood-gates have opened.

"I got fired from my job. I know you hated that I worked there, but it was good money, better than minimum wage, and I got fired because I spent so much time helping out at home. And I'm so fucking mad at you!"

I look up to the sky, whimpering. "And you know what else? Your friend Vince? He's really great." It's hard for me to swallow, my mouth dry even though I can't stop crying. "He said he loved me, but I can't believe it. I'm a train wreck, so why would he want me?" I use the cuff of my jacket to wipe my face. "I'm in this catch-22. I want to make my life better, but I can't, so when I finally get something good, I mess it up."

I bend down, my hands in my hair. "It doesn't even make sense. Nothing does, and I'm here talking to a stone. Ugh!"

"Hey."

I gasp and wheel around at the greeting, falling back on my butt in the process.

Nell extends a hand to help me up. "You okay?"

"Fine." I stand and brush myself off, about to ask why she's here, but why wouldn't she be here? She was in love with my brother.

"You don't look fine," she tells me.

I lift my head up, meeting her gaze, and she offers a sympathetic smile and a tissue. I wipe my face then blow my nose before conceding, "I'm not fine."

She moves closer to me, not touching me but obviously offering comfort. "The first step is to admit it." When I glare at her, she laughs. "It's true."

We stand in silence for a while, me, her, and my brother's grave. "So...you come here often?"

"Every couple of weeks. I like to bring flowers." She holds them up as evidence then places them down. "Could use a little color around here."

I snort in amusement. Nell is actually kind of funny. I watch her fidget with the fall-themed bouquet, placing it so it doesn't cover anything from Lara and Lucy, while also pushing away any remnants of dried flowers or weeds. She rights herself and smiles at me. "Want me to leave? I can come back if..."

I shake my head, gazing down at my brother's name in bold, block letters. "No, I think I'm done yelling at him."

"I yelled at him too," she says quietly. "After I cried, I got angry. Now, I come and bring flowers and can sort of smile about it." When I curl my lip, she touches my arm. "It sounds trite, but it's my journey. Yours is different."

"Yeah, I know," I say dryly. "I read it in one of my pamphlets."

"They put it in the pamphlets because it's true."

I scowl.

"When you make that face, you look like him. You have the same crease between your eyebrows. Right there..."

I glide my index finger over said spot.

"He told me a lot about you," she says.

"Really?"

"Yeah. I think he was envious of you."

"Envious?" My voice squeaks out the words. "Of me?"

She nods, reaching out to touch the top of the headstone before turning away. I follow her, trekking back toward where I'm parked. "I don't know if you know this about your brother, but he was a great pretender."

Internally, I let out a huge guffaw.

"He pretended to be more confident than he was, made up for it by being overly extroverted, you know? Always the life of the party, inviting people out, leading karaoke after dinner."

I know all of this already, but I don't interrupt. She wants to say it, and I want to hear it.

"He had to try to be what he thought people wanted from him. You don't. That's what he liked about you—you were you. He was a people pleaser, but you don't care what anyone else thinks." She pauses. "In a good way."

This part is new to me, and I lean against my car, listening to Nell.

"He said your parents were a bit overbearing, especially your dad."

I bite the inside of my lip. Overbearing? Mom, maybe. But Dad? Could have fooled me. And maybe that was the difference between us. My brother felt he had to prove himself, while I didn't. At least, not until recently.

"He ended up giving in, doing whatever to placate them, but not you. He said you always followed your own path, and that took strength he didn't have."

This time, I laugh out loud. "He did not say that."

She smiles. "Well, no, not those words exactly, but it was the basic sentiment."

"Ray would never say I was stronger than him. Ever."

"He thought it, though." She lifts one shoulder. "You want to go have some coffee or something?"

"Right now?"

"Yeah."

Over the summer, when Nell had tried to talk to me, I avoided her because I didn't want to bear the burden of whatever it was she needed from me to get over Ray's death. I was wrong in that moment—I was wrong in a lot of moments—and nothing has made it more clear than waking up in jail.

This time around, I need someone. Or, in this case, Nell. She sticks her hands in her jacket pockets, the petite features of her face serene, and I could use some of her serenity. "That would actually be really great. Thank you."

NOVEMBER 30

I've been absent on my social media for a long while. It wasn't a conscious decision but an accident. An unplanned yet necessary break. Remember when I said I hit rock bottom? That wasn't it.

I don't recall the actual layers of the Earth from high school science, but here's a quick tutorial. The first layer is the one we live on. The next is the one we lie down in after our bodies have fulfilled their purpose. Then the layer after that, it's a pit of despair, rocky and hard, but not bottom. Because after that is the hot, sticky slide of embarrassment and self-loathing into the true bottom.

It is darkness. A blank mind. A pain behind the eyes and a thumping in the temples. Hitting the bottom is an incorrect analogy. It's more like crashing into the bottom. It's a cartoon fall so fast and hard, your body leaves an impression, and the only thing you can do is stare back up into the spaces that tricked you into believing *this time is it, there is nowhere left to go.*

But as they say, you have to truly hit bottom in order

to find your way back to the top. I'm definitely not back at the top, but I'm working my way there.

Thank you, everyone, for the nice messages, worrying about my absence. I read them, and I'll try to reply to them all individually, but consider this my apology to you and appreciation of you. I have a lot of mea culpas to make, and don't worry, I'll disclose all the dirty details once the dust settles. Thanks for sticking with me on this journey so far, friends. It's only up from here.

#Grief #Journey #Epiphany

CHAPTER 30

After weeks of self-reflection, one of the things I've come to terms with is my tendency to make snap judgments about people. It's not one of my better qualities, and I'm working to curtail that, even if my judgments are not always wrong. For instance, I knew when Paul Sandino escorted me to the nurse's office in first grade, after I fell during recess, that he'd end up helping the world, and, lo, social media tells me he's working in some special lab for HIV medication.

I also knew the first time I met Shayna that her personality was as fake as her eyelashes. In hindsight, it's probably why my brother was attracted to her, two lost souls trying to find an anchor. Unfortunately, they couldn't help each other, and now that Ray's gone, Shayna's out there waving in the wind, attaching herself to any post she thinks is steady. That means Todd is out, and Bryson is in. I'm tempted to leave a comment on the picture of the four of them at Thanksgiving dinner together, but I don't want to hurt her. Not really. I only want her to stop doing what she's doing. In the end, she'll only hurt Lucy and Lara.

My judgment about Nell, however, was totally wrong. I tap the heart button underneath the picture she posted of the two of us shopping at six in the morning on Black Friday. After I admitted that I'd never gone, she somehow convinced me to tag along with her. Why we had to go so early, though, I don't know. No one actually shops in stores anymore. We weren't beating a crowd for Furbies or laughing Elmos.

But I had a lot of fun with her. With an understated sense of humor, she's considerate and thoughtful, not the horrible person I assumed she was for having an affair with a married man. One late night over a pitcher of sangria, she explained how much she loved my brother. She believed he was *the one*. She said she tried to ignore it, forget about him, but couldn't. Not like he tried very hard either.

"Should I force myself to let him go and be miserable, or should I fight to make it right, as best I can, for the man I love?" she said, and I couldn't argue otherwise.

She showed me the timeline she'd made with Ray, saved on her computer in an orderly table. It outlined months of events they could accomplish with the best interest of the twins in mind: when he would move out of the house, when he would introduce Nell to the twins, when and what family counselor they would all see, when Ray and Nell would get married. It was hopeful then, but now it's a digital reminder of a future left unlived.

Nell, for her part, does the best she can, loving a ghost. "It's what we have in common," she told me over coffee the day we ran into each other at the cemetery. "Ghosts are perfect in their absence. They remain faultless in our minds. That's the hard part. I'll compare every guy I meet to him, and you'll constantly compare yourself to him. Hard to compete with someone who can't fail."

She was exactly right.

It took me months to get there, but I finally stopped making Raymond an excuse not to move forward with my life.

With a good word from Aunt Joanie, I found a job. It's a terribly boring administrative position, where I mostly file papers and answer phones, but it's a salary and benefits. I even opened a retirement account. Nell let me sleep on her couch for a few nights until I found a little apartment, the third floor of a townhouse. It's covered in old yellow wallpaper and the stove only works half of the time, but it's a step in the right direction. I also found a counselor to talk to, Maryanne, and I go every two weeks. It's not like I assumed it would be. There is no couch or deep psychoanalyzing, but there is discussion of my anxiety, and she helps me figure out solutions so I don't become overwhelmed by it.

I'm figuring out my life, except for the most important part, Vince. I haven't told Maryanne about him yet, not sure where to begin. Back when I was a fourteen-year-old kid hanging on his every word or when he walked through my parents' front door the day after my brother died or the kiss on the baseball field. Or his hand on my neck or the party with Patch or the night we shared a bowl full of ice cream in my parents' kitchen. Our story is full of fits and starts, and that's my fault. I know the only way back to him is to once again start, but with myself first.

I close down Instagram and toss my phone into my purse. I told my mom I'd be at her house in fifteen minutes, and I'm already late. As I speed down the street, Christmas decorations blur together out of my window, blow-up Santas and snowmen, wreaths on doors, and trees in windows.

With Dad permanently living in the city now, Mom

decided to sell the house. She said it was too big for one person, and a little too much to live with the memories. She didn't say which memories, but it's not hard to guess. As I pull into the driveway, I'm overcome with sadness that soon the house I grew up in alongside Ray will belong to another family. I never thought I'd be so attached to stone and brick, but I cry through all of George Michael singing "Last Christmas" and some of "Jingle Bell Rock" before shutting off the car.

Maryanne tells me not to shy away from the journey, rather to embrace it. I'm supposed to give myself the freedom and respect to grieve, and I have to give it to others as well. I can help my mother work through her own grief, but I don't have to add it to my own. I should be a model, Maryanne says. So that's what I'm trying to do.

The front door's open, and I let myself in, stepping out of my boots before striding across the carpet. I unwind my scarf and take off my coat, leaving them on the sofa in the living room. All the decorations are already packed up, the pictures, lamps, books, and the oil painting of Tuscany that used to hang above the fireplace.

"Mom?"

"Up here," she answers, and I follow her voice upstairs. She's in the hall, taping an empty cardboard box together. Two are already stacked up and labeled behind her, and she looks good, healthy.

After my episode in the city, I was too embarrassed to go home. I was afraid to face her, knowing I'd hurt her. Neither one of my parents had ever hit me in my life, and while her slap was physically painful, it wasn't nearly as bad as what I said to her. With Nell's help, I rehearsed my apology, but when I finally went home, I didn't get to deliver it. Before I spoke even one syllable, Mom towed me in for a hug and didn't let go. We both cried, for what seemed like hours, and when I finally tried to apologize, she stopped me, her hands on either side of my face saying, "I know. Me too."

And that was it. We haven't brought it up since. Now when we talk, we try to move forward. It's not easy, especially when she gets weepy at the mention of Ray's name, but she's been acknowledging my own loss too.

"What do you need me to do?" I ask her.

She readjusts her headband, keeping her newly trimmed bangs away from her face. I talked her into them since I recently got mine back, but she hates hers. Oops.

"I packed up the guest bathroom," she tells me. "Wanted to wait until you were here to go through the closet."

I pick up a box and shuffle to the guest room, which used to be Raymond's bedroom. The closet became storage for all of our old belongings we didn't take with us when we moved out. Mom doesn't have to voice the reason she waited for me to do this part. When I open the closet door, I'm met with the ordered chaos of old boxes and big plastic bins stacked on top of one another. Some are open, spilling out Barbie dolls and high school yearbooks.

"I can't believe you kept this," I say, picking up a scruffy pink Care Bear.

"I can't believe *you* didn't keep it," Mom says, coming up behind me. She takes it from my hand and runs her fingers over the rainbow on its belly. "You loved this thing." She smiles to herself then gently pushes it back into my hands. "Maybe you can give it to your child when you have one."

I start to laugh but stop because of the love and hope that cross her features. I never imagined myself as a mom—I never imagined a lot of things that have happened—but life's thrown me a curve ball before, and it might again. I give Cheer Bear a squeeze and set it down to grab the bin on top of the pile in the closet. Mom sits on the floor, a box on one side of her, a bag on the other. "This is for things we want to donate," she instructs, patting the box. "And this is for trash," she says, holding out the bag.

"What if we want to keep something?"

"Put it in a separate pile, but you need to take whatever you want home today."

I open the small bin to find it's filled with school assignments, art projects made out of noodles or clay, a notebook of stories I wrote as a kid, and other mindless things. Everything from it except the notebook of my scribbles goes in the trash, and I open another one, this one toys. We chitchat while inspecting each item, deciding whether to donate or trash them.

"I made reservations for Christmas dinner."

I glance up to my mom. "Oh?"

"Your grandmother doesn't like the idea of going out, but what else are we going to do? I'm certainly not going to cook anything."

Her voice is so much surer than it's been since February. She's gained some of her no-nonsense attitude back. I used to bristle at it, but now I'm glad for it. My mother had always been a type A problem-solver, but after Ray died, she lost all of that. She couldn't problem-solve her way out of her son dying. I don't think it's all back yet, and maybe it won't ever be, but she's happy now. As happy as she can be.

I think divorcing Dad has a lot to do with it. And, in some sick way, it's good. It's forced her to wake up. Dad didn't fight with her over assets. It's been mostly painless. I suppose after burying a child, divorce might be like a walk in the park. She'll be moving in to a small condo close to one of her friends and a short drive to Nana and Pop's apartment, and I'm happy for her.

I pull down another box, this one of Raymond's trophies and knickknacks. "The girls might like to have these," I say, holding up two small derby cars from when he was a Boy Scout. "Do you want any of this stuff?"

Mom's eyes water as she shakes her head, and I push the whole box next to the trash bag. It's a shame to throw it all away, but there is no value in it for other people. "We have our memories," I tell my mother. "That's what's important."

She agrees with a slight nod and brushes her hand over the gold figurine on top of a skinny baseball trophy.

I open another box to find it filled with our old baby stuff, little booties, thin blankets, finger- and footprints from the hospital. Watching Mom gingerly touch each item breaks my heart all over again, and I have to turn away to keep from crying. I open another box.

We work like this for another hour until the closet is empty and sorted. With both of us here, it's not too terrible deciding which of Ray's stuff is important enough to keep and which old Blink-182 CD could be thrown out. When we finish, we carry the piles downstairs and the two full bags of trash out to the bins next to the house.

"Thanks for helping," Mom says as we stand by my car.

"Of course. Do you want me to give Dad's stuff to him?" I ask, referring to a small pile, including Ray's framed high school diploma and a few pictures.

She props her hands on her hips. "You're going to see him?"

"Well, I was thinking of it, yeah." The idea of following through has my stomach in knots, but I've been over and over it with Maryanne. If I want some kind of closure, I need to talk to him too.

Mom's shoulders rise with a deep breath, and she softens. "I guess if you're going, you might as well…" She hands the pile to me then hugs me and kisses my cheek before pulling back sharply. "What in the world are you washing your clothes with?"

I pull my sweatshirt up to my nose. "Huh?"

"It smells like…an animal or something."

"Oh, that," I say with a grin. "I went to a shelter to go pet some animals today."

"What?" She practically convulses in horror.

"I went to a shelter to play with the animals. They need love too, you know."

She wrinkles her nose.

"I'm considering adopting a cat. His owner moved and couldn't keep him."

"Oh, Cassandra." She braces her hand on her throat in horror.

I lift a shoulder. "His name's George, and I thought it was destiny…George St. George."

She makes a sound in the back of her throat like she's allergic to even the thought of George.

"He's really sweet, you'd like him. He's old and fat."

She closes her eyes, waving her hand like she can wave the idea of him away. "No. Cats shed everywhere. They sit on the furniture, and they're—"

"They sit on the furniture?" I repeat with big eyes. "How dare they?"

"Don't make fun."

"Maybe you should think about getting an animal to keep you company," I ponder out loud, and she shoos me away.

"No. Absolutely not. No."

It only makes me laugh more. "Okay, I'll get you one for

Christmas. Not a cat, but maybe a rabbit or something small. A guinea pig!"

"Cassandra, I swear, if you bring one animal near me..."

I don't hear the rest of her threat because I close the car door. I drive away, eyes in the rearview mirror where Mom's hint of a smile is reflected back to me.

DECEMBER 31

Happy New Year's Eve, friends! I've never been so happy to say goodbye to a year. I don't expect next year to be any better, but I do hope it's not as bad.

To be honest, I've drunk two glasses of champagne already, and my friend and I are watching the old stop-motion Rudolph movie with the baby New Year. And I'm weepy. As always, my brother is on my mind. In a few hours, I'll be able to say, "My brother died last year." And that's an appalling line. But then again, anything can happen next year. I could win the lottery. I could finally reach my dream of hosting a game show. Or, at the very least, be a contestant on one. Who knows. The world is my oyster.

Anyone have any big plans for this year? I'd love to hear them!

#Grief #NewYear #NYE #ByeBitch #Champagne #BubbleCry #CallMePriceIsRight

CHAPTER 31

I never took stock in making resolutions, but it's a new year, a new me. On January 1st, I sat down to write a list of goals, and maybe it's my start of morphing into my mother—I don't know—but it felt good.

1. Meet with Dad. Do not take no for an answer.
2. See Lucy and Lara at least once a month. Read books with them.
3. Buy a paper calendar and make note of birthdays.
4. People like birthday cards, buy them.
5. Write a book.
6. Tell the people you love that you love them.

So far, I've crossed off number four, but it's only the second week of the new year. For someone who doesn't usually follow through with a plan, I'm doing pretty well, particularly since I'm about to cross off number one.

Arguably, the toughest one.

With my laptop open on the train, I take my mind off the nerves I have about seeing my dad by working on the book.

I'd started journaling daily at the suggestion of Maryanne. I tried to argue I already have my posts, but she insisted I needed to document my day-to-day life as a way of observing growth. At first, it felt kind of immature, like a little girl writing in her diary. But after a few days, I ended up looking forward to it. It's become a form of meditation, to inventory my day, digest it, and then let it go.

The thoughts that most often shaped my days weren't about my brother or family. They were mostly about missing Vince. Or sometimes about Dale, the guy who works next to me, who is the actual worst. Him and his sunflower-seed crunching and constant sniffling. Get a tissue, Dale!

Looking back over the last few weeks, I found a story of struggle and progress. Along with my social media posts, I wrote an outline for a book. It's part memoir, part advice column, and hopefully something people could commiserate with or find humor in. I'm almost like a real adult, all because my brother died. Or, maybe, in spite of. I'll never know, but I am grateful the roller coaster has slowed down for now, and even more grateful that Raymond St. George rode with me for part of the way.

I work through a few notes a critique partner gave me in the time it takes to get to Penn Station, and I load everything up in my purse. The memory of the last time I was here is still fresh in my mind, even though it seems like ages ago. So much has changed in so little time. For a while there, my life was frozen, but recently, my days are moving like dog years. Playing catch up, maybe.

It's cold, and I wrap my scarf almost all the way up to my eyes to guard against the wind whipping between the skyscrapers. I scurry up the ten or so blocks, passing the Empire State Building on the way, and it reminds me of the one time I went to my father's office for Take Your Kid to Work Day. I was ten and spent most of the day with his secretary, but after he finished, he took me up to the top of the Empire State Building and then bought me an ice cream cone. Besides the fact that he's top management of a global accounting firm, I don't know much more about what exactly he does.

When I arrive at the tall, silver building on Lexington, I hope I'm not turned away. I didn't call ahead or make an appointment because I don't want to give him the opportunity to make an excuse, but the man at the front desk barely takes his eyes off the video on his phone as he signals me on after I sign in.

It's the middle of the day, and the elevator is blessedly empty, allowing me time to silently freak out. I wiggle my hands before wiping them on my pants. I'm sweating, and I remove my hat, coat, scarf, and gloves, holding them all on my arm, which doesn't make me sweat any less. When the elevator doors open again, I trip and drop everything on the floor.

"Whoops, sorry," I say when someone steps around me as I pick up my gloves and hat.

"Cassandra? What are you doing here?"

I wing myself upright, thrown off my mental game. I practiced what I wanted to say to my father, in the tone I wanted to say it in, but he takes me by surprise now, and I let out a startled, "Hi."

Dad's arched eyebrows and flapping chin tell me he's dumbfounded too. "Why? What...? Why are you here?"

I get myself together, stand taller, and answer, "I came to talk to you."

He lifts his arm to peek at his watch. "It's two in the afternoon on a Thursday. You need to talk now?"

I shrug. "No better time than the present."

He rolls his eyes at me but doesn't move. The elevator doors can't close with us at this impasse. "You know this is where I work, right? You can't simply come here whenever you please."

I don't apologize or move. I'm not going to. I came here to talk to him, and I will.

After a short standoff, he relents with a sigh. "Fine," he grunts, checking his watch again. "I have a meeting in ten."

He spins on his heel, out of the elevator and down the hall. His strides are so long, I have to hurry to match his steps until he stops at the end of the hall to open a door with his name next to it: Stephen St. George, Director, Analytics.

I tap on the sign. "Fancy."

He ignores me and sits down in the black leather chair behind his desk, reclining slightly, his hands folded across his stomach, a power pose.

It's been months since I've seen him, and not much has changed, except maybe a few gray hairs. His suit is cleanly pressed, and he doesn't smell like alcohol...yet. It makes me want to take a stab at him. "Divorce looks good on you."

His chair creaks as he sits up. "You came here to poke the bear?"

I huff. "It hasn't worked with you so far."

He leans forward on his desk like he's going to negotiate with me. "Still you continue."

"Mom says my stubborn streak is from you."

"Hm." He wipes one hand over his mouth and chin, gazes down and then at the wall behind me before meeting my eyes. "How's your mother?"

"Settled in the condo."

"Good." He fiddles with his tie, and I know from recent experience I don't have much more time with him being uncomfortable—able to be cracked open—before he changes back into the bear he is. I have to go for it.

"I'm sorry about what happened that day," I start, knowing he'll understand I mean the day I lost it on him and Mom. "I'm not sorry for telling you how I feel, but I am sorry how it came out. It wasn't the right way to express myself."

He casts his eyes down again, and I wait for him to say something. He doesn't utter a word, doesn't even let out a breath.

"I'm trying to...make amends, I guess."

No response.

If he's not going to interact with me, I'm not sure what else to say. In all of my rehearsals, I didn't plan for silence.

"I think, um, I think we're all pretty messed up from Ray's death, and we need to grieve in whatever way we have to, but I'm tired of fighting with you and Mom. This is hard enough as it is."

He blinks his gaze up to the ceiling. His throat works on a swallow, and when I think he's going to speak, he doesn't. Instead, he wipes at the corner of one eye before tilting his head toward me, waiting for me to go on. The quiet show of emotion dents the armor around my heart. He's not a robot.

I wonder what it is he's thinking right now, but he'll never tell me. I wish he would.

"You and I never got along, and it's okay," I acquiesce, working on *that* particular understanding for weeks with Maryanne. It's been challenging, to say the least. "I wanted to come talk to you to see if we could move forward, maybe create some kind of relationship that's different from what we had. Better." I clear the lump from my throat. "Unfortunately, I'm the only kid you have left, so it's me or nothing," I say, forcing my voice to be light and teasing.

His face is blank. He doesn't think I'm funny.

"So, what do you think of...my offer?"

He considers me, picks up a pen, then promptly sets it back down before stacking some papers. "Yeah, sure."

I perk up. "Yeah?"

He tips his chin toward his door. "Talk to Lisette for my schedule."

"Oh." I know what that means. It's a brush-off. It's an *I'll call you* after a first date. My own father's ghosting me.

"Welp." I leave the bag of Ray's belongings I brought for him on the floor. "We saved these for you, if you care." I don't want to expend one more second of energy on this man and pivot to leave, but on the way out, my eyes snag on a picture. It's a framed 8 x 10, placed in the middle of his floor-to-ceiling bookshelf. I stop to admire it.

It's an old family photo. The four of us on the boardwalk at the beach. Mom and Dad stand behind Ray and me, and I must have been eleven or twelve years old at the time. We're all smiling. Dad has on a tattered baseball hat, and Mom's wearing a neon-green top. Ray's nose is all freckled, his hair shaggy and curling at the ends, while I'm sunburned, my fingers up in a peace sign. We look truly happy.

"It's my favorite," Dad says gruffly behind me.

I turn over my shoulder to find his attention is on his computer screen. I'm not sure what to make of the statement or the fact that he even has this picture up. Just when I think I can hate him, I can't, though he doesn't raise his eyes or make a move to me, so I see myself out.

As Lisette types away on her keyboard, she glances up to offer a friendly hello. I wave at her. I'm not going to bother checking my father's schedule. If he really wanted to work on our relationship, he could tell me his schedule himself or, hell, offer up any other idea.

I stick my arms through my coat and begin to put on my scarf when my dad calls out from his office, "It's good to see you, Cass."

His head poking out from his door reminds me of Ray with the way it's cocked to the side. He offers a flat, closed-lip smile, and I guess it's better than nothing. Like Maryanne told me, I don't know what he's going through. I can't control what he does, but I can control my reaction to it. I change my mind and make an appointment with Lisette before heading to the elevator and back outside to the subway entrance so I can travel uptown.

Professor Row agreed to meet me at a diner in Harlem, and I arrive early to get some writing done. With a steaming cup of coffee and my laptop open, I pour my emotions from the last hour onto the page. My fingers fire across the keyboard, a steady staccato, my hands typing the words before they're even fully formed in my mind.

I didn't think I was allowed to grieve, I write. *Faced with an incredible loss, everyone goes through the same emotions. The sadness, anger, denial, it's all the same, really, but I didn't think I was permitted to experience those things when my brother passed away.*

I don't have children. I don't know what it's like for my child to die, but I witnessed the suffering of my parents. They both bore that worst-nightmare scenario physically. They still do. The evidence is in the lines of their faces, the gray strands of hair, the hunched shoulders. My brother stole a piece of me when he died, so what must it feel like for them? Their whole self dying? It has to be terrible for them, I thought. More terrible than it is for me.

I'm not married and don't know the intricacies and nuances of marriage, but if what I feel for the person I love is any indica-

tion, losing your partner must take the wind out of your sails. I suppose it might be like you're a boat stuck in the ocean, endlessly floating, not steered in any particular direction. To go from having daily routines, inside jokes, and support to suddenly nothing—it must be terrible, I thought. More terrible than what it is for me.

I'm a fully grown adult—sometimes—with the ability to comprehend complex ideas. I don't need my father or mother to hold my hand anymore, not like little kids who lose their parents. The innocence of a child shouldn't be interrupted by something so dismal as death. I think of all my twin nieces are missing by not having my brother around. Because they're so young, I hope they're somewhat shielded from the emptiness inside, but when they get older and my brother isn't there, what will they feel then? When he's not there to teach them to drive a car, take a picture at graduation, walk them down the aisle at their weddings, or for any other day, special or not, that he isn't there for. I'm sure they'll be quite familiar with the missing link in their life and family. And it must certainly be terrible. More terrible than what it is for me.

My brother and I were level, in a way. We had always gotten along, we were great friends, and there was nothing left unsaid between us. I felt like my loss wasn't as big as everyone else's. I saw the relationships my brother had with others as more impor-tant than mine. Therefore, I couldn't grieve. I didn't deserve to. I thought I needed to be strong for everyone else. But by putting others' grief ahead of my own, I unintentionally made it worse for myself. I self-destructed. And, sadly, I think it may be true for a lot of people who experience the death of a sibling. The putting others ahead of yourself, not the self-destructing part.

What you experience with your sibling during your time together can span from black eyes to fits of laughter to screaming matches to "Hey, give me five bucks for a beer." The connection between siblings is established from birth, and even though it can often be tenuous, it's undeniable. We may not be burying our parents, children, or spouse, but our loss is just as great. Different, but significant. It's a pain that deserves moments to say, "I'm not okay."

I've learned it's okay not to be okay, and we need to take time to heal. Otherwise, we'll be useless to those people we think we need to help in the first place. Take time to scream into your pillow, cry, or get drunk in public, whatever works for you. Although, I would suggest avoiding anything where you might end up puking on a train or waking up in a jail cell.

CHAPTER 32

A coat of fresh white snow covers the ground and rests on top of the headstones. I brush it off Ray's then kick the bottom of the stone. "What's up, bro?"

No one else is out at the cemetery today, probably because of the weather. I didn't want to come today, and I certainly don't want to memorialize the anniversary of my brother's death. I'd rather celebrate his life, but it's Valentine's Day. And I have a special mission.

"The girls made these for you," I say, presenting the homemade Valentine's cards to the stone. I have to take off my mitten to open the first one. It's a giant red construction paper heart folded in half. "This one's from Lara. She drew a dog, I think. Or maybe a horse. It's hard to tell." I spin it around to study it from a different angle. "It says 'I love you, Daddy. Please tell Jesus to send me a puppy.'" I laugh. "Okay, so it's definitely a dog she drew." Lucy's card is flat with a bunch of rainbows and hearts all over. "'Dear Daddy, I love you. Happy Valentine's Day.'"

I place them on top of the headstone under a rock and put my mittens back on before sticking my hands in my pockets. "The girls both got some kind of stomach bug, so they asked me to bring you the cards." I try to push as much of the snow away as possible. "The weather will probably soak them into mush, but..."

I clear my throat, a puff of white air forming in front of my mouth. "The girls are good. They're already talking about being in first grade next year. Crazy, right? Shayna's single for now, and I like her a lot better when she is. She's got a Rosie the Riveter vibe going on, woman doing for herself. It's good." I blow out another puff of white air. "Mom's all right. I mean, she's an absolute wreck today. I can't even talk to her, but I know she had a friend or two with her today. I can't be around her when she gets all... It sounds bad, like I don't support her, but I need to deal with my own stuff."

It's silly to talk to a stone, and I laugh at myself. "You're a real jackass for ignoring me, you know." My skin's dry from the winter temperature, and when I frown, I fear giant chasms will form. "Last month, I went to confront Dad. It didn't go well, but it didn't go...horrible either. We've emailed each other a couple times. We're supposed to be meeting for dinner next week, so..."

My voice dips as my chin trembles. "I don't know if you're keeping track of what everybody's doing, but I think you'd be proud of me. I made a list of life goals a while ago and got to cross everything off on the list. Everything but one, and I thought you'd be proud." I drop my head, crying. "I wanted to tell you that, and I want you to be proud of me. I hope you are."

I wipe my face, the tears hot against my cold skin. "I—" I sniffle. "I grew up a lot since last year. Bet you didn't think it was possible, huh?" I wipe at my eyes again. "One of my professors from Columbia's been mentoring me on my writing, and I got a literary agent and everything. Hopefully, a publisher will want this book I wrote about you. Well, it's not about you per se, more inspired by you than anything. Don't get too excited." My smile fades and I fidget. My feet can't stay still. "It's crazy to think all these good things are happening to me, and it's all because you died. I had to climb out of the hole I fell into, but I did, and now I'm living on my own, getting regular paychecks. I even have benefits and a retirement plan like a real adult." I bite my lip. "Sometimes I wonder what I'd be doing if you were still here. I'd probably still be a lost boy wandering Neverland." I shrug. "I don't know."

Bending over, I succumb to a racking cry that's difficult to breathe through. I still can't believe I am here, talking to a grave. I haven't seen my brother or heard his voice in a whole year. I made it through the longest, hardest year of my life, and all I get for it is to stand here, where he's buried. It's cruel.

"I m-miss y-you," I stutter after a minute of concentrating on my breaths. In my nose and out my mouth, I let the sorrow wash over me. "I m-miss you a l-lot."

Straightening, I take off my mittens. They're soaked from wiping at my tears. "I had my makeup done," I say, rubbing my index fingers under my eyes. "I'm gonna ask Vince to forgive me, and now I have to do it with a raccoon face because I'm crying over you." I sniff a few times, my chest expanding on full, deep breaths as I roll my shoulders back. "I thought about doing it on a different day, but it *is* Valentine's Day, and I refuse to have this made-up, Hallmark holiday be completely ruined all because your heart happened to crap out on it." I lower my attention, watching snowflakes land on my black boots for a moment. "I hope he doesn't completely hate me. If he does, I may have to take

February 14th off my calendar permanently, and then what would I use for an excuse to eat chocolate all day long?"

I knock on the side of the headstone. "All right. I don't plan on coming here a lot. It's creepy and weird, but I guess I'll see you around. Don't be afraid to flicker my lights or something. I promise not to scream too loud. I love you, you dumb jerk."

I smile and wave, out of habit, I guess, and then return to my car.

I was right. I am a raccoon. I try to fix myself, but it's useless. I drive to the drugstore and head straight to the cosmetics aisle. If I'm going to meet Vince, I refuse to do it with smudged makeup. I snag only the essentials: foundation, powder, bronzer, blush, eyeliner, and mascara. And cover-up. And ChapStick. It's not my usual brands, but it'll do in a pinch.

By sheer luck, there's a small display of bagged chocolate-covered pomegranate seeds by the counter, and I purchase it all, then shuffle back to my car. Butterflies multiply by the minute as I apply a new face with trembling hands. I haven't seen Vince for months, and I'm not sure what he'll say.

Or if he's even moved on. I wince. The idea of him with someone else breaks my wretched heart, and it gives me pause, rethinking if I want to go through with this plan. But I can't give up if I want to cross this final goal off my list: number six, tell the people you love that you love them.

And I love Vince.

With an application of my signature color lipstick, I start my car and begin the heart-pounding ride to Vince's house. I run up to the front door before I can lose my nerve and ring the doorbell. I wait a few seconds and then ring again. I don't hear any movement in the house, not even Gracie.

"Stupid," I whisper to myself, thumping my forehead with my hand. I only know of one other place he might be. With a little less haste, I get back in my car, gather up whatever courage I have left, and head straight to the Underworld.

The parking lot of Mancini Funeral Home is packed, and I take the first spot available. With my nerves bungling my brain, I scuttle to the side door, closest to me, open it, and—goddamn it—interrupt again.

"I'm so sorry," I say to the people around me. A couple of the rows in the front, by the casket, are full of mourners, while a few other people are scattered throughout the room. I try to back out, but my foot catches on a chair leg, and I stumble. "Oh, sorry." The man I bump into gives me a bland look as I hurry to get the hell out of here.

"Cass."

Someone tugs at my elbow, and I already know who it is before I turn around. "I didn't mean to walk into the middle of this," I tell Vince in a whisper. "My brain is like..." I wave my hands by my head. He curls his arm around my waist, pressing against my back so I'll move forward. "I'm sorry. Can we talk?"

When he doesn't answer, my pulse quickens to light speed, and if I thought my brain wasn't functioning before, it goes into overdrive now. I pull away from him. "We have to talk."

"No," he mumbles out of the corner of his mouth, his focus on the front of the room. He moves me closer to the door in the corner, by the hall that leads to his office, but I can't stop staring at him. He looks the exact same, except he's grown his hair back out. I want to push it away from his temples, smooth it between my fingers. For a while, I'd been able to touch him whenever I wanted to, but I can't anymore. I lost the opportunity.

"I'm sorry I hurt you," I whisper hurriedly.

"Not now, Cass. We have a viewing going on," he says with a gentle shove so that I exit the room.

"Please, Vince? It'll just take a minute." My voice rises at the end, and he holds a finger up to his lips, his hazel eyes meeting mine for the first time since I crashed into his funeral home for the second time. I glance around the room. No one's paying attention to me, so I sidle up next to him, making sure to keep my voice down. "I've been doing a lot of thinking, soul-searching, and I came to apologize. I did use you. I'm sorry. I didn't do it on purpose, but it's no excuse. I took you for granted, and I feel awful about it. I didn't—"

"Shh." He cuts me off with a severe hush and tugs me outside the door into the hall.

I try again, whispering, "I didn't realize then what I was doing. I was falling in love with you."

Vince's body is always in motion, tapping fingers, head tilts, bouncing legs. His body is always buzzing with energy, not overt but more like an even, constant rain. It's soothing. But now, he's still next to me. The only signs of life are his blinking eyes.

"I'm working," he says and glances at his watch then crosses his arms. He doesn't tell me to leave, so I don't. I stand next to him, impatiently waiting, and he occasionally tosses me an annoyed frown. I want to apologize again, but I'm afraid to make the situation worse.

I can do nothing but watch a slow, steady line of mourners speak to the people in the front row before approaching the casket. I'm a morbid voyeur. Even with my angst about Vince, it's impossible to ignore the life and death in front of us.

Finally, when there is no longer a line, Vince turns to me and says, "Wait here." I do as I'm told, and he walks back into the room, bending down to a person I cannot see. After a moment, he stands and opens the back doors as if to usher the guests out of the room. "On behalf of the Bryne family, thank you for coming today. The funeral service will be held tomorrow morning at St. Mary's Episcopal Church at ten a.m."

He makes his way to me back in the hall and spares no time or minced words. "*You* left *me*, Cass," he says in a harsh, low voice. "*You* didn't want to give me time. *You* didn't want to talk about it. *You* didn't want to do anything." He aims his index finger at me and then himself. "You said I was nothing to you and left, just walked out. But now you expect me to fall at your feet? You want me to pretend you didn't break my heart and disappear?"

"No!" At his raised eyebrows, I slap my hands to my mouth even though I can't help that I already yelled. "No. I don't expect you to do anything."

He folds his arms and angles his body to block my view of the room behind him, although it appears the guests are filtering out. "Then why are you here?"

"To apologize. I know I have terrible timing, but you knew that about me already." I smile, hoping he does too. He doesn't. "I said horrible things to you. I don't want to make any excuses, but I need you to know where I was coming from."

He doesn't stop me, so I continue. "I was really messed up. Even before Ray died, I was messed up. His death made me crash, but the train was already coming off the tracks. But when you showed up at my door, none of that mattered.

When I was around you, I was happy, and I didn't know how to handle it. I didn't know how to be good for you when I couldn't be good for myself."

Vince curls his bottom lip into his mouth. It's what he does when he thinks.

"I hurt you, and I did it on purpose. I said you didn't mean anything to me, but I lied to you and to myself. You mean a lot to me. You mean everything." Tears well up, and I let out a maniacal laugh. "I can't stop crying," I say, wiping at my eyes. "This was the second time I put on makeup today."

I tip my head back to meet Vince's gaze, and his mouth is angled down, his shoulders soft and curled toward me. He nudges my hand away from my face to replace it with his own. His palm smooths down my cheek, and I lean into its warmth.

"I love you, Vince. You're sweet and patient and funny and kind. God, you're so kind, and I'm sullen and bitter and sarcastic. I'm perpetually late and—"

"And I'm always early." He blesses me with my favorite uneven smile as he bows toward me, like we're forming a crooked little heart of our own. "We can even each other out."

"Yeah?"

He nods, and I hold on to his hand with both of mine, afraid if I let go, he'll change his mind. But then he bends to kiss me, and everything I've been missing for months disappears. His lips ease my fears. His arm wrapping around me promises we'll be okay.

I lift onto my toes, bringing myself as close as I can to him. If I could, I'd saw him open and climb into his chest, live inside his heart for the rest of my life. After all, it is my home.

"Oh!" I push away from him. "I almost forgot." I retrieve the small plastic bag from my purse and hand it to him.

His brows furrow. "Chocolate-covered pomegranate seeds?"

"Remember I told you about Persephone and Hades?" I open them when he doesn't and pull out one of the little chocolate balls. "She stayed in the Underworld because she ate the pomegranate seed." Then I pop it into my mouth, grinning.

Vince releases a big belly laugh and throws his arms around me, lifting me up. I laugh too, my feet off the floor, and he kisses my neck and cheeks, repeating, "I love you."

My wretched heart grows wings at those words, and I press my lips to his as my heart flies above me.

"Ahem." A purposeful cough sounds, and I am smacked with reality. I barged into a funeral service to tell a man I love him. Vince's body tenses as he releases me to the floor. His face is beet red, and he slowly spins around. I peek out from my place in the hallway, behind him.

A group of people are staring at us. They're gathered at the door like they've been eavesdropping. But they haven't. We've been loud.

Curious eyes scrutinize us.

"Ladies and gentlemen," Vince says in his most professional tone, "I apologize profusely for my inappropriate behavior. It is not my—"

"No," a distinctly feminine voice says, stepping between two bodies in the small crowd.

I cover my face with my hand, mortified. I don't know if I should run to Vince's office, say something, or pretend I'm here to mourn and take a seat. I can't decide, so I only squeeze Vince's hand.

"Don't apologize," the woman says, moving to stand in

the doorway. She's tall with short gray hair, and her tawny skin has a pallor that I've seen in my own face, but she's smiling. "My father died two years ago, and my mother has missed him every day. They were married for sixty-four years. She said they were soul mates." She motions for us to come into the room, and the small crowd parts for us as we amble to the aisle in the middle of the chairs. Everyone's attention is on us as this woman speaks only to Vince and me.

"Mom read romance novels voraciously, even more so after Dad passed, and this..." She settles one hand over her lips as her voice wobbles. "This moment between you two, it was the perfect way to send my mother off to meet my father."

Vince bows his head, and I think he's tearing up from the way he skims a knuckle over his eyelid. I peel away from him to meet the woman. We embrace, both of our smiles watery. She's a complete stranger, but in this moment, we are bound together by love and death. I hold her hands in mine.

"I hope you can find peace in your grief," I tell her.

She squeezes my fingers, fat tears rolling down her cheeks. "You've already given it to me, darling." Her gaze drifts over my shoulder then back to me. "Now, go get your man."

So, I turn around and go get my man. Applause breaks out all around as I wrap both arms around Vince's neck and kiss him with every bit of love I have in my heart.

Persephone is staying in the Underworld, but it's okay.

I'm okay.

FEBRUARY 14

It's Valentine's Day today, and I spent more time than I'd like to admit browsing the candy aisle. Three years ago, on this day, I received the worst news of my life. In the 1,095 days since, it hasn't changed. It's still the worst news of my life—hearing my brother died—and it's still hard for me to believe it's real, to imagine my life without him. Every day, at least once a day, I have a thought about something, usually inane, I want to share with my brother, so I do. I tell him I can't believe our mother is on a dating website. Or that I had another fight with my fiancé about how he never remembers to close the bathroom door and the dog keeps making a home in there among the toilet paper the cat rips up. And that said fiancé wishes I'd go to some of the baseball games for the team he coaches, but baseball is really boring.

I also ask my brother to keep my secret—although it's not so secret anymore as I'm about to tell you, my internet friends—that my fiancé isn't my fiancé anymore. He's my husband now since we went to city hall last week. Surprise! We're still having a bigger ceremony in April, but I needed something for myself. Partly because it was giving me anxiety, and partly because my brother's not here to be the man of honor.

But with every voiced thought, I'm met with silence. What's that saying? Insanity is doing something the exact same way every time but expecting different results...

I am by no means in a rush for my life to end, yet if there is anything my brother's death has taught me, it's that there is an end. There is an end to what sometimes feels like endless human agony, and that is what makes all of this...whole being alive thing kind of beautiful. My brother is gone, and I hate it. It causes me pain every day, but that same hole in my heart, that thorn in my side, reminds me to spend every day soaking it all in. For as long as I'm here on this rock, I will live and enjoy and find a way to smile even when it all sucks, because one day, it'll be gone.

I look forward to the time I finally receive an answer from my brother when I ask him how he's doing. Maybe we'll croak it to each other when we are reincarnated as frogs or blaze the answer across the sky as shooting stars or speak in tongues as angels with wings. I don't know. But one way or another, I will hear from him again. And until then, I'll bear the pain because it's a reminder of how much we loved each other.

This isn't a romantic Valentine's Day post, but it is a reminder to take care of your heart, because when you love someone, you give them a piece of it. And most importantly, if you're lucky enough to receive a piece of someone else's heart, hold it close. Their heartbeat is in your hands. It's their life, for the love of Zeus, take care of it!

As always, I want to hear about your experiences with

grief, so feel free to comment, and make sure to pick up a copy of my book *Life, Love, Death, and Other Awkward Conversations* at your favorite indie bookstore.

#Grief #GoodGrief #ValentinesDay #HeartHealth #MentalHealth #GetHelp #ShopLocal

AUTHOR'S NOTE

The worst day of my life was December 15th, 2015. My older brother and only sibling died suddenly of a massive heart attack. Hours earlier, I had signed the contract with a literary agent, and as I sat at my parents' kitchen table, my mom told me, "You're brother will be so proud."

I never got to tell him.

My brother and I are three years and ten days apart. A month before his death, he had just turned 33. I had turned 30. He had two little kids, a full-time job as a teacher, and he coached football. I was trying to make a go of it as an artist and worked multiple part-time jobs to pull my weight. I was a lot like Cass. He was a lot like RJ. But while there are quite a few similarities between this story and my real life—including things in this book that were straight up lifted from my personal experience—it is not *MY* exact story.

It is *A* story. One that I wrote to explore how lost I was and still am, even years later. Mourning a sibling is very lonely. I think it's quite impossible for anyone to understand, if they have not had to do it. When it happened to me,

I had never, ever met anyone—more accurately, a young person—who had to bury a sibling. And it was horrible. Not only was I irrevocably changed, but so was my family and my place in it.

I couldn't talk about it because I didn't know how to articulate what I was feeling. Not that I wanted to because no one seemed to be able to understand what I was going through. Not my friends, not my family, no one.

Like Cass, I struggled to come to terms with my new life and to find ways to cope with the loss. Unlike Cass, my parents showed me what true love and strength were, and they still do. I don't have a Vince, but I do have my husband, who I have only grown to love and appreciate more because of how he consistently holds me up when I can't stand on my own. I have my wonderful sister-in-law and my nephew and niece, who were so young when they lost their father, yet are growing into smart and loving young adults. I am #blessed for amazing friends who support me and for a perfect little seat in my shower for when I want to cry.

Because, of course, I'm a Scorpio. I only cry in the shower.

There are no words to accurately describe how much I miss my brother. Every. Single. Day. But writing this book has helped express what I can't and often don't want to. But I do believe we have to get it out. All of the ugly, hard, draining feelings, we have to exercise them. And writing is my way of doing that.

If you have had to experience what it means to become a forgotten mourner, I am truly sorry you are part of this club. It sucks. But I am with you. I understand. I am here for you.

Whether you have ever grieved anyone or have yet to be touched by the inevitable pain of this wild and beautiful thing we call life, thank you for coming on this journey with me. Thank you for allowing me into your hearts. I hope it brought you some joy and maybe a little bit of healing, if you needed it.

WHAT ELSE?

For bonus contest in Vince's POV, use the QR code to have it delivered straight to your inbox!

If you enjoyed Love at a Funeral and Other Award Conversation, you're going to want to check out How to Ruin a Wedding, out now in Kindle Unlimited, paperback, and audio!

ACKNOWLEDGMENTS

Indie publishing is a wild ride. Thank you, reader, for coming along with me.

I guess I would have to first thank my brother for...dying. Without which I would not be going to therapy or have written this book, so thanks, bro.

I'd also like to thank the two men who inspired Vince. The first is Mikey, my neighbor growing up, who I had a crush on, because I had a crush on all the boys. I appreciate him hugging me so tight at my brother's funeral, it felt like he was holding me together, and for telling me it was okay, that I'd be okay. There is also my friend, Connor O'Donnell, the handsomest funeral director to walk the planet. He answered all of my questions, is built like a tree, and has a great smile.

Big shout out to my ARC team and those wonderful readers who DM or text me their thoughts on my books while reading. It never fails to pick me up.

If you'd like more information about me, you can find it at https://sophieandrewsauthor.com/

ABOUT THE AUTHOR

Sophie Andrews is a contemporary romance author who writes steamy books that will leave you smiling. As a millennial, she's obsessed with boybands, late 90s rom-coms, and will always be team Pacey. When she's not writing, she's most likely trying to wrangle her children or drinking red wine. Or both at the same time.

ALSO BY SOPHIE ANDREWS

Tangled Series

Tangled Up

Tangled Want

Tanged Hearts

Tangled Beginning

Tangled Expectations

Tangled Chances

Tangled Ambition

Single Dads' Club

The Rehearsal Fling

The Nanny Tenure

The Dating Pact

The Bartender's Baby

Stand-Alones

How to Ruin a Wedding

Love at a Funeral and Other Awkward Conversations

www.ingramcontent.com/pod-product-compliance
Lightning Source LLC
Chambersburg PA
CBHW021242190726
48289CB00005B/1443